LOVE SWIPE BLACKMAIL

LOVE SWIPE BLACKMAIL

NITISH BHUSHAN

Anecdote
Publishing House
For the love of quality reading!

Anecdote
Publishing House
For the love of quality reading!

anecdotepublishinghouse.com
champreaders.com

Anecdote Publishing House
2nd Floor 2/15 Lane no. 2 Ansari Road, Daryaganj-110002
Email: info@anecdotepublishinghouse.com
Website: anecdotepublishinghouse.com

Published by Anecdote Publishing House

Third Edition 2025
ISBN 978-81-95251-85-8
MRP ₹ 350

Book Promoted and Marketed by Champ Readers Pvt. Ltd.
Edited by Mansi Kashyap and Meraki
Cover design by Amitesh Tandon
Layout by Graphic Tailor
Printed by Thomson Press (India) Ltd, New Delhi

Dedication

The book is dedicated to my father, **Shri Chandar Bhushan**, who battled blood cancer against all odds in the year 2017-18. While cancer won the battle with him, his battle with cancer won the hearts and minds of the amazingly dedicated medical staff, relatives, and friends alike! Most of the original manuscript was written while I was by his side in the hospital, during nights. He had no idea what I was up to, so, like a caring parent, he would always advise his child not to overwork, but to sleep and rest. Till his last breath, he lived like an emperor, leaving those of us in his wake to learn from his life.

Contents

Acknowledgements

Thanks to:

Nishi, my wife, who never agreed with me on any of the earlier drafts so that I could keep on improving the story and its contents. Rumour has it that she hasn't agreed on this draft either.

Anju a very dear family friend who liked the storyline and gave detailed inputs on what would work well and what wouldn't, and who just wouldn't let me give up on writing the book.

Aditya for being my beta reader and giving me a thumbs up after reading the initial draft.

A big thanks to all the publishers whom I did not hear from—they inspired me to work harder.

Sagar Azad, my publisher from Anecdote Publishing

House, who has been a pillar of strength, encouragement and support.

Mansi Narula Kashyap, my editor from Anecdote Publishing House. We have taken her valuable suggestions in this edition. I admire her patience & skill.

Meraki, for diligently finding out things that we all missed. She is an absolutely brilliant proofreader with one thousand eyes for details.

My friends, Rajath and Ajay, for standing by me during all the tough times. Amrita, Nitin, and Swati—for helping me with the name of the book. Special thanks to Swati for suggesting the cover for the first two editions and for running through the draft and identifying errors that I missed.

Amitesh Tandon for the top-class effort in designing the cover for the third edition.

Shubhra my sister, with whom I braved our toughest times together.

Living without a life partner is hard. I have no words to speak for the unbridled energy, courage, strength, determination, and wisdom that our mother, Smt. Kiran Bhushan brings into our lives.

Statutory Warning

This book is a work of fiction, and the blame for any resemblance to any person living or dead is totally on the Lord Almighty. ☺

Advance Reviews
(Pre-release of edition 1.0)

Highly captivating book. It's a dramatic love story wherein you feel emotions, confusions, desires and the dilemma of this madly in love boy, Ravi. I loved the bond he shared with his friends and his dedication for his love. The story is full of unexpected twists and turns which keep us glued to the plot. Author's sense of humour and wit is well portrayed in his writing. The book has the quality that one wants to make one read cover to cover.

Ms. Anju Nagpal, Meerut, India

A page turner with a good mix of love, friendship, humour and suspense. It is engrossing from page 1 and takes you on a thrilling roller coaster ride with the characters' adventures/misadventures. What I also liked about the book was that the characters were relatable. Just what the doctor ordered to beat Covid-19 blues.

Ms. Swati Sankhla, Food Blogger - Perth, Australia

Advance Reviews
(Pre-release of edition 1.0)

Highly captivating book. It's a dramatic love story wherein you feel emotions, confusions, desires and the excitement of this madly in love boy Ravi. I loved the bond he shared with his friends and his dedication for his love. The story is full of unexpected twists and turns which keep us glued to the plot. Author's sense of humour and wit is well portrayed in his writing. The book has the quality that one wants to make one read cover to cover.

Ms. Anju Nagpal, Meerut, India

A page turner with a good mix of love, friendship, humour and suspense. It is engrossing from page 1 and takes you on a thrilling roller coaster ride with the character's adventures/misadventures. What I also liked about the book was that the characters were relatable. Just what the doctor ordered to beat Covid-19 blues.

Ms. Swati Sukhija, Food Blogger, Perth, Australia

Early Reviews
(Pre – release of edition 2.0)

सरल, सहस, सहज और प्रवाहमयी भाषा में लिखा यह उपन्यास आप एक बार उठा लें तो पूरा किये बिना रख ही नहीं सकते। कुल मिलकर हम इस उपन्यास के बारे में यही कहेंगे - शिकवे गीले हैं प्यार भी है, तकरार भी है तो मनुहार भी है, खोने का मलाल है, दोस्ती की मिसाल है, दोस्तों का आपसी प्रेम बेजोड़ है, कथानक में गजब का मोड़ है, सस्पेंस है, रोमांस है, थ्रिल है, परेशानियों में भले हों घिरे, बावजूद इसके सब चिल है, सच्ची प्रीत है, सत्य की जीत है, हिंसा न तोड़-फोड़ है, उपन्यास बेजोड़ है। खूब रंग जमायेगा और सराहना पायेगा, नितीश जी को अच्छी पहचान दिलाएगा, वाह वाह क्या बात है, वाह वाह क्या बात है, ऐसे ही लिखते रहो हमारी शुभकामनाएं आपके साथ हैं।

Dr. Sarika Mukesh
MA (English) PhD (English)
Associate Professor & Head English Department
VIT Vellore Vellore, India

A good book is one that makes the reader feel. It takes the reader on a compelling journey. An interesting story weaved around dating apps, love and blackmailing. There is itself an escapade in the very beginning of the story which draws up a thrilling scene. The story reflects the current circumstances of every human's daily life. The online dating app, love and true meaning of friendship can be seen in the story which makes the book interesting and more fascinating. Loved the way the writer builds up suspense right from the start. Narration is also smooth which makes the book an easy and quick read. The author clearly meets the reader's expectations through the story.

Ms. Seema Ghosh

Educator, Motivator, Legal Activist, Social Activist, Writer

Kota, India

Nitish, what I am saying is you are indeed a wordsmith. Your book is quite like a whiff of modern romance with all the modern traps and temptation to stray! I enjoyed the book and am impressed of your handling of the different strings. I found that timelines were quite easy to follow and once I got that sorted in my head, I could easily go back and forth. Very entertaining take on the trouble dating apps can spring on. I hope to see Bollywood taking it up!

Congratulations on a well written engaging book!

Ms. Vasundhara Dharmaraaj
Formal Principal in–charge IHMCT&AN Bangalore

A remarkable tale about a most insightful journey seeded in a hospital during the author's father's treatment. It is a surprising story full of magic and wisdom; the quest to fulfil one's destiny. I recommend Love Swipe Blackmail to anyone who is passionately committed to claiming the life of their dreams today. It is really an unabashed delight and an inspirational wonder. A rare gem of a book, it will most certainly touch the very core of every heart earnestly seeking its own destiny in the journey of life.

Dr. Deepak Kumar Shrivastava
INELI India and South Asia Mentor
Divisional Librarian and Head, Government
Divisional Public Library Kota, Rajasthan
Name considered in IFLA WALL OF FAME
Kota, India

CHAPTER 35

Shock!
(Six Months into the Future)

Bhanu called up Raaj, "Raaj, where are you?"

From Bhanu's tone, Raaj knew that this was not just important, but also urgent and ultra-critical.

"Office, Why? What happened?"

"Ravi was trying to reach you, but was unable to get through."

"I must have been in the basement parking lot, seeing off Suchita. We were discussing something. What happened?"

"Ravi called up. I don't know what has happened yet, as he did not say anything apart from, '*Pick up Raaj and come to my flat, immediately. I will explain everything later.*' And then he disconnected the call."

"I am done for the day, anyway. Was planning to meet Simi. But I guess I can join you. Will start in ten minutes. You?"

"I am on my way, already."

In the next forty-five minutes, they arrived at Ravi's place. It was clear from Ravi's tone, during the call with Bhanu that the matter was serious. The seriousness was amplified when they reached his flat and saw him pacing back and forth in the drawing room. Raaj went to the kitchen and fetched three pints from the fridge. Bhanu and Raaj sat on the couch, waiting for Ravi to open up.

"Yaar, it was post lunch in my office when I got a ping. I thought it was a…chuck that. You remember when you made me delete my original profile on Sofu?" he looked at Bhanu.

"Yes," Bhanu replied.

"Well, someone from the past is back, and with a blast!"

Both Bhanu and Raaj had question marks on their faces.

"You guys remember Mahek, the one who was in Dubai with Vandana?"

"The one you found extremely hot and all?" asked Raaj.

"Yes. Well, she texted me today."

"Did I not ask you to delete your damn profile?"

"And you know that I did, in front of you both!"

"Then how come?" mumbled Bhanu. "By any chance, did you leave your number with her? I had explicitly told you not to be in touch with her, at all.

Why did you?"

"No, I did not. It beats me how she got my number?" Ravi scoffed.

"Beats me too!"

"Okay would you now tell us what she wants?"

"She texted from her number that she wants to meet me. I told her that I don't want to! She warned me to follow her instructions; otherwise, she would talk to Vandana."

"What?" screamed, a shocked Bhanu.

"Shucks!" Raaj amplified his volume in disbelief.

"Exactly!"

They were silently gulping down their beers. "This is tough," Raaj broke the silence. "But didn't she tell you when she had connected on Sofu that she hadn't used her profile pic or her name?"

"Yes, she did. So?"

"So you could have just told her that you don't know who she is, you don't know who Ravi is, and that someone else had just used your profile pic."

"It occurred to me later, but by then, it was of no use."

"Besides," said Bhanu looking at Raaj, "she directly got to the point. I don't think she would have bought that lie from you." Then, turning towards Ravi, he asked, "Can you show me her text?"

Ravi showed them the exchanged texts.

Unknown number – Hi Ravi, how are you doing?

Ravi – Very well, thank you. Who is this?
Unknown number – Mahek. I want to meet up with you.
Ravi – Mahek? Who Mahek?
Mahek – Mahek from Sofu.
Ravi – I do not know any Mahek. Stop playing games.
Mahek – Shall I ask Vandana to allow you to meet with me?
Ravi – Who are you?
Mahek – That is not important. What is important is that you follow my instructions.
Ravi – What instructions?
Mahek – I will tell you when we meet up.
Ravi – Don't do this, please.
Mahek – This needs to be done. I will set up a date and time with you. If you keep on following my instructions, you are in safe hands. Good day!

Both Raaj and Bhanu realised the soup that Ravi was in. "I got totally mind-numbed! I can blow my brain on the wall," said Ravi, "and you guys have any ideas on how I should handle this?"

There was a pin drop silence in the room. Usually, Bhanu was quick in firefighting, but that day, even he was silent. Or was he contemplating?

"Let us take a step back," said Bhanu in a calm, calculating tone. "You were in touch with her a few months ago. And at that time, you had mentioned your real name on your Sofu profile. You had also used your real picture as a display image. She knew your name then. She even knew your face. Is there any way she could have known then that you were going around with Vandana?"

Ravi was processing what Bhanu alluded to. Raaj was in deep thought.

"But hold on," continued Bhanu before Ravi could process it, "had she known it then or had she been a good friend of Vandana, she would have already alerted Vandana! But she did not do it! That means she is not thick with Vandana. Then why is she reaching out to you now? I mean, what could be the trigger?"

"Valid points, *mishti doi*. In fact, I have a few more thoughts," added Raaj. "If Ravi never gave his number to her, how come she got the same? And why is she reaching out to Ravi now?"

"What do you mean?" asked Ravi.

"Raaj wants to say that Mahek has sourced your number from somewhere or someone else." Bhanu clarified.

"Quite correct," said Raaj. "Have you shared your number on any of the social or professional sites?" he questioned Ravi.

"Um…Nope. I am hundred per cent sure I have not left my number on any of the social media sites."

"How are you so sure, Ravi?"

Turning towards Raaj, Ravi answered, "While you guys were on your way here, this thought did cross my mind that she knew me by face, and also knew me by my name, so I re-checked all my social and professional accounts but did not see my number mentioned anywhere. Also, I googled my number. It shows no reference at all."

"Which means..." Bhanu mulled, "that she indeed sourced your number from someone. Ravi, what have you done to her? It takes a lot to source someone's number and stalk them."

Ravi had been tense due to his message exchange with Mahek that had somewhat retarded his ability to analyse the situation. Bhanu's and Raaj's line of thinking was getting him somewhere.

"Bhanu I don't remember troubling anyone so much that they would be so motivated to come after me. There's one more thing. How could she have known that I was going around with Vandana? I mean, I never told her that on Sofu."

Now this was a troubling thought, indeed.

"Ok, let's recap what we know and what we don't. And then you can try and fill the blanks, Ravi. I will list down what we know. Raaj will list down what we don't. Is that a fair start?"

Both Ravi and Raaj nodded.

"So, we know that Mahek is Vandana's colleague," started Bhanu, "and we also know that she knows you and Vandana are a couple. She has your number. You did not give her your number. Your number isn't listed anywhere, so she could not have gotten it from social media. Clearly, and if she hasn't gotten your number from somewhere, it means she has got your number from someone. She knows she can hurt you. She wants something from you. In short, she is blackmailing you for something."

"What we don't know is how she got your number," started Raaj, "or from whom she got your number, why she wants to meet you, we don't know her motive—is it sex, is it money, is it both sex and money? If it is none of these, then what? We don't know how she knows that you and Vandana are going around. She hasn't yet told you where and when she wants to meet you. Now, that could be because she herself might not have planned that far ahead."

"Man, this is challenging," said Bhanu, excited to solve a mystery and also concerned that this was happening in his best friend's life.

Ravi fell silent after listening to all that. He was thinking, contemplating, and reflecting on what his friends had so far analysed. After a few minutes of silence, he said, "You wanted me to fill the blanks, didn't you? I cannot think of anything."

"This is no challenge, Bhanu," retorted Raaj. "This is calamity."

CHAPTER 1

Life Comes a Full Circle (Present Day)

Ravi and Raaj were at Bhanu's place having dinner. The three friends would gather at each other's place once a week so that they could have three meals together. The friendship was thick, and the gravy they were enjoying was even thicker.

"I am a great fan of this chef who cooked this dish. Look at the boneless mutton pieces and the super thick gravy! Huge...and they just melt in your mouth, man! I just love this chef!" Raaj was singing praises for the chef who had cooked the mutton gravy.

"Yeah?" asked Ravi, "Even more than Simi?"

"Oh, there is no comparison to how this chef touches me and how Simi does," the praise for the chef was still running large in Raaj's mind. But the laughter of his friends at his statement made him realise what kind of touch his naughty friends were talking about!

"You guys are *haramkhors*, I swear," said Raaj sheepishly.

"Don't blame us, you big fat oaf. Food is always the first thing on your mind," retorted Bhanu. "Some eat to live, but you run the road the other way around. You take pride in living to eat."

"YOLO brah, YOLO."

"Of course we all YOLO," said Ravi to Raaj, "but we all eat thrice a day, right? With you, every meal is like the first meal of your life. I am glad God didn't make any clones of you, otherwise not just animals, humans would also become an endangered species."

"Yeah yeah, you cannot make love, so all you can do is to make fun!" Raaj gave it back to Ravi, royally and winked at Bhanu. Now it was Bhanu and Raaj's turn to laugh off, while Ravi sheepishly ate the humble pie.

It was Wednesday, so they could not have a long night. After dinner, Ravi and Raaj quickly left.

At 28, Ravi had never been intimate with a woman! It is not that he didn't have a girlfriend now, or earlier. He did. In fact, he had his fair share of lovely and loving lasses. While driving back home, he was thinking of Suchita. They both graduated in engineering from the same college. Not sure what tickled him at that time to think about her—maybe her caring nature, or the fact that she smelled really great whenever they were together? Or the fact that outside his window he could see the rain fall, and Suchita and he used to be more or less together in Bengaluru whenever it rained! Bengaluru rains can be really lovely, any Bengaluru dweller will tell you that. To young college-going lovers staying far away from their homes, surviving on their parents' hard earned money, in a city that had natural air conditioners on from May through October every year, rains were just what were needed to snuggle and snog and feel and hold and move and go wild and, for some, of course, ding-dong!

Ask people living in Bengaluru about it—they say rentals in Bengaluru are high not because of better quality of life or superior infrastructure, or higher-than-average salaries, or lower-than-average crime rates, but because of this natural air conditioned weather supplied by God without charging anything, but maybe expecting a little bit of love, gratitude, and preservation in return. Coming back to rain…well, that's the mating season for most animals, isn't it? Humans obviously do not conform to such rules—they ding-dong anytime two things match—he wants it, which is true most of the time, and she agrees, which is what he waits for, most of the time!!

Ravi's thoughts went into a flashback—the day they bunked a class—a lecture on a boring subject, delivered by a boring professor in a way that would make even the word 'boring', appear more interesting. Most of his classmates had sworn to hang themselves rather than suffer any more of Prof. Saraveshwara

Venkatanarasimharajuvaripeta Srinivasaraghavendra Ramalakshmanaiyah's lecture, but the love for their own lives and the instincts of self-preservation never allowed them to bring themselves to committing it. So while Prof. SVSR was teaching the rest of the class a very boring subject, trying to make it as happening as the poor sod could, Ravi and Suchita were at Ravi's place. Suchita hailed from Tamil Nadu and Ravi was a Punjabi from Delhi. Over the time he had spent with Suchita, he had come to love her filter coffee, and that day was the day when Lord Indra was shedding the combined tears of all the generations of students that had been taught, the generation of students that at that moment were being taught, and the countless generations of students that were yet to be taught by Prof. SVSR. Man, the scientific instrument to measure the volume of tears had not yet been invented, not even by the divine and famed Vishwakarma.

Suchita had lovely, deep, energetic, bubbly, naughty, doe-like, bright, sharp, sparkling, intelligent, expressive, luminous, playful, cat-like, emotional, mesmerising, penetrating, seductive, shining, soulful, twinkling or such eyes! That's what happens when we are in love, right? Everything in our partner looks so extraordinarily gorgeous—absolutely laden with the most loving adjectives! Rain, filter coffee, private confinement, and a promise from his classmates with whom he shared the flat during grad days that they wouldn't be coming back at least till 6 in the evening (the time was 11:00 a.m.) had all the ingredients for a love-filled ding-dong. To top it all, Suchita was looking very seductive, wearing a body-hugging top and denim, and was also looking seductively at Ravi, hoping that he would make the first move(s). Only that Ravi wasn't sure! No, it was not that Viagra wasn't readily available, or that Ravi ever needed that. He was at an age where a young male could easily help himself a few times a day with the capacity to do it even a few more times afterwards. Well, the hands might get tired, but no, that's not the point. The problem was not being endowed with the erectile function, but not knowing what to do with it! And here was a setting where everything was in order—a girlfriend madly in love with her boyfriend, moments safely private to them, the nearest distraction seven hours away, classmate's drawer filled with many varieties of condoms, and the girlfriend being turned on, in very close proximity to Ravi, conveying through her expressive eyes to Ravi to make his move(s). Funny guy, Ravi. He told her—Marriage first!

You know how some guys are just plain lucky! And the world is just so jealous of them. Ravi was one such lucky guy. What do you think happened to him after he said that? It is the kind of moment that boys dream of, beg for, plan (no, they don't plan, they conspire) for, hope for, and pray for. Well, she couldn't believe that a man could say so in such an enticing situation. She had utter disbelief in her eyes and kept on staring at him, wondering whether what she had heard and understood was exactly what he had said. In those few moments, she processed a lot of data—love, commitment, their individual careers, marriage, kids, emotions, intimacy—not necessarily in that order. She gave Ravi such a tight and warm hug that he was overwhelmed.

Suchita and Ravi had ended their relationship mutually, so why was his train of thoughts running on the track of his past? The answer lay in the taunt that Raaj made at him—Ravi could only make fun, not love.

Vandana, Ravi's current love interest, would never allow him anything more than a passionate snog. Okay, really warm hugs as well, but nothing beyond that.

A few days ago, he had received a WhatsApp joke from Raaj:

What is the shortest love letter a girl can write to a boyfriend?
Okay.

Ravi laughed when he saw that, and wondered when his '*okay*' moment would come?

When Suchita, the prettiest lass he had been in love with, offered him intimacy, he had declined citing high morals. Now that he wanted intimacy, his girl declined him citing higher morals. Life comes full circle, they say. This was one circle he just did not want at this stage of his life! Especially with his two besties Raaj and Bhanu teasing him occasionally about his (no) sex life. Quite honestly, Bhanu has had his fair share of ding-dongs, and while Raaj might not have too much to report home in this area, they both scored ahead of Ravi, with Raaj keeping count and Bhanu losing his.

Ravi, a virgin at 28!

At 28, he was a handsome young man who had received advances from some of his lady colleagues as well. But so far, he has been able to resist every distraction to concentrate on Vandana. Vandana was the gorgeous young woman whom he had fallen in love with about two years ago. Well, who the eff remembers these precise dates anyway? Okay…maybe some do, but then most men don't, and Ravi was the *most men* in this department.

Vandana and Ravi met at Raaj's home. She was Raaj's colleague, and headed the content design team for a top-notch marketing firm in Delhi. Ravi liked her quite a lot and the chemical was strong. I apologise, their chemistry was strong. She was such a combination of beauty and boldness that Ravi didn't know whether he should think from the grey matter in his skull or somewhere else, when he first saw her. At first, he thought it was the gin and tonic that was making him think like that, but when he overheard another young man say—"*Kya maal hai* yaar", he realised that he wasn't wrong. Not only did he realise that he wasn't wrong, he also realised that what he felt for Vandana was 'something,' given the hint of jealousy he felt when he heard '*maal*'.

So the question at that time was how to approach this *maal*?

CHAPTER 2

Approaching Vandana (Two Years Ago)

"Raaj…."

"Hm?"

"Raaj, when will you come out? Are you relieving yourself or making yourself happy? God knows you might be doing both."

"Bullshit. What's your problem man? Let me clear my intestines first. Last night was a heavy party."

"O like hell it was a heavy party! Party wasn't heavy, you were stuffing yourself with food. Of course, where else do you think it will go? Into your small stomach only *na*?"

"Shut up, Ravi. I have a big stomach!"

"That is the mix of your hide and the fat around it. Your big stomach is no bigger than your fist!"

"Don't yap bro. I am reading the newspaper, crapping, and smoking all at the same time. Can you imagine the havoc this conversation is wrecking on my concentration? I cannot concentrate on your nonsense too!"

"Is this nonsense? Through opening in your door I can see how strongly you are in love with the needle of a tool that you gloat over…"

"Why are you obsessed with my size? You should be looking at a different biology."

"Can't you rest it for a day and just come out?"

"What's your problem, jackass?"

"Raaj, I want to talk about Vandana…"

"Vandy…?" Raaj cut Ravi short and then laughed his lungs out, "Ha ha ha ha ha ha…"

"Now why are you laughing?"

"Ha ha ha ha ha ha…"

"Bugger, don't tell me you are cooling off yourself thinking of her. *Saale*, I will kill you."

"*Nikamme* you kill yourself. And Vandy is a good friend of mine. I was helping myself thinking of someone else. Man, what a nymph she is. Hold on for two minutes, will you? And just shut up! Do not speak. Do not even think. Your thinking is very noisy too."

Ravi complied. He knew he had no option, for he had to take help from Raaj to reach out to Vandy. '*Big fat oaf,*' Ravi said in his mind.

"I heard that," said Raaj aloud.

"Wha… Ho… How could you hear that?"

"Don't you think that I cannot read your pea-sized brain."

Ravi had to be careful, otherwise Raaj wasn't going to help. And while Ravi would call Raaj a big fat oaf, the fact remained that they weren't themselves an Asterix & Obelix kind of pair. If Raaj was Obelix, Ravi was a smaller Obelix, or Obelix in his teens, if you may call! If on a scale of 10, Raaj was an 8 on size, Ravi would be a 5 as seen by him, and 7.5 as seen by Raaj.

"Bro, listen to me. Vandy is a complicated case," said Raaj, "Her extremely gorgeous looks come with a sharp tongue and an ego that can make Mt. Everest look like a pigmy. Will you be able to manage?"

"Get me introduced to her and leave the rest to me."

Ravi had always been confident about reaching out to good-looking girls. All his girlfriends (two in number) had been stunners so far. The other thing common amongst all his girlfriends had been that none of them had dumped him! It was always mutual. He had tremendous self-confidence, presence of mind, chivalry, ability to strike really good conversations, above-average cooking skills, and the biggest thing that girls of that age would like—he wasn't a leech! He would let them do their own thing.

When he saw Vandana, he had 10,000 guitars playing in his mind at the same time. Maybe a few tambourines too, along with bongo drums supported by clarinets, saxophones, pianos, flutes… do the details of the musical instruments matter here? To Ravi, what mattered was a single meeting with Vandy.

The daughter of an ex-army officer (Armoured Corps), Vandana was indeed a stunner. She had worked hard, all her life, and was extremely disciplined – as per the values taught to her and her elder sister by her father, Brigadier Raghav Sharma. Vandana and Raaj both worked with Stellar Creatives and reported to the same boss. Stellar was a well-established ad agency with offices all over India. In NCR, their office was in the Cyber Greens in Gurgaon. Raaj was in sales, while Vandana was a content designer for both online and offline advertisement. More on Vandana and Raaj for later; currently the issue is how to make Ravi and Vandana meet.

Ravi's leech-like persistence with Raaj in this matter helped. Raaj agreed to set up a meeting between the two, but it had to look like a 'Luck-By-Chance' meeting. It was agreed that the meeting would be held in Cyber Hub in one of their posh restaurants. Raaj would take Vandy out for lunch on some pretext, Ravi would happen to drop in there, and the rest would be easy…or that's what they thought!

CHAPTER 3

Bhanu's Chill Pill to the Hulchul in Ravi's Dil (Present Day)

"Bhanu, do you feel what I am thinking is right?"

"I think it is appropriate," replied Bhanu to Ravi.

"You mean to say that it may not be right, but it is appropriate. Yes?"

"It is appropriate, that's all."

"Bhanu, stop being a lawyer with me! Stop playing with words!"

"I told you, it is neither right nor wrong. It is plain appropriate."

"This is the reason I do not listen to you. You have completely confused me."

"No. You are in this state because of your own silly habits and thought processes. I have nothing to do with it. I am very clear that what you are now thinking is damn appropriate. Hell with right and wrong!"

"*Mishti doi*, explain it to me if it is so clear to you." Ravi would pretty often call Bhanu *mishti doi* (Bengali for sweetened curd).

"You bloody intellectually illiterate, morally confused, language retard jackass. Pay attention! When we talk of right and wrong, we are conversing in the realm of judgments. We are being judgmental towards the judged! Whereas when we speak of appropriate and inappropriate, we are speaking in the realm of practical reality. We are talking about what is suitable or what fits a purpose. Got it now?"

"Only somewhat."

"Ok, let me try again. The context of right and wrong was ingrained in us by our parents, grandparents, and every other person elder to us when we were way too young. This judgment system was just told – that it is so… why something is right and why something is wrong was never explained properly with reference to all the contexts."

"Hmm…" said Ravi, albeit with a hint of not fully being able to understand what Bhanu was saying. Bhanu was a lawyer, so he was good with words. But at times, it was purely magical. And the way the conversation was heading, it appeared that he was getting into his element.

"Bro… understand this. Would you kill a man with whom you have had a quarrel?"

"Now why would I do that just because of a quarrel?"

"Exactly… but if you were in the Army, would you

kill the nation's enemies?"

"Without the slightest doubt," replied Ravi with Punjabi overtone and pride, and military heritage. His father, grandfather, and great-grandfather had served in the Indian Army and Royal Indian Army. His great-great-grandfather and forefathers had served in armies of various princely states of Punjab, or so his father was told by his great-grandfather, and his grandfather was told by Ravi's great-great-grandfather. Basically, they had warrior blue blood in their veins for as many generations as they could remember.

"So, it is not right to kill a man just because of a quarrel, but killing a man who is your enemy is appropriate, not just because you have to follow your superior officer's orders but also because if you don't kill that unlucky jackass, he will kill you. In the interest of self-preservation, therefore, you'll kill him."

"*Vakil* sahib, you are really good with words, and you are really good with explaining. I knew you alone could help me with the mental soup spill that I am in."

"Hmmm…issue sorted?"

"Yes."

"Cool. All the best."

After Ravi exited Bhanu's place, Bhanu quickly called Raaj, "I have explained to him. Seems like he's convinced. He is coming to you. Just see that he doesn't deviate now."

"Done."

CHAPTER 4

Meeting with Vandana (Two Years Ago)

"Ravi…," said Raaj to Ravi over the phone.

"Raaj, I am a bit caught up right now."

"Are you sure?"

"What do you mean?"

"Because I had set up something for you with Vandy...in case it is important for you?"

"*Haramkhor*!" Ravi murmured.

"Boss, you wanted me to fix up a meeting, right?"

"Yes."

"So I have fixed it up. Our standard place 12:30 p.m today."

"Seriously?"

"Yes. And of course, I haven't told her anything about you. So keep it like that. Like we planned, you will have to drop in by chance. I will introduce you two, and then it is up to you…"

"I understand that, but..."

"Don't be such a sissy. You think getting her time is easy? She is loaded with work. On top of that, she was so suspicious when I asked her for lunch. What do you want me to do now?"

"Raaj, that is fine, buddy. But Anup is here in the second half."

"Oh shucks! That oaf?"

"Yes."

Anup Chaddha was Ravi Malhotra's boss who was touring India at that time. He was based in the UK and had roots in Delhi. Sort of a globetrotter, a high achiever and a high-profile VP, he was a tough taskmaster. His plane from Dubai was landing in Delhi at around 4:00 p.m. and he would be in office by 6:00 p.m. Thereafter, he would review Ravi and a few others and then they would all go out for drinks and dinner. Since Anup was coming in, Ravi was working on deck.

"This is complicated. What do you want me to do now? I cannot cancel the lunch."

"Couldn't you have checked with me? I am caught now between the devil and the deep sea."

"O hello... I am not your secretary or something. And you think Vandy is easy to come by? She had ten questions to ask me about this lunch. You know how women are!"

"Ok... 12:30, you said?"

"Yes."

"I'll be there."

"No. At 12:30 p.m. Vandy and I will be there. You walk in at 12:40 or so."

"Done deal!"

Vandana was still not sure why Raaj had asked her out for lunch, but Raaj was able to make her agree by giving her a convincing story. He had told her that he wanted to discuss a few things related to work and career and since he valued her advice, he wanted to speak with her. Also, there was a tricky customer issue that he wanted to discuss. Since they lived in different parts of NCR—Vandana was in Dwarka and Raaj was in Gurgaon—it would be difficult to meet and discuss after office hours given the traffic and all.

At the appointed hour, Raaj was walking with Vandana towards the restaurant. On their way, they were having a little social chit chat about families, friends, schools—you know the basic talk. Raaj was telling her about how naughty he had been in school and colleges where he had studied. Vandana, on the other hand, was telling him about her tomboyish nature at school and how she later learned the value of discipline from her father.

Raaj had graduated in Commerce from Delhi and post-graduated in Business Administration from Pune. Vandana, on the other hand, had done BBA from Delhi and post-graduation in Mass Communications from Pune. They both realised that they had studied in different colleges of the same university. Raaj and Ravi had been classmates in post graduation, but Raaj never got the opportunity to tell Ravi that Vandy was from the same university, and that too from a college that was just a stone's throw away from theirs.

Vandy and Raaj had just finished ordering food when Ravi walked in and was walking past Vandana and Raaj's table with a waiter, apparently posing to see the manager. He purposefully avoided looking at Vandana and Ravi.

Such a dog, thought Raaj and smiled to himself.

"Ravi," said Raaj, "what are you doing here, buddy?"

"Oh hi…Anup is in India today and wanted to sit with all of us in the evening. Since this place is close by, I thought to check with the…" and then he stopped in between, apparently having noticed Vandana with Raaj. "Hi Vandana," Ravi greeted her.

"Hi," and she squinted as if trying to recollect where they had met, "We met at Raaj's party, right?"

"Yes, we did. How are you?"

"I am fine, how about you?"

"I am good as well. Um...listen, why don't you guys carry on, while I sort things out with the restaurant manager," offered Ravi, "then, if you don't mind, I will sit with you folks for a few minutes and leave. I have a presentation to prepare."

"Sure," said both Vandana and Raaj.

Raaj's head was turned towards Ravi even as he was walking away to meet the manager.

"You planned this all, right?" asked Vandana, shaking Raaj's hand resting on the table.

"I planned what?"

"This! The meeting with Ravi! You think I am a fool?" Vandana exclaimed, leaning forward and staring firmly at Raaj.

"Vandy, are you crazy? I don't manage Ravi's calendar. He happened to be around just as we were settling in. In case you haven't noticed, I didn't even invite him to our table. I am here to talk to you about what I have on my mind, but Ravi has invited himself. What did you want me to do? Say no?"

Vandy leaned back. Raaj had a point. Besides, he was a good actor and was able to partly convince Vandy. Boys of course will be boys. These are things they do for each other out of sheer brotherhood.

Vandana had resumed her calm demeanour but did not trust Raaj fully. It was her instincts, maybe! In fact, she had recognised Ravi in an instant, but acted as if she was trying to figure out where they had met. She remembered how Ravi had been looking at her at the party at Raaj's place—with puppy eyes! Alas, he didn't have a tail. Otherwise, it would have been wagging all the way from Gujarat to Assam. And had he not been drinking at that time, he would have been drooling for sure. With all those thoughts still in her mind, she found Ravi walking towards them and pulling a chair.

"Hey guys, deal done with the manager. We needed a

corner where the eight of us could sit down and socialise post work, today evening. Our VP of Sales is here, so…" said Ravi, while sitting down. "I hope I am not bothering you both. If there is something you guys are discussing, I'll get going. Otherwise, I am hungry too."

Raaj did not utter a word, trying to prove his innocence. Vandana, still circumspect, did not have much of a reaction but she offered Ravi to join them for lunch out of sheer courtesy. After ordering for Ravi as well, they all sat discussing. Raaj discussed with Vandy about the issue that Raghu and Raman, a law agency, had raised on creatives designed by their agency, recently. Raghu and Raman were amongst the big five customers of Stellar Creatives. That account was handled by Raaj, and Raaj was reviewed on a weekly basis, by their supervisor, Jamshyd Wadia. Jamshyd was very nasty when it came to customer complaints. So Raaj, in a way, was doing a favour to Vandy by telling her what to expect, something that Vandana acknowledged. That apart, he also mentioned a fictitious offer that he had received from a competing organisation.

Amidst all of this, Ravi didn't know what to do, and how to enter the conversation. Vandana picked up on the fact that Ravi was indeed sitting blank.

"Ravi, I am sorry that we are discussing the intricacies of our work here," said she, "but that is how we had planned this lunch. But you are Raaj's friend. I am sure he must have told you about this offer. What do you think about it?"

'Damn you, Vandana,' thought Ravi. She was clearly trying to stump him here as he did not know the context in which Raaj had set up his own meeting with Vandana. Being an astute salesman, Ravi could think on his feet. So his answer was very different from his original reaction of surprise, "Yeah, we were discussing this yesterday and the day before, but Raaj was pretty much confused whether he should take the new job or not."

"What is the confusion, Raaj?" asked Vandana.

"You," replied Ravi.

CHAPTER 5

Eating Bhanu's Chill Pill (Present Day)

Ravi reached home. Raaj was waiting for him. They had planned to watch a movie that night, and Ravi had all the equipment for it—Bose home theatre connected with a projector hung on the ceiling, focused on the wall ahead making for a 10 ft. wide screen. What else could two bachelors ask for? Of course, a few wheat beers (both of them loved Hoegaarden) and some chicken-shiken.

"How was your discussion with Bhanu?" asked Raaj.

"Lovely. The lawyer cleared all my thoughts. Now I know why he is so bloody rich. *Sala*, he convinces very well."

"What did he say?"

"Raaj honestly, his words were heavy, but the meaning was light. He said what I was thinking was right. He meant appropriate, not right."

"Right and appropriate?"

"No. Not right, yet appropriate."

"How?" asked Raaj, but then, before Ravi could utter a word, Raaj said, "Never mind." Raaj probably did not want to take a chance at all. What if their discussion meandered on a different route? It would then be difficult to convince Ravi again, and apparently Bhanu had done a fabulous job!

"You want me to play the movie or will you change and come?" asked Raaj.

"Let me change and come," Ravi said and went into his bedroom.

Raaj took this opportunity to text Bhanu, '*Fab job vakil sahib, he was bloody convinced. He hasn't asked me anything about it, so I am not touching the topic at all.*'

Brilliant – replied Bhanu.

But my suggestion is, you come here. You know he will have the final apprehensions. - texted Raaj.

On my way. - texted Bhanu.

Ravi came out after taking a bath and went straight towards the fridge to get the Hoegaarden bottles and chicken with green chutney. There was a fast food joint nearby, and Ravi had ordered food on his way home after meeting Bhanu. He had picked up the chilled beer from a nearby liquor shop and stored them in the fridge as soon as he entered his flat. Raaj and Ravi both had spare keys to each other's flats. Raaj was already there when the chicken vendor came for the food delivery.

"Cheers, man!" said Ravi, "To clarity and to appropriateness!"

"Ha ha ha ha, cheers indeed! I am glad you have found a way to beat your FOMO!"

"*Achha,* before we watch the movie, Raaj, how will I do it? I have never done it before."

"What, sex? The way it is done, you innocent pup. Do I have to teach you that?"

"*Array,* no… not the sex. How do I get a girl? Now that my dilemma is over, I need to know the mechanics. And you know I am not in for sex workers."

The bell rang. Bhanu was at the door. "I thought I would join you guys," he said.

"Why not?" exclaimed both Raaj and Ravi.

Ravi and Vandana had met at Raaj's place two years ago. It took Ravi some quality chase before Vandana gave him her approval. The first person to know about it from both sides—Ravi's and Vandana's—was Raaj. Then, of course, many friends and classmates on either side got to know the same. Over a period of time, their families came to know of things and everyone was in agreement. Both sets of parents had mentioned only two things to both of them: "Decide when you want to get married and just be careful that you don't rush into things (read that as ding dong—of course no parent would say it in so many words), since both of you are away from your parents and living in the same city."

Vandana had a very balanced lifestyle. Brought up under her father's discipline, she would get up early in the morning and, on alternate days, go for a run. On the other days she would sweat it out in the gym. She had been into sports during her school, grad and PG days. Vandana pretty much sweated it out with boys in school and graduation—whether that led her to become a tomboy or her being a tomboy led her to play sports with boys is left to anyone's imagination. She would pick up a fight or two with the boys and would more or less beat them to a pulp. Her sportiness, her workouts, and her discipline had helped her develop an attention-grabbing figure and a very commanding presence. By nature, she was ambitious, determined, motivated, perfectionistic, and short-tempered, and she could not tolerate lethargy, nonsense, or anything that was gender-biased.

Ravi, on the other hand, brought up by a disciplinarian father and a traditional mother, was happy-go-lucky, intelligent, good at making conversations, chivalrous, clear-headed (when he did not face a dilemma—he had only two dilemmas, one of which is easy enough to guess), inclined towards arts and crafts, and politically right of centre. In school, he had been the clown of his class. He was also athletic during his schooldays, but had padded up in his grad and PG days. Yet, he looked good and had charm, somewhat—Rishi Kapoor style! The similarity with Rishi Kapoor did not end with the kind of physique alone, but also extended to his romantic disposition.

Ravi was always the first one to kindle romantic intimacy. In moments private to them, they would hug and kiss and maybe do a few things more, but Ravi's traditional upbringing had set a limit in his mind which he found difficult to cross. That was his first dilemma! Six months after they started going around, they had both informed their families and secured their respective parents' approval. And they were committed to each other, which made Ravi think that there was no harm in taking intimacy to the level next—making love—but then, what about the values inculcated during his upbringing, and what about the advice his mother and her mother gave independently to both of them ("Be cautious")? He wanted to take that step, and every time he thought of doing so, his mother's words echoed loud in his mind. This dilemma continued for quite a few months till he finally let his hormones get the better of his thoughts and decided to talk to Vandana about it.

One fine day when he and Vandana had reached the limit of their intimacy, he tried traveling that extra mile, but Vandana held him back smilingly, telling him it was only a matter of time, after which she would be his. Ravi smiled and backed down, deciding to raise it some other time. He didn't just raise it one other time but raised it many other times; however, Vandana's reaction was the same—this much and no further. This gradually led to discussion, debate, argument, spat, quarrel, days of silence, apology, making up, hugs, kisses and then… again discussion, debate.... In the background, of course, Ravi's desperation was getting accentuated by the proud stories that Bhanu had to share about his intimate escapades and the fact that Raaj and Simi used to make love pretty often. Raaj and Simi met through family friends at a common wedding (same old Punjabi wedding story) and were going to get married in a few months. Theirs would be an arranged marriage, yet, their meeting had led to love-making before marriage. This knowledge would screw up Ravi even more—Raaj and Simi being a couple who fell in love after their marriage was fixed and making love, whereas Ravi and Vandana, having fallen in love first, followed by familial commitment, yet to attain the pleasures of intimacy, which were being held by Vandana's sheer determination of crossing the line only after marriage.

And, that was where things turned trickier. Ravi had won over his first dilemma, but his second dilemma had started. Ravi, Raaj, and Bhanu were discussing it.

"Shall I ask Simi to talk to Vandy?" volunteered Raaj, "Women have a way of talking and convincing."

"Are you mad? Are you stupid? Did you loan all the stupidity that ever existed in the universe while taking birth? Vandy will take my happiness left, right and centre if she gets to know that I have told you all this. Have you given leave to your grey matter?"

"I am trying to help you and you are calling me names. Bloody jackass."

Before their argument could transform into unarmed combat, Bhanu intervened, "Ravi, what Raaj is saying is right. Women indeed have a way of communicating that we men can never develop. They can converse without speaking and we cannot. Remember one thing: a man gives love to get sex. For a woman, it is the other way round—she gives sex to get love."

The last two statements shut up Ravi and Raaj. The words were light, but the meaning was profound.

"Having said that," continued Bhanu, "I know it will be difficult with Vandana. She's very proud of herself. You would be robbing her of her pride if Simi talks to her. She would never see this in a good light that Raj suggested all this. She would see this as a breach of her privacy engineered by the very person charged with protecting it."

"So what should I do?" lamented Ravi, "Now even *bhai* cries."

"*Bhai*??" asked a stunned Bhanu, "When did uncle have another male child? You only have a sister, as far as I know."

"Bro, that's what he calls his hand," said Raaj, and

both Raaj and Bhanu burst into laughter.

"Yeah, yeah. Laugh it off, you jackasses! I am getting boils on my hands. How much can a man help himself, bro?"

"We did discuss this, Ravi. There are so many ladies who want to have casual sex. Find them. How else do you think I survive?"

Bhanu had no girlfriend. But with his exceptional social skills, he was able to… you know…

"I hope your cobwebs are sorted," asked Bhanu.

"You are single, ready to mingle. It's easy for you, but I am going around, for love's sake!" Ravi gritted his teeth while he reached the end of his speech.

"Yes, but as you have realised, you cannot have the cake and eat it too, at least not yet." Bhanu then placed his hand on Ravi's shoulder and said, "*Dekh*, you tried enough. You aren't getting chicken biryani at home; you might as well have salad outside."

Bhanu had already turned Ravi in this direction earlier. He knew that all Ravi needed now was a little push in the same direction. This discussion was to him that final push. So now the question was, how to source someone willing to do it? Ravi was clear—no prostitution.

"Haven't you heard about dating apps?" asked Raaj, sipping Hoegaarden. The movie was still not on; this conversation was important.

"Tell me."

"Which world do you live in man?"

"You think I have time? Anup keeps us so busy that the only thing we can do apart from running his errands is to breathe."

"Download the Sofu app. Sofu stands for social fun. And get started," winked Raaj. They started the movie after this.

CHAPTER 6

Meeting with Vandana Contd. (Two years Ago)

"I wonder how, since Raaj has never told me so," exclaimed Vandana.

Raaj, on the other hand, did not know what expression to wear. He was jittery about what Ravi would utter next. Vandana could never be the reason for Raaj to not leave Stellar. She wasn't Raaj's type. Besides, Vandana knew that Raaj was going around with Simi.

"The faith he has in your capabilities to deliver your products and services to the customers he sells to," replied Ravi.

"Really?" asked Vandana, "How come Raaj never shared that with me?" looking questionably at Raaj.

"I told you I have so many things to discuss with you, Vandy," mentioned Raaj sheepishly.

"Yeah, but some time ago, you only mentioned to me how folks at Raghu and Raman were pissed with me, whereas now you are mentioning that my dependability is not letting you make a career choice. I mean…are you sure? It does seem a little far-fetched." Vandana had that seriously suspicious look in her eyes. She had smelled a rat; the only problem was that there were two, and what was going to happen in the next few minutes would make it seem like the restaurant was full of rats!

"Vandana, try as you might, you will never be able to keep all your customers always satisfied, right?" stated Ravi.

"Mm hmm," said Vandana, "you do have a point."

"Just like you two, I am in the services industry—IT sales, to be precise. And we keep facing this day in and day out. Our customers clearly do not expect the sales folks to deliver services, but they expect those who are supposed to, like this Project Manager I know—one customer finds him good, another finds him average, and a third finds him completely useless. What can one do?"

Vandana knew that Ravi indeed had a point. And Raaj was happy that Ravi had been able to divert the discussion somewhere else.

"So, as difficult as it might be for you to believe it, Raaj had mentioned on a lot of occasions that you are one hell of a parachute for him, and that if he doesn't get a colleague like you in the new firm, he may lose his existing customer relationships and might find it difficult to build newer ones," mentioned Ravi.

By this time she had started enjoying her food. "Too palatable," said she, enjoying her morsels, "Ravi, your friend here was telling me that you and he were classmates in your PG days. How was he like there?" asked Vandana, changing the topic.

"Oh, Raaj was always a darling. Sincere, soft-spoken in front of girls, rash and brash amongst us. Teachers would see in him—a cute student. Very intelligent, but scared of exams. A friend you could always depend upon. A majority of my two years in PG were spent at his place. I just love his family—his mother Neelam aunty ji, such a Godly woman, his fauji dad, Brigadier sahib…such an inspiring uniformed officer, his dog, the Great Dane Buzo Khanna…"

"Buzo what??" asked Vandana bursting into laughter while Raaj sheepishly smiled.

"Buzo Khanna…"

"You really called his dog that? I mean, did Buzo have a surname?"

"He had all the traits of Raaj—big, lazy, intelligent, always active around women, wanting to be pampered. You should have been there and seen the way he would stick out his neck so I could caress and pat it. Bloody monster of a pampered, gentle dog. Well, what else would you call that big horse? His hugs would kill us. He was as big as any of us, the ferociously loving beast that he was. Would just love whatever we would cook for him, mostly non-veg."

"By the way," said Raaj, correcting Ravi, "he was a Doberman, not a Great Dane."

"But Danes are big, how can one confuse a dobby with a Dane?" asked Vandana.

"He was big even for a Doberman," mentioned Raaj, "We would jokingly call him a Dane, but he was a dobby."

"Whatever was his breed … his name was Buzo Khanna."

They all laughed again.

"Raaj and I were a team. In fact, there were more of us in the gang, and we used to call ourselves the *Bhaizone*."

"The what?" exclaimed Vandana, slightly amused.

"The *Bhaizone*, our gang's name. There were other guys, too. We were intelligent most of the time, brilliant at other times, but naughty, always!"

"*Bhaizone*? Ha ha ha ha!" laughed Vandana.

"Oh, there is more. The flat we had taken on rent was called *Bhainiwas*. And Raaj's bike was called *Bhaibike*. We even printed a T-shirt with *Bhaizone* printed on it…designed our logo and all. We still have the tee," mentioned Ravi with a sense of pride.

"Really? You were a bunch of creative guys, it seems. But naughty? I never felt Raaj was like that."

"Terribly," replied Ravi, "but if you honestly ask me, I think, between Raaj and me, I was naughtier. We would take *pangas* with our professors—standard stuff!

Bunk classes at times, take some lessons to heart, some to hand, and others to fart."

Fart...? Fart...?? Fart...???? Both Vandana and Raaj were wondering whether they both had heard what they thought they had heard. Raaj knew that Ravi could have a loose tongue at times, but he always took care in front of ladies... and wasn't this a special one? He was trying to chase her. Are these really the words you use while chasing? But Ravi had a lot to share so he went on, and the thought about the fart diffused in Raaj's and Vandy's mind... well, like a fart!

"Good to know about you guys...," said Vandana, and was going to say more but Ravi cut her short.

"That's not all, Vandana. There's lots more. You would of course relate to this... when you spend two years away from home and with friends, there's always lots more," mentioned Ravi, rather mysteriously.

"A-haan," said Vandana, "like what? Love stories and heartbreaks?"

"Yeah, some of that too. In fact, we used to loiter around and become Tigers in front of that ladies' college."

The moment Ravi said that, Raaj sensed trouble. Raaj knew what Ravi was talking about, but Ravi did not.

"Ladies' college? What ladies' college?" asked Vandana.

On their way to the restaurant, Raaj and Vandana

had discussed that they had studied in two different colleges of the same university. Raaj and Ravi post-graduated from the College of Business Administration, while Vandana post-graduated from the College of Mass Communication. Since Mass Com had more ladies than lads, it generated a lot of interest from neighbouring colleges. CBA was the closest college. It's needless to say where the CBA boys were found during most of their break-time. But Ravi was not aware of this.

"Array yaar we had that Mass Com college close to ours. All lovely lasses used to study there, surrounded by some of their sissy male classmates. Bloody jokers, all of them."

"Ravi…," said Raaj softly with a hint of nervousness, knowing fully well what was going to come next, and also knowing very well how Vandana would react to it.

Vandana was quick to interject, "No, let him say it; let's hear him out. I am interested to know."

And that gave Ravi all the encouragement he needed.

"*Kuchh nahi* yaar," started Ravi, "so as I was telling you, we had this Mass Com college pretty close to ours. It had some really hot chicks studying, most of them really looked dumb, if you ask me."

Raaj was getting a little more nervous here…

"They had an air about themselves, as if they were God's gift to mankind. I mean, I really don't know what kind of course was taught in mass communication. Was that even a course? We saw most of the girls there only hanging around, being chased by boys with big bikes and big cars. Of course, some of our classmates too went after them, but the ladies clearly had a liking for guys with money. You should have seen them sitting in the university canteen. Yap yap yap yap yap yap always! Gosh, they would never stop. Very pretty, but totally useless gangs…"

"Hmmm," said Vandana, interjecting Ravi. Ravi hadn't realised that every word he was uttering in sharp criticism of College of Mass Communication and its students, was making Vandana's expression change—change for the worse!

"Oh, we have such hearty stories from our campus days. Leave that. Tell us, what have you done?" Ravi asked Vandana.

By now, Raaj was searching for a pillow to hide behind. Restaurants have no pillows, even a napkin would do. Alas, the one he had was soiled.

"I was a mass com student," said she with a cunning smile, surprising Ravi. She further mentioned the name of the university while standing up from her chair. Ravi was now shocked! And then she mentioned her year of passing out. Ravi was now horror-struck, realising that their year of passing out was the same, and didn't know where to duck. Vandana was now standing tall opposite to him, arms folded, eyes angry, voice raised, but within the limits of civility.

Ravi was still sitting on his chair, his right arm raised towards Vandana. He gestured to Vandana to sit. A sheepish smile on his face, he wanted to request her to sit down and even opened his mouth. But Vandana had other plans.

CHAPTER 7

The Sofu App (Present Day)

Ravi was in a review with Anup Chaddha. There were others from India as well. It was a one-to-many Video Conference. In the last two years, Ravi had become sales head for enterprise customers of Cyber Dynamics. Cyber Dynamics was based in India, headquartered in Noida. Their offshore data centers were in NOIDA, Gurgaon, Pune, Chandigarh, and Hyderabad. Anup was based in the UK and oversaw sales across the globe. Ravi reported to the Regional Director, North. Anup used to conduct his review with his direct reports every fortnight, and once a month he would ask his direct reports to get their direct reports as well. Two years ago, Ravi used to report to Anup directly when the post of regional director was vacant; now, Shalini Bhattacharya was in between Ravi and Anup. So, at the conference from the North, were

Shalini and her two DRs—Ravi (Enterprise Sales) and Salma Khan (Government Sales). Apart from them, other Regional Directors were also present.

Shalini had been fielding Anup's questions pretty skilfully till now. Not that she had expected any problems; the last quarter had gone well, the current quarter was proceeding well, and the next quarter too looked promising. While discussion was on with the North team, their video feed display on Anup's V Con screen was much larger than other regions. This enabled Anup to read their faces clearly. An inattentive colleague could irk Anup to no end. And for some reason, Ravi, otherwise attentive, was focusing on something below his table and seemed as if he was fidgeting with something in his hands.

"Can we all know what is in your hands that is keeping you so busy, Mr. Malhotra?" asked Anup.

"Er…What, Anup?" uttered a surprised Ravi, flustered.

"How would I know? While Shalini is busy presenting plans for this and the next quarter, and the directors of the rest of the regions are intently listening, your attention seems to be grabbed by something that conveniently lies below your table. What is it?" barked Anup.

"I am sorry for irritating you, Anup, but I was expecting an urgent message from a customer; I was only checking if I had received it," said Ravi, bringing up his mobile and keeping it on his table. He had managed to lock its screen.

"Well, we have this review only once a month. I am sure your customer can let you be with me, for these precious few moments."

Ravi knew not to argue, especially when Shalini was also staring at him in anger.

"Sorry, Anup," said Ravi.

But Anup hadn't had his fill and wanted to take it a little more!

"That's easy to say, Ravi. But let me tell you this—I am not very happy with your funnel. While Shalini has the region under control, which goes on to show that some of us do really work to earn our salaries, you are being subsidised by the good work happening in the public sector, and in parts of the private sector where Shalini has control."

Both Shalini and Ravi knew this wasn't completely true, but they also knew that any argument against Anup would only ensure a further downhill tread.

"Anup, I will work on it," said Ravi in a tone of conciliation.

"You would only be doing a favour to yourself Ravi, not me."

"I understand, Anup."

"Do you?"

Before he could say anything, Shalini gestured to Ravi to shut up. And he did. She also gestured to him to lower his gaze, and he did.

After the review was over, Ravi asked Shalini, "What was wrong with that road roller?"

"Well, quite frankly, he was indeed over the top, but you know him more than I do. You know what tickles him and what pricks him. Why did you have to be such a prick?"

"I was being a prick? Come on, Shalini, you know better," Ravi whined.

"What were you doing, by the way? I know that you weren't expecting any message from any customer."

"I had downloaded a game app…was just testing it," remarked Ravi sheepishly.

"Crazy, you are," said Shalini, walking out of the V Con room.

Ravi was of course bluffing her. He had downloaded Sofu and was seeing who all he had matched with. He was sending invites to girls he felt would be good for… ding-dong. There was a whole variety of them, as he would find out in the days to come—professionals on travel, students trying to make a few extra bucks, wives unhappy with their husbands, wives wanting to try something different, professional sex workers, confused ones, those searching for a life partner, those out to cheat lusty men off of their money, those who chose words of English language so obscure that you would wonder what the eff they wanted to convey, those who had put up their snaps, those who had put up their kids' snaps, those who had put up some other women's snaps, those sure, and then those not sure…you know the whole list. But our hunter was sure. He was looking for someone with whom he could explore intimacy.

So he was sending invites to connect with them to see what kind of response he would receive. He hadn't received even one, since this morning. On top of that, that fat oaf Anup had screwed him over, and to make sure an example was set, Anup gave him the lashing when all regions were on the call. Both these things had made him edgy by lunchtime. And after lunch, what happened in the men's room made him a laughing stock. He went to the urinals, holding his future in one hand and possibilities in the other!

"Which tool are you using more, Ravi?" asked a colleague relieving himself in the adjacent urinal, blessed by Ravi's presence.

"I am sure it's the mobile," said the guy relieving himself in the urinal on Ravi's other side.

They laughed like crazy and Ravi was embarrassed. He finally decided to stop looking at his phone and checking it only when he heard a message tone/beep from the Sofu app. But can you picture a dog's tail? It always wags when a basic instinct such as hunger or mating is being satisfied. Humans have no tail and Ravi was no exception to this rule, yet his mind was wavering today. The anticipation, the excitement, the charm, the possibility of a kill, the possibility of a quick fix!

Oi Bhanu.- texted Ravi.
Kya hai? - asked Bhanu.
Does this app work?
Which one?
The one you and Raaj told me about.
Of course it does. I have used it, at times.
I am getting no response, yaar.
Every dog has his day, wait for yours.
As of now it is time to go home.
Ha ha ha.

The day was coming to an end. Ravi wasn't sure about getting a response. He shut his laptop and walked towards the metro station close to his office. He would get off at Sikanderpur and take the yellow line to his home.

Before boarding the metro, he checked his phone again. Still no matches!

'This is a crap app,' he thought to himself and boarded the train full of bodies! Alive bodies. From Sikanderpur he boarded the yellow line to Huda City Centre. Still no message! Still no matches!

Upon alighting from the metro, he booked an Uber sharing cab that is considered very cost-effective. And to his luck, he was sharing the back seat with a very beautiful lass who sat tight-lipped.

'This is as bad as it can get,' he thought to himself, 'first Anup, then the nonsense in the toilet, and now this app. Totally crappy app, totally crappy Bhanu…'

And just then, a sound came, 'ting'—the notification of a match!

CHAPTER 8

Meeting with Vandana Concluded (Two Years Ago)

"Lovely lasses...," reiterated Vandana, "mm hmm. Sissy male classmates! Dumb looking hot chicks having an air about themselves, mm hmm... Girls hanging around with boys who had big bikes and cars... Your classmates went after us, but we girls had a liking for guys with money... WOW! Sitting in the university canteen most of the time going yap yap yap... Very pretty but useless?"

"Listen Vand..." Ravi tried interjecting but was cut short.

"No, now you listen to me, Mr. Know-it-all. I think I've heard enough of you," said Vandana, bending forward and resting her fists on the table, standing in a commanding position. She stood like a matron over a pair of rule-breaking hostelers discovered in the corridor late after acceptable hours.

"Listen," she paused, "and listen very carefully, Ravi. I do not care what you think of the world around you; most of it is due to your ignorance anyway. You are clearly amongst those who gained education at the cost of knowledge! Do you even know what the mass com syllabus is all about—project work, hours and hours of being in the field, trying to work in teams, combined effort, collaborative assignments? But why am I telling you all this, anyway? You are more bothered about the lasses out there. Clearly, your priorities weren't studying, but grapevine, bird-watching, bird-chasing, and all that third-rate, boyish mumbo jumbo."

"You may be right," continued Vandana, "about some girls falling for the charms of big bikes or big cars...Ravi, but some of us were out there to STUDY!"

"Vandana..." protested Ravi.

"Like I told you earlier, Ravi, this is where you listen and I speak. Allow yourself to be enlightened."

Ravi knew that this was actually the time to keep shut and wait until she had vented out her anger and had nothing left to say. Vandana of course hadn't noticed that while Raaj was finding all this a bit awkward, Ravi was somewhat regaining his composure and turning calmer. He had a smile on his face that wasn't mocking Vandy but admiring her. Ten thousand guitars were playing in his mind when he first saw her, remember? Rest assured that a few hundreds of them were again playing in his mind. Maybe this was the result of Cupid's inverse law of falling in love—the more enraged his lady love was becoming, the more engaged he was feeling towards her.

"Did you ever see me around the campus, Ravi?"

"Not that I remember..." replied Ravi, trying to recollect.

"Not that you remember. How can you? When you, I am sure, were amongst the crowd that was either chasing girls, or staring at the boys who had the guts to do so in their big cars or on their big bikes, for I am sure you had neither."

Raaj laughed at this. Ravi actually would never go checking out girls in the mass com campus as he was going steady with Tara, his girlfriend from MBA. But he sure did check out the bikes and cars. And Ravi indeed had no ride; he would borrow Raaj's bike whenever he had to go out with Tara.

Vandana gave that angry look to Raaj that said, 'I'll deal with you at work, later.' Then, facing Ravi, she continued, "You said you really didn't know what was taught in mass communication or if anything was even taught! So here I am in front of you, proud of what I was taught, proud of where I am, and thankful to my alma mater. I hope that gives you an idea."

By now Hari, the restaurant manager, was observing what was going on—a matron was scolding two school kids. He was turned towards their table. He was close enough to see what was happening, but far enough not to hear. Vandana ensured that her voice was low but firm!

"Very pretty, but useless girls? Very pretty, but useless…Can you even begin explaining what you mean by that? Does it not make you sound like a sexist MCP?"

Ravi raised his hands once, trying to genuinely protest. But his action was feeble against an opponent who was formidable.

"Lower those hands," said she, raising her right hand and right index finger, "you must have been on campus for two years, assuming you did not fail either, and of course you mentioned that you do not remember seeing me. Wondered why? Because some of us were out there to make our careers, not to be chased by suitors. And even if there were some who did, how can you paint everyone in the same colour… not that it matters to me."

This is where Ravi thought he had to speak up. All this while he was thinking how to retort to this admonishment he had received. Since all his attempts till now had failed, he had to try something different. So he stood up and, with both his hands holding his ears, said, "Sorry". His tone was firm, his gesture reconciliatory, and his move surprising. Vandana was ready to hear an argument, and was anticipating it and even preparing logic in her mind to trash it. But the apology left her defenceless. She kept on staring at Ravi for a while, in indignation and surprise, her arms folded. That wasn't long though—a few seconds, perhaps. Gathering herself and her thoughts, she turned towards Raaj and said, "I'll see you at work. We need to talk. Do not think I did not see through your 'Luck-By-Chance' lunch meeting!" And she stormed out.

Ravi turned around, watching her figure disappear, and Raaj was staring at her, half-standing, half-sitting, wondering what to expect next.

"You have killed me! You saw her threatening me, you dog?" barked Raaj aloud.

"Relax, Raaj, we will think of something. But I loved her, man. What a fiery girl! I loved her attitude, her performance."

"Yeah, like you are the one who has to face her in the office. Boss, you have no clue of her wrath."

"Of course you can take it for your best friend."

"Dog!"

"Bro."

"Bloody dirty pig. I am not bothered about the argument you two had, but how did she see through our game?"

"She's smart, no doubt. She's much smarter than others. That's why the stiff upper lip."

"She's smart," Raaj mimicked Ravi, "Jackass, she had both of us on a platter."

"Oh, chill yaar Khanne, you get unnecessarily stressed. Let us sit and discuss. I am sure we will be able to cover ourselves. Let's also plan our future moves."

While all this was happening, the restaurant manager Hari walked over to Ravi and asked, "All well, sir?"

"*Unhe aata hai pyaar pe gussa, Hari, humein gusse pe pyaar aata hai.*"

CHAPTER 9

The First Ting Tong (Present Day)

The girl sitting next to Ravi seemed to notice the message tone on his phone, but chose to ignore it. Ravi, of course, wanted to check whom he had matched with, but was shy of opening the app with a lady passenger sitting next to him. The excitement was killing him and he wanted to check what the message was and whom it was from. His mind at that moment was filled with a lot of questions: what would she look like—hot/suggestive; would she be a married woman or an unmarried one; in the images she would have put up, would she be in saree or western or casuals; would she be a working professional or a student or a housewife; where would they meet—his place or hers; would they have to plan to travel out? Ravi was apprehensive of accessing the app with a girl sitting next to him. He decided to check in the cab service app where the lady was getting dropped off, and possibly, after she alighted, he would check the Sofu app. Or, if luck favoured him, maybe he'd get dropped before the lady.

As per the cab service app, he was getting dropped after the lady. The lady's destination was about 15 minutes away, and after that was Ravi's.

'I can wait for 15 minutes when I have waited this long!' thought Ravi.

The cab was moving at a normal speed, and everyone was enjoying listening to the Radio65 music, when...

"What…?" yelled Ravi.

"Ouch…" cried the lady next to him.

At that moment, she was over him; the coffee she was drinking was spilled all over his legs. His trousers were badly stained and legs slightly scalded. The driver had to bring his cab to a screeching halt turning right, as he saw a cow in front of his cab who seemed to have appeared from nowhere. The lady was sitting right behind the driver and Ravi was to her left. The sudden screeching of brakes and the hard-a-starboard turn generated centrifugal forces that flung the lady hitherto in inertia flying towards Ravi. And the same force flung Ravi towards the door. Ravi got it badly from both sides – the door and glass on his left and the lady on his right. In addition, he had coffee over his thighs and the lady's elbow jabbing into his ribs!

"*Abey dekh ke chala* yaar," Ravi yelled at the driver.

"Sir, I am sorry but the cow sprung out of nowhere," said the driver. And saying so, he stepped out of the car to see if there was any damage to the car as he had heard a sound upon stopping. The thud came from the right side of the car. When the driver had taken a hard right, the right front wheel had slid into a pothole and that had created the thud.

While the cabbie was busy inspecting his cab, the lady turned to Ravi and said, "I am so sorry for hurting you, but it was all of a sudden."

'It's okay, I understand you weren't at fault, but the coffee has completely screwed my pants."

"I am so sorry."

"That's okay. I have to only go home; it's good I am not headed for a meeting."

"What do you do?"

"I am in sales in an IT company. You?"

"I am in aviation. I work as ground staff with an airline."

The cabbie was in the cab by now.

"Is everything okay with your cab?" asked Ravi.

"*Haan sahib*," replied the driver with a smile, "*baal baal bach gaye*."

"How come you did not see the cow?" asked the lady.

"Ma'am, my wife was calling on the other phone, I was only disconnecting that call when this happened. Please do not provide negative feedback on the app," said the cabbie, folding his hands.

"I do not have a problem," said the lady, "for I am not hurt much, but it is he," said she pointing towards Ravi, "who is injured. Do not multitask while driving."

"Sorry ma'am, sorry sir, the call was actually important. I thought of dropping you both, before taking the call..."

By now, vehicles piled behind had started honking madly and a traffic policeman was aggressively waving at the cabbie to drive and get lost.

"Ok, please start moving, otherwise these guys will all eat you up. You are between them and their destinations now," said Ravi. The cab started once again.

The small accident had taken Ravi's attention completely off from the Sofu app. Ravi and the lady started talking about how narrowly they had escaped being hurt, with all the traffic moving behind them. They talked about their work, offices, travel routines, etc. and exchanged their numbers. The cab stopped outside her house. They bid each other farewell, and the cabbie turned his cab around, looking at the map for the exit route from the lady's colony.

There was a message beep on the driver's cell as soon as he turned around, which meant another pick-up was scheduled on the way to Ravi's destination. That beep reminded Ravi of the message waiting for him in his mobile.

'I have time to check it before that other pick-up,' he thought and hurriedly checked his app. The girl who accepted Ravi's invite looked good. In fact, she looked hot. Young, less than 25 years of age, fair-looking and tall. She had put up a few profile pictures and Ravi wasn't able to decide which one was the best of them.

In her status, she had mentioned that she was studying in Delhi University, though she did not belong to Delhi, and was looking to make some friends.

'Yay,' thought Ravi, 'finally some luck.' Ravi had a car, and he saw no reason why he couldn't show her around the city and other places too.

'*Hi*,' he sent her a message. Suddenly, the cabbie's phone rang—the person whom he was supposed to pick-up had called and was coordinating with him about their location.

Ravi waited for a while, staring at his mobile, but did not get any response. Meanwhile, the cab reached in front of the new passenger's house. He entered the cab and sat next to Ravi. 'Shit,' thought Ravi, 'can't use my cell again. Let me check where he has to go.'

Apparently, Ravi and he were traveling to the same destination as per the cab service app's map.

'Beat me,' said Ravi to himself.

A trail of thoughts occupied his mind, 'Just when I was about to get lucky. First Anup laid me, then after waiting the whole damn day I got the message of a match. As soon as I got the message, I was in a sharing cab with a lady. Then we met with an accident and now, just when I have sent the message and am waiting for a reply, this guy jumps in. Cannot check the app again; will look awkward. After all, it's that kind of app that needs to be accessed in privacy.'

And he would have no privacy at least till he reached home. Those ten minutes seemed to be the longest minutes of his life. The cab was passing through Hong Kong bazaar in sector 57, Gurgaon, headed towards their common destination. All Ravi could do was fume in his head. And he knew that even with all the fuming there was nothing else he could do.

Meanwhile, the other passenger got a call on his mobile. He received his call and looked the other way. This gave Ravi all the opportunity he needed. He went back to Sofu to check on any updates (he had put his phone on silent once they resumed their journey after the accident). There was no response and there was no new connection as well, but there was something that sent his heart racing faster than Usain Bolt and slightly slower than the speed of light! The app showed that the distance between him and her was less than a hundred metres.

'Hullo… Is she my neighbour? Someone living very close by or maybe on the floor above or below?' He rummaged through her pics once again but could not recognise her.

Meanwhile, the other passenger's call ended and he put his phone back in his pocket. Ravi quickly locked his phone's screen, his mind racing even faster than his heartbeat.

Thankfully, they had just arrived at their common destination. Both men seemed to be in a hurry to leave. The cabbie first concluded the other passenger's trip. That frustrated Ravi even more. The other man was a cash passenger, whereas Ravi was an e-wallet passenger. The cabbie could have easily concluded his trip first.

'Today is so buggered-up,' he thought again, 'how could it get more buggered-up than this?'

Well, Ravi was about to find out.

As soon as the guy left, the cabbie asked Ravi, "Sir, shall I conclude your trip as well?"

"Quickly. I have no time. As it is, you have spoiled my mood and wasted my time," Ravi was in an obvious hurry.

"Sir, where is the need to hurry when I have an answer to your problem."

"What?"

"Sir, do you need girls? Tell me what kind you need and I will send someone over. You can pay me now."

"What?" yelled Ravi. This 'what' was louder, stronger and more surprising than the previous what.

"I operate the account of the girl that you connected with sometime back, sir. I was scared that you might think it was the other lady who was in the car when I picked you up because the location would have shown that you are at less than 100 metre distance from her."

"That's right, why did the location not show me the distance then? Or maybe I never noticed. I just saw it some time back."

"The accident that almost happened with the cow happened when I was organising Reshma for you, sir."

"Reshma?"

"The girl whose profile pic is there."

Ravi was shocked. He just did not know where this day was headed to, or now, the night!

CHAPTER 10

Salvage! (Two Years Ago)

Bhanu, Raaj and Ravi were sitting together.

"Have you seen *Satte pe satta*?" asked Bhanu.

"Yes," replied both.

"*Wo hawa ke thande jhonke ki tarah ayee, aur toofaan ban ke chali gayee.*"

All three burst out in crazy laughter after that. In that epic movie the character played by the legendary Amitabh Bachchan invites to his home the character essayed by Hema Malini, under a false pretext. Hema Malini's character uncovers that pretext and she fumes out.

"I will have to really think of something smart here. Just being persistent with her won't work. She is a smart girl," remarked Ravi.

"Correct," said Raaj, "for she won't view persistence as persistence. She'll view it as pestilence. And please do not ask me to set up another meeting for you. She has already seen through the game."

"What happened in the office after this 'chance meeting'?" Bhanu asked Raaj.

"She gave me an earful. Though she also said that she admired the love I have for Malhotra."

"How did she see through the 'chance meeting'?" Bhanu asked.

"I think our reaction of meeting 'by chance' wasn't convincing enough," said Ravi, "plus Raaj had never gone out with her earlier. She is a smart one, Bhanu, a very smart one. I'd love to woo a woman like her. What a beauty, what brains!" Ravi exclaimed as he said that.

"Do you have any plan in mind, anything whatsoever?"

"I don't know, Bhanu. I screwed up last time so badly that I don't think I can ask Raaj to set up a meeting once again."

"I have said that already, and by the way, Malhotra," said Raaj, "she even asked me to forewarn her if you would be coming to any of the parties or get-togethers in which I invite her."

"Meaning dogs and Malhotra not allowed," quipped Bhanu.

They all laughed again.

It was a serious matter. As serious as what possibly JFK went through during the Cuba crisis. After all, three *chaddi*-buddies were discussing the tight spot one of them was in—matters of the heart! Are matters of the heart any simpler than the complicated games of statecraft that state leaders play? We are talking about two very determined parties here—Ravi and Vandana. Both parties would not back down—Ravi from wooing her and Vandana from shoo-ing him. Raaj could not set up a meeting. He had lost his leverage with Vandana due to this kind of an act. Any patch-up attempts by Ravi or Raaj would only meet abundant hostility from Vandana. Worse, Ravi did not have Vandana's number, and Raaj steadfastly refused to share it with Ravi, fearing the result of Vandana's resolve.

"You are in a tight spot, Ravi."

"Stop stating the obvious, Bhanu. This is the moment when you contribute an idea."

"That is what I am trying to do."

"By stating the obvious?"

"No, duffer! By defining the problem. Once you have a crisp problem definition, finding an answer becomes easy. Ok..." said Bhanu, turning to Raaj, "so let us revisit all aspects, and Raaj, you predict the outcome possibilities since you know her the best."

"The problem statement being Vandy won't meet Ravi?" asked Raaj.

"No," said Bhanu, "The problem statement being how to make Vandana and Ravi meet up. Rest I am sure our bro will manage. Will she meet with Ravi one-on-one if Ravi wants to offer an apology?"

"And who will carry that message to Vandy?" asked Raaj.

"You," said Ravi, smiling and winking.

"FO bro, why does it always have to be me, in your case?"

"Guys, focus yaar," said Bhanu.

"The answer is 'unlikely,'" said Raaj.

"What if Ravi sends her an email?"

"And who will give him her email ID?"

"Oi Khanne, you really think I am that stupid?" Ravi mocked Raaj, "I know your email ID. That tells me your mailing syntax, which is first name underscore second name at company name dot com. So I can guess her email ID and send her an email."

"Ravi, don't do anything like this. You may be smart, but she will unnecessarily smell me behind all this."

"Better smelling you behind than smelling your behind," Ravi cracked up at Raaj.

"Yuck!"

"Hmmm," said Bhanu, "what if Ravi calls her?"

"I am not parting with her number. Don't think such crazy things at all!" Raaj wanted no complications with a supportive colleague.

"But I can always ring the board line."

Bhanu looked at Raaj, seeking his opinion.

"That could work…" said Raaj after thinking for a while, "but there is no guarantee that it will be successful."

"We have to take chances here, don't we?" asked Bhanu.

"Yeah, but I am sure we can think of something better."

The three went into silence, quietly sipping their drinks.

"Is there any other common person between you and her, apart from Raaj?" Bhanu asked Ravi.

"I do not think so," replied Ravi, thinking deeply.

"How about sending her a LinkedIn invite? Upon her response, Ravi can always start a dialogue," suggested Raaj, "and LinkedIn is not a social networking platform, it is for professional networking. It will appear better than sending her an invite on FB or a follow on IG or a connect on Snapchat or a text on WA or a text on TG."

"Good idea, but I doubt it will work in this case."

"What if I accidentally bump into her?"

"You'll be ignored big time," said Raaj. "Besides, how will we plan this? No more accidents or chances, please."

They were all sitting at Ravi's place that weekend, Raaj and Ravi sipping wheat beer and Bhanu drinking his Vodka. All three of them were in a fix. Despite their collective brain power, they were not able to conjure an idea that had a high probability of securing a meeting between Ravi and Vandana.

"Ok… you guys keep thinking. I am going to the loo. My bladder is bursting," Raaj said and walked towards the loo, gulping down the last few sips.

While Bhanu and Ravi were silently sipping their drinks and thinking what next, Bhanu received a text from one of his girlfriends.

Hey Bhalu. (this one used to call him Bhalupratap).

Hey sweetness.

Wassup?

Bromancing with my BBFs.

Tum wahi karo, aur main chali.

Where are you off to?

Ravi was getting distracted by all this texting, "Bhanu, what's this, yaar? Keep your cell down till we get an idea."

"*Array*, it is her. Besides, Raaj is freeing himself of the load in his bladder. Give me a few moments."

"What is she saying?"

"I am waiting for her text."

I am off to Bengaluru tomorrow morning for three days. Some conference. Can we meet before that? Tonight, at my place?

"She is off to Bengaluru for three days, Ravi. She wants me to meet her tonight."

"Will you?"

"Of course."

Sure. I will be in before dinner. He texted back.

Cool.

"Bloody hell," barked Bhanu, "Why did it not occur to me earlier?"

"What?" asked Raaj who, by now, had come back into the conversation.

"Does Vandana travel for work?"

"Yes, she does. Why?"

"I mean, does she travel out to other cities?"

"Of course she does, Bhanu, when we need to make client presentations or some other meetings… Wait!! Are you suggesting that Ravi & Vandana meet at some kind of official travel? You mean Luck-By-Chance Travel Now, huh?"

"Wouldn't that be a good idea?" asked Bhanu.

They were all mulling over it—Vandana and Ravi meeting in a hotel where they are both staying while on work-related travel. A different city, a different place, a fresh setting! That might just work. The only thing left to do was for Raaj to figure out, in stealth mode, Vandana's travel schedule and share it with Ravi. This wouldn't be too difficult, but of course, Raaj had to exercise caution.

After finalising this idea, Raaj went to the kitchen to get some more snacks. They had two rounds of drinks yet to be gulped, and drinks would need support from snacks.

A brainwave hit Ravi, and he picked up Raaj's phone.

CHAPTER 11

Keep Trying (Present Day)

"Ha ha ha ha ha," both Bhanu and Raaj were laughing when Ravi narrated the cab incident to them over a conference call. Raaj suggested to him to keep his cool and keep trying, while Bhanu advised him to possibly make better choices. He, of course, shared shreds of wisdom gathered from his vast experience in this matter.

'How to possibly make better choices on Sofu?' Ravi was thinking while moving around in his apartment when he got a call from Vandana. That evening, Ravi was supposed to pick her up and take her out to the airport since she was flying to Dubai for a three-day conference. The plan was to pick her up from Dwarka, take her to Aerocity for dinner and then drop her at T3. Ravi had time, but was hurrying up. Traffic between Gurgaon and Dwarka could range anywhere from difficult to hazardous on the navigation scale. Of course, between difficult and hazardous, the scale had other ratings like uphill, challenging, chaotic, dangerous…

It took him about thirty minutes to change into casuals—light blue tees, blue denims, brown loafers—and have a very generous helping of 'cologne rich' manly-smelling deo. Blue was his favourite colour and cologne his favourite smell. He had planned to take Vandana out to JW Marriott that day. Once in his car, he connected his phone to his car stereo via Bluetooth and called Vandana.

"Hey, R."

"Hey, V."

"You, on your way?"

"Very much, darling. You ready?"

"Not yet, but by the time you're here, I guess I will be."

"Cheers to that, girl."

"How was your day?"

"Well, Anup screwed me first in the review. Frankly, more my fault than his; I was fidgeting with my phone while the lord was viewing me on VC from a continent away."

"I have told you so many times to respect authority. Why don't you?"

"I was awaiting a customer's important message," lied Ravi, "and he caught me doing that."

"What did Shalini say?"

"Well, she was more supportive, but I know I shouldn't have done that. How was your day?"

"Hey… let's save the conversation for our drive and dinner. Otherwise you'll reach here and I still wouldn't be ready," said Vandana smilingly.

"Sure, V," said Ravi and disconnected the call.

On the way to Dwarka, he was thinking that perhaps for the first time he had lied to Vandana like this. He had of course lied earlier as well, but those reasons were different—he had lied to her that he wouldn't be able to turn up on her birthday only in a bid to surprise her by turning up later with the whole jing-bang. Or when he told her that he would be busy at work whereas Raaj and Bhanu were coming over for a 'boys only' night. Those were sweet lies, loving and caring lies. Even during the boys' night out, they did not do anything immoral, unethical or illegal. Just a boyish get together. But this was a major lie. Somewhere, he had a mild feeling of guilt, which was however overpowered by the excitement of an adventure, of trying something new.

With these thoughts in mind, he reached SkyRise apartments, Sector 23, Dwarka, where Vandana lived. The security guard informed Vandana that she had a visitor. Upon Vandana's permission, he let Ravi in. Ravi parked his car in the visitors' parking and went up in a lift to the fourth floor. Vandana had left the door open in anticipation. Ravi walked in to see that she was collecting the last few things. She saw Ravi walking in and ran towards him. They hugged and kissed each other and she went back to hasten up, collecting the last few things. Ravi was spellbound seeing how breathtakingly beautiful she was looking in peacock blue kameez and parrot green salwar that she was wearing with a chunni that had colours and shades of both the kameez and salwar. The kameez and chunni also had peacock feather designs printed on their borders, and the neckline of the kameez had the same peacock feathers, albeit in a much smaller size. Plus, she was wearing mojaris; light brown in colour with dollops of blue and green blobs. The kajal in her eyes was magnifying the light in them a thousand folds. Her complexion? Very fair! And to top it all, she had maroon matte lipstick and a big, round, maroon bindi on her forehead that had a small green roundel on top of it. Ravi couldn't take his eyes off her.

'My god, she looks so beautiful,' thought he, 'If only she would allow me to…'

"No…" she said as if reading his mind, lowering her face but maintaining eye contact and the 'mischief caught' smile on her lips.

Ravi gave her the puppy look, shrinking his eyes and pursing his lips. Vandana walked up to him and placed her index finger on his lips, looking at him with glowing eyes and a victorious smile. Then, in the next instant, she gave him a very warm hug. Ravi reciprocated the hug with equal warmth and heard her whisper, "Just a few more months, Ravi. Wait na! I will be all yours."

And then they broke the hug slowly. Ravi moved her trolley while she carried her bag in her hand. In the car, on their way to Aerocity, Vandana was narrating how her day went—she was talking about her meeting with a client at their office. The client had been very angry about a mistake that one of her team members had made. She had pacified him, heard him, empathised with him, and committed that in the next billing cycle, her team would give in one man week extra. She was narrating how, in the end, he had gone back like a happy customer. The icing on the cake was when Suchita Ramakrishnan had lauded Vandana in front of the entire team.

Ravi was with Vandana in the car, but in his mind he was elsewhere. In his mind Vandana and he were somewhere in the hills where clouds kissed their feet. Sun was rising and very mellow, as if only to give light and warmth but not heat. The grass around them was all green, the atmosphere heady with mixed sweet scents of blooming flowers nearby. It was as if nature had complimented Ravi's most recent emotion about his lady love in the vision that was created in his mind. They were the only two humans around in this vision—a waterfall nearby flowing into a river, snow-capped mountains in the near distance, the breeze slightly chilly. In his vision, Vandana was wearing the same salwar kameez that she was wearing for real, sitting next to him. In addition, she was wearing a green and blue cardigan with maroon linings. They were sitting on a bench, lost in nature and each other's company, and he was caressing Vandana in the most romantic way.

"Oi…" Vandana snapped him out of his vision, "are you even listening or not?"

"Well… Yes… yes… of course, I am. Why?"

"Mr. Salesman, I have never experienced you this silent. Plus, do you notice where we are?"

Unmindful of the surroundings, Ravi had brought them to Centaur—the prime hotel of the yesteryears.

"OMG," said Ravi, "Brought you to the wrong place; let me turn the car."

"No… I think it's a better idea. Hardly anyone comes here. We can have a quiet coffee. But where are you lost, Ravi?"

They walked in and ordered coffee.

"I am lost in you, V. Madly, terribly, most lovingly. Totally smitten and in full submission. You are shining bright like a Goddess. You are looking so pretty that it feels like I'm falling in love with you once again. I have never found you this beautiful except on that occasion when we first met and you literally had Raaj and me together."

Vandy was smiling. She was also blushing, which was showing in her eyes and on her cheeks that were turning cherry red. "Come on, R, I ain't even that beautiful. I think you are just going to miss me and that's why you are feeling like this." She held his hand and said smilingly, "You really are embarrassing me now. You take good care of yourself. I want my loving boyfriend back to myself when I land back."

"Not so, Vandy. You know I don't lie to you…" Before Ravi could complete his sentence, he heard the ting-tong of Sofu. And Vandana's flight was still a good four hours away!

CHAPTER 12

Reconnecting with Vandana (Less Than Two Years Ago)

Ravi was at work making a proposal for an Indian MNC, Indus Heavy Engineering (IHE), which had a presence in 12 cities across India and 7 more in the US, Europe, and Australia combined. Ravi had worked his arse off to get to this stage with IHE. This was the first time IHE had considered Cyber Dynamics for a service they wanted. Ravi had gotten in touch with them about two years back. Back then, they were in the seventh year of a 10-year contract with a much larger IT MNC, YPN. It had taken Ravi only about three months to have the first meeting with Inquilab Singh. In the meeting he had gotten to know what a stellar job YPN had been doing. Also, since it was a major European MNC with about 45 years of history, going with YPN had been a no-brainer for IHE.

IHE was in the business of making heavy engineering

products for companies—EPC, steel, food processing, petroleum, atmospheric gases, etc. It had four plants in India and three abroad. IHE's contract with YPN had been signed in the era of enterprise data centres that required a lot of on-site support from IT manpower. YPN provided onsite manpower for data centres and end-user support management. It had provided two service desks—one to handle Australia and India, and another to handle Europe and the US. Remote support was still nascent then, so operations were manpower-heavy.

Over the last five years, the world has started moving towards virtualisation, hyper convergence, cloud, mobility, information security, automated support, etc. But as Ravi was realising, no matter how strong the reason for a change, no matter how strong the reason to modernise and automate, bringing in change in a behemoth was never going to be easy. Professional insecurities, vested interests, and low clarity on new technologies were the biggest hindrances. Besides, for the owners as well as the senior management of IHE, if things in IT were comfortable and moving with a reasonable smoothness, they were fine with it.

Ravi had gotten in touch with Inquilab about two years ago on LinkedIn. A few messages were exchanged, and after three months of relentless chase, he gave time to Ravi to meet up. Ravi had been able to strike a good rapport with his customer in the very first meeting, leading to more meetings, thereby learning quite a lot about IHE. The IT team was headed by Isaac Mathew, CIO. He had been with IHE for 25 years now and knew in depth all IT initiatives ever taken by this company. Ajit Mishra was the Chief Information Security Officer, Shakti Singh was in charge of end user support, Salim Ilahabadi was the Head of IT Governance, Ashok Kumar was Data Centre Manager, and Inquilab Singh was Head of Enterprise Applications. Anup Chaddha then, and Shalini Bhattacharya much later, had advised Ravi to leave IHE alone since it was deeply committed to YPN, but Ravi had both the perseverance and tenacity to go after a heavily entrenched competition and a very inert customer.

About two months ago, IHE had realised that their industrial designs were being leaked out, and they had not been able to identify the leak properly. But the commotion that had been created had led the thievery to stop at that time. Forensics was expensive and, more importantly, IHE didn't have the software for it. YPN had suggested a top-of-the-world solution, the cost of which was very prohibitive. Inquilab had shared all this with Ravi. Ravi had since long been pitching in Application Security, Data Centres on Cloud, Digital Rights Management, Data Loss Prevention, Privilege Identity Management, etc. Inquliab felt that it was something that the organisation wanted. Plus, if he could bring in a solution that was cost-effective, easy to deploy and cloud-ready, he would go up a few notches in the eyes of Isaac. But given that the matter was of Information Security, any unsolicited move would bring him in the cross hairs of Ajit Mishra, the CISO. Ajit's relationship with YPN had been rock solid. Of course, there had been ups and downs, but Ajit and YPN had both helped each other in times of professional need. So both Inquilab and Ravi knew that dislodging Ajit wouldn't be easy.

Inquilab had set up a meeting with Ajit for Ravi after finding the right opportunity. During one of the lunches, Ajit had appeared really concerned about information security and had mentioned that YPN is moving slowly on this. It was then that Inquilab had mentioned Cyber Dynamics. Ajit was apprehensive about an Indian IT firm understanding the scale of complication and its business impacts, but Inquilab had been able to softly nudge him into committing time for Ravi.

Ravi had reached IHE's office in Connaught Place in Delhi at the designated hour. Inquilab met with him and took him to Ajit's cabin. Ajit was a burly fellow, about six feet tall. He weighed clearly more than a quintal and was a man of a very serious disposition and good manners. He stood up for Ravi while shaking hands, but the handshake came without a smile. Ravi immediately understood that this had to be a no-nonsense meeting. If he failed to make an impact now, re-entry into this account would be tough, and Anup would have his arse anyway, having told Ravi to stay away from this account.

The discussions were indeed heavy, completely technical. Ravi pitched his company well, answered most of the queries, took note of the concerns that Ajit had, took down points that Ravi could not address and promised to do a follow-up meeting along with a technical expert. After the work discussion went to Ajit's taste, the atmosphere lightened up. Tea and snacks ensued.

Ajit's phone was on the table in vibration mode. They were still in the meeting, almost concluding their discussions, when the call came. Ajit had clearly synced his phone numbers with his email profile, for the image of the caller appeared as the call came. Ravi saw the image, recognised the caller instantly and was very excited to hear what would happen next! In the heart of his heart, he was hoping that Ajit would take the call in front of him and not disconnect or ignore it.

Ajit looked at his phone and a smile appeared on his face—the smile foxed Ravi but gave him the hope that he would take this call. Ajit picked up the phone, still deciding whether to accept the call or not and kept on his banter with Ravi and Inquilab.

Ravi's heart was pounding blood in his veins at the speed of sound now! He could feel and hear sonic booms emanating from his heart, bursting in his ears like a few atom bombs going off together. More importantly, Ravi wanted to know how the caller was connected with Ajit Mishra and how Ravi could derive any help from the situation that he was in.

Ajit, almost in two minds, wore an apologetic look on his face and, looking at Ravi, whispered, "Family, I have to take this call."

"Of course, sir, please go ahead. Do you want me to step out?"

"No, no. Be here." Saying this, Ajit answered the call and said, "Vandana *beta*, how are you?"

CHAPTER 13

Maybe Jackpot (Present Day)

Ravi was in a terrible fix. His love was sitting in front of him, in her most mesmerising version, and Sofu was doing ting-tong on his phone!

'This is going to be my most difficult conversation ever,' thought Ravi to himself, 'I so want to spend all this time with her, yet I want to see what's in store for me in the app. And her flight is a good four hours away.'

"So, what are you going to do in the next three days, R?" Vandana's question snapped Ravi out of his mindspace back to the restaurant of Centaur.

"The same that I'd do any other day, V. Why would these be any different, except, of course, for the fact that I am going to miss you badly and madly." Ravi was smiling as he said that out of genuine love for Vandana. And Vandana knew that he loved her deeply and madly. Every time either of them went away on travel, Ravi stayed in touch over text. In the beginning, the texts had come in at a ferocious frequency. Vandana had to ask him to text less lest he/she miss out on work-related developments. Being a working couple, they'd get on call once in a day whenever either was traveling and share with each other how they spent their day at work or otherwise. There was so much they used to share, right from the first tea or coffee of the day to the last morsel/drink they had.

What took place between Ravi and Vandana was the same thing that happens with young lovers: long hours of texting, chatting, calling each other, especially after the day is over. Discussions that go right up to 2 or 3 a.m. and then waking up late in the morning realising the time lost. Smiling to themselves remembering whatever pieces of the conversation they can from the last night and looking forward to the next lovey-dovey conversation.

"That apart, everything else is going to be the same. There are a few deals that we are going after. Will try and close them," Ravi said, looking at the waiter who was bringing them coffee and sandwiches.

"Yeah, all the best! You know I do not enjoy these conferences much, R."

"Come on... you are off to Dubai. Shop till you drop. You women love shopping."

"That's what I am going to do. Have squared it off with Ramakrishnan too."

"Who's Ramakrishnan?"

"My new boss. I told you na, Jamshyd had resigned a few months back. Now it is Ramakrishnan."

Ting-tong.

Ting-tong.

Ting-tong.

The Sofu app cried out thrice. Ravi didn't know whether these were three different connects, or three messages from the latest connect, or three reminders of the unchecked new connects that had happened when Ravi was driving into Centaur.

'Gosh, four hours!' he thought again… 'Oho, it is 3.5 hours!' he thought, checking his watch. 'Oh, bloody hell… Why did I not think of it earlier; it's just 30 to 45 minutes… Her flight is 3.5 hours away. I have to drop her much earlier than that. That thought gave him excitement and his brain started secreting dopamine, otherwise known as the molecule of happiness.

"Who's messaging so much, Ravi?"

"Must be one of my friends' groups. You know all these groups; as night approaches, they become awake. Chuck all that. Let me put the phone on silent. I will check messages on my way home."

"No, you will check them once you reach home. No checking messages while driving."

"Ok, milord! By the way, have you planned what you will shop for?"

"Nah, I will go there and see."

Their conversation continued over coffee and sandwiches. All the while, Ravi had Sofu on his mind. After the first experience, he had been praying to get something more substantial. And he had been wondering whether the ting-tongs were more substantial this time around. Vandana had told him where they would be putting up and the fact that it was going to be a relaxed conference. Check in on Day 1 and leave for a city tour to begin with. Conference followed by dinner in the second half. Day 2 was going to be a conference in the first half followed by free hours post lunch. Day 3 was meant for concluding remarks followed by a guided tour to some prominent malls, and a drop to the airport. All this had gone way above Ravi. The dopamine in his mind was keeping him super excited and focused on ting-tong.

Then, Vandana got up and proceeded to the ladies' room. 'Mauka mauka,' the song that had been played during the last two cricket World Cups, played in Ravi's mind. Ravi unlocked his mobile as he saw Vandana walking away and he hurriedly opened the app.

"Sir," said the waiter coming close to Ravi, "anything else?"

"No," said Ravi hurriedly without even looking at the waiter, "get the bill please."

Opening the app, he saw that he had connected with two ladies—Sana Khan and Aditi Saxena. Sana had left two messages. He read those and closed the app.

'Yes... Finally!' thought Ravi.

By the time he settled the bill with the waiter, Vandana had come back to her seat.

"Time to go," she said, looking at her watch.

"Yeah. Let us walk to the parking area."

Close to the car, Vandana gave Ravi the warmest hug and the most passionate kiss. Ravi's brain had already been secreting dopamine, but this hug and kiss was a massive top-up. Some part of his brain was receiving heavy showers of dopamine. He was on such a high he just wasn't letting Vandana go. Vandana held Ravi by his arms, withdrew herself and exclaimed very softly, "Baby, if you hold me like this, how will I ever go?"

"Babe," said Ravi, complaining.

"Let me come back and we will spend time together."

"Even then you will leave me wanting for more," winked Ravi.

They both laughed, sitting in the car. From Centaur, T3's departure area is about 10–12 minutes of drive, accounting for slow speed at CISF post. Close to the departure gate, Vandana started looking out for other colleagues and spotted them without difficulty. It was a group of twenty folks leaving for Dubai. And a group as large as that was also as boisterous.

"There they are," said Vandana, turning towards Ravi. She saw him sporting a very serious look on his face looking at the group.

"What happened, R?"

"You said Ramakrishnan was your boss," said Ravi, looking at Ramakrishnan standing about 50 feet away with the group.

"Yes, Ramakrishnan. That's what we all call her."

"You never told me it was Suchita Ramakrishnan."

CHAPTER 14

It's Tough to Crack Vandana (Less Than Two Years Ago)

"Raaj, did you do this?"

Vandana was furious. At 11 in the morning, she was standing at Raaj's desk, holding her phone in her right hand, flashing it right at Raaj's face. Raaj squinted his eyes looking at the phone but couldn't make out anything as the phone's screen went blank.

"I did what?"

"Don't act innocent. Look at the screen."

"Look where, Vandy? The damn screen has gone blank."

Vandana turned the phone towards herself and realised that Raaj was telling the truth. She unlocked the screen and went to her call logs.

"Look at the call logs. Look at the very first number. Do you understand now?"

Raaj looked at the number and told her that he

didn't recognise the number.

"It is Ravi's, Raaj. Now who else but you could have given him my number? Why would you do that?"

"Vandy, no. And you got to trust me. I did not share your number with Ravi. He is my BBF, but that does not mean that I share your number with him without asking you. I'd never do that. What happened? Did he reach out to you?

Vandana kept looking into Raaj's eyes, trying to ascertain the truth. Her father used to tell her and her elder sister when they were kids that people's lips can lie but their eyes cannot. So all you've got to do is read their eyes with all the skill.

"Vandy, come on, you've got to trust me. Tell me what happened. If Ravi has done anything silly, I will roast him myself."

After concluding that he was indeed telling her the truth, she gestured to him to follow her. They went to the meeting room where they both sat down and Vandana shared, "I got a call from Ravi about ten minutes ago."

Raaj's jaw dropped wide open.

"He wanted help. The cheek of this guy!"

"What help?"

"Ajit mama is the CISO of Indus Heavy Engineering. Apparently, Ravi happened to be in a meeting with Ajit mama when I called Ajit mama. Ravi saw my pic flash on Ajit mama's phone, and just before taking my call,

Ajit mama told him that this call was from a family member. He didn't call me immediately after the meeting, but he called me today. So I was wondering if you gave him my number."

"I didn't, Vandy, you need to trust me."

"I do now. Then how, how?"

"Right now, even I don't know, but I will find out from him."

"And will you let me know?"

"Vandy, you're putting me in a spot!"

"Why would you care if it isn't you that parted with my number?"

Raaj paused for a while, and then, after giving it due thought, said, "Vandy, you are right. But he's my BBF. I cannot be stabbing him in the back, just like I wouldn't stab you. At the same time, you've got to understand that he's not your adversary or enemy. He's a very determined and resourceful fellow whether it comes to his professional or personal pursuits. Keeping your anger aside, won't you admire him as a professional?"

"You think so?"

"Think objectively, Vandy. He knows he messed up with you the first time. Yet, when he saw that you were somehow connected with his customer, he called you. That takes courage."

Vandana cooled down and thought about what Raaj was saying. "Thinking like that, I think what you are saying makes sense, Raaj. His position was awkward. And yes, the way our last meeting ended I never thought he'd have the courage to call back. And yet he called up."

"That's what I was saying, Vandy. But leave courage aside for a while. I am wondering how he got your number."

"Raaj, I hate him for it. But then, as you said, he is a resourceful chap."

"What did he say when he called you?"

Vandana smiled when Raaj asked that and then narrated the conversation to Raaj, which opened as follows:

Ravi – Hi, Vandana, this is Ravi.

Vandana – Ravi who?

Ravi – Raaj's friend, and please do not disconnect the call. I need a big help.

Vandana – You will have to come up with something a lot better than that. How dare you...

Ravi – It is about Ajit Mishra. Do you think we can speak with tempers under check?

Curious, Raaj asked, "My God, he straightaway jumped to the point?"

"Honestly, Raaj, I do admire that rascal's guts now that I am narrating the conversation to you."

"So, what happened next?"

"He told me about the meeting he had with Ajit

mama and how perseverant he had been in tracking them down for two years—all his trysts with Inquilab. And not to miss the jibes from Anup about IHE. I don't know, but if all you sales guys are like this, then your job isn't easy…"

"It is not easy at all, Vandy. And I am glad you are saying so. It takes years and years to build your name as a sales professional and gain the market's trust and respect. Till then, we are beaten around by our organisation, customers, and others in the value chain alike. So what did he want with your mama ji?"

Vandana smiled, "Actually, I had thought he'd want me to put in a word. But he surprised me by not asking for that. He wanted to know more about mama ji—his likes and dislikes, professional background, the story of his growth, the kind of person he is, etc. so that he could draw a mind map about mama ji and gain professional closeness to him."

"See, I told you. Ravi is a consummate professional. When he decides to go behind something, he plans it big time, tries to gather all information about a person no matter how insignificant as it may appear. You know, even I have learnt a thing or two from him. He is so close to some of his customers that it's like he knows what happens inside their bedrooms."

"What? Really? And how would you know that? I mean, he broke their trust? I mean, they must have confided in him, and he shared all of that with you just because you are his best friend? That's not a good ethic, Raaj."

"Vandy, why are you ever so ready to burn him? I didn't say he knows what happens inside their bedrooms. I said it's like he knows what happens inside their bedrooms. It's a metaphor, Vandy. Why are you so biased against him?"

"He is such a boastful character, Raaj. I remember very clearly the first meeting. What was he trying to prove in that meeting?

"What are you trying to say, Vandy? What are you accusing him of?" asked Raaj, angrily.

Vandana, taken slightly aback at his reaction, retorted, "I don't know why you are getting so worked up."

"Why am I getting worked up?" asked Raaj angrily and, getting up, continued, "You keep on accusing my friend for no crime he committed and you want me to remain silent? Vandy, what's up with you? You are normally pretty logical with things. In this case have you flushed out all logic?

"Raaj, you know he was being disrespectful that day."

"Not to you in particular, Vandy. Besides, he had no chance to know that you were from Mass Com college."

"That apart, Raaj, just because he didn't know that I was from that college he cannot talk nonsense about it, and you know I have a point."

"Yes, you do. I give you that. I know all of it went horribly wrong that day, but please understand that he was trying to impress you?"

"What? How? Why?"

"You have no clue the lengths to which he went for that meeting with you at the restaurant."

Vandana remembered something, but kept shut as she wanted to know it all before reacting. And to know it all she had to keep Raaj in play without letting Raaj know about it. "What are you talking about, Raaj?" she feigned being flattered and surprised at the same time. Raaj had little or no clue what was in store for him.

"You guys first met at my place. Remember?"

Vandana nodded.

"That was when he fell for you and had multiple discussions about you with me. *Dimaag kha liya tha usne mera.*" Raaj then narrated the conversation Ravi had with him while Raaj had been in the loo, skipping the expletives. Raaj was continuing in an agitated and excited state of mind. He was partly angry because Vandy thought low of an otherwise nice guy and Raaj's best friend, and partly because she didn't know the extent of planning that Raaj himself had done to set up the meeting in the restaurant in Cyber Hub.

After Raaj was done explaining everything, Vandy spoke up, "Now you listen to me, Raaj Khanna. You are BBFs of each other, I admire that. And while your friend is a perseverant, determined, gritty go-getter as you tell me, you are no more than one foul, lying git."

"What? How dare you, Vandy?" Raaj was completely taken by surprise, not knowing Vandy had smartly made him take off all of the onion's peels.

"How dare I? How dare I? You remember I asked you many times whether the chance meeting was not by any chance but planned, and you never admitted. Now you tell me that it indeed was. I was so right."

It now dawned on Raaj that Vandy had played him.

"You guys planned it to the tee. What did you say—he's a very determined and a resourceful fellow whether it comes to his professional or personal pursuits."

CHAPTER 15

Maybe Jackpot or Major Confusion (Present Day)

"You know her?" asked Vandana.

"Doesn't the name ring a bell, V? Try and recollect."

Vandy had to dig deep into her memory. "OMG. Is she the one I think she is?"

Ravi nodded.

"Ha ha ha ha ha ha. Then I am happy that I am taking her with me to Dubai." Saying that, she walked out of the car and took her luggage out. Ravi also stepped out to fetch the luggage trolley for her. By now Vandana had waved to her troupe. The troupe waved back at her. Most people in Vandana's team knew that Ravi and Vandana were a couple. And this was a young team, so when they all waved at him, they did so with an excitement of waving at a colleague's beau. It gathered Suchita's attention. She focused in the direction where

Vandana was, and realised the excitement was because of the man next to her. After a moment's pause she recognised Ravi. By now Vandana was giving a goodbye hug to Ravi. Suchita gathered what was going on. She chose to just smile at Ravi and give him a light wave. After this, she turned towards the entry gate.

"R, you'll wait for me? Miss me?"

Ravi and Vandana were in the final chat before she left for her flight. With the 'miss you', 'love you', 'take care' over, Vandana started walking towards the entry gate as well. The airport guards were gesturing aggressively to Ravi and others who had come to drop their loved ones, hated ones, and others, to move away. Ravi managed to stay till he saw Vandana go inside the entry gate, turn towards him for a final wave, and proceed into the airport. Ravi hurried back to his car and drove away. Since the airport was a zero-tolerance zone, he did not want to take any chances checking his mobile till he was at a safe spot. He sped towards Aerocity and parked his car in one of the lanes. He had been lucky today with a few matches. Sana, Aditi, Sabia, Mahek and Samiksha. These were messages that he had received almost an hour to an hour and a half back while he was with Vandana.

'Jackpot!' thought Ravi.

Sana was out in the face with her profile on the Sofu app, mentioning very clearly the rules of engagement.

1. Time wasters out of my way.

2. Chat with me on my IG handle @kamini_hawt. I use Sofu only for establishing a connection, not for chat.
3. My e-wallet number is mentioned below. Pay 1,000 bucks to show your seriousness and then WhatsApp me on the same number.
4. Do not expect any answer till you pay.
5. I share my naked pics when you pay. For anything more, you pay more.
6. Short service: 6,000. Full night: 15,000.
7. Be decent, be chivalrous and be a man.
8. I get, I give!
9. Mutual respect

'Wow,' thought Ravi, 'how bloody professional. And the pics look good too. In fact she is sexy. She's hot. Looks like a good deal for someone who is into paid sex, but not for me. Let me quickly check others while I delete this one.'

Meanwhile, he got a text on WhatsApp from an unsaved number, the notification of which appeared on top of the mobile screen. Really not wanting to be bothered right now, he ignored it. Sofu was solid jackpot today.

Sabia was an airhostess with a foreign airline. She was based in Mumbai and would fly to foreign cities from Delhi or Mumbai, based on the flight her airline took. She had put pictures of her in uniform and pics of a lot of foreign locations. On her profile was the message: 'Hey guys, I am in Delhi for tonight. Flying off to Europe tomorrow afternoon. Anyone care to show me around the city? A good conversation over a cup of coffee or cocktails could take us to clouds. Text me.'

Ravi was wondering whether he should text either of them or both of them before moving onto the next messages, or go straight to the next messages. The greedy pig in him made him go straight to the next messages.

Mahek had a beautiful picture. And her DP (display picture) carried a quote – '*Leaping without looking at what lies ahead takes guts. Are you ready?*'

'Man… she is daring AF!' thought Ravi.

More WhatsApp text notifications came from an unknown number. Ravi continued to ignore them and moved to Samiksha. Samiksha was a lusting man's sweetest and horniest dream come true. She had pics, lots of them revealing a lot about her barring the face and the barest essentials. Her pics had left very little to imagination, but whatever was left to imagination would transport an aspiring man into the very plane of his imagination. 'Try me' – was her status.

Aditi had mentioned that she was looking for a serious relationship leading to marriage. Ravi decided not to go ahead with Aditi at all since that was not what he was looking for. He was clear that he would marry Vandana, so why waste someone's time?

Three more messages from an unsaved number made Ravi take notice. 'Let me check,' thought he. When he checked, his heart reached his mouth. He just didn't know where to start – Sana, Aditi, Sabia, Mahek, Samiksha, or… Suchita!

***

Meanwhile, a chat was developing on Sofu between a man somewhere and a woman somewhere else.

A man somewhere – hey, thanks for accepting my invite.

A woman somewhere else – cheers dear. Thanks for sending me one.

Man – what do you do?

Woman – you really wanna know or you are just building a conversation?

Man – what do you think?

Woman – can't say. So many creeps on this app.

Man – and you're sure I ain't one of them?

Woman – can't say. You have been behaving well till now. Maybe you'll turn into a creep later.

Man – maybe!

Woman – yes. Maybe.

Man – so what do you do?

Woman – can that rest for now? There are so many other things to discuss.

Man – yes there are. What do you want to discuss?

Woman – I'd like to see your imagination here. Let us see whether you are indeed different.

Man – and who will be the judge of that?

Woman – me of course.

Man – ah the advantage you women carry.

Woman – of course. There are so many of you chasing so few of us. Come on, impress me.

Man – must you make it tough?

Woman – are things that come easy worth having?

Man – maybe worth having, but not worth relishing and enjoying.

Woman – we're reaching somewhere now. And I must say you are proving yourself to be different till now.

Man – huh ☺

Woman – come on now tiger, do not give up.

Man – wasn't giving up 'Ms. Hard-to-come-by'.

Woman – sarcasm?

Man – isn't that your first name?

Woman – oo, anger?

Man – no, mocking you.

Woman – wasn't lost on me. But come to think of it practically boy, will sarcasm or anger take you anywhere? I am telling you I am just about beginning to like this conversation and we will reach somewhere, I am sure. Just don't ruin it like other jokers.

Man started thinking, 'I'll have to be smart and patient with this one. This could be good. This could be worth it.'

Man – ok let us talk about something else.

Woman – anything but personal details darling.

Man – where are you?

Woman – India.

Man – come on! Don't you mock me now.

Woman – he he. Two can play the game.

Man – Ok what are you up to right now?

Woman – chatting with you silly.

Man – listen, I respect you and all, but I am trying to build a conversation here, and if you aren't game lemme know.

Woman – I told you, I was looking for your imagination.

Man – my imagination can be wild.

Woman – try me.

Man – what if it agitates you?

Woman – well, what if? That's the risk you carry, not me.

Man thought to himself, 'she's bloody smart. I got to give her that. In all this I am getting agitated, but I am also enjoying this. Clever woman, she's unhinging me. Let me throw it back at her.'

Man – that's true. So let me not talk about my imagination as yet. Let me be guided by your choice. What is it that you'd wanna talk about?

Woman fell silent for a while. Man started wondering to himself what was happening. He had even met with someone cerebral on this app after a long time. Finally, here was a lady he'd love to meet, if not flip-flop. While he was thinking so, he got a message.

Woman – what do you do?

Man thought, 'Now she's letting her defences a little low.'

Man – and you wanna know that mutual basis?
Woman – means?

Man – I just asked you the same and you buggered me off. So if I answer this, would you quid pro quo?

Woman – ok.

Man – I help people make their writing impactful.

Woman – you edit?

Man – You bet.

Woman – I should have guessed.

Man – how about you?

Woman – I repair.

Man – mechanic?

Woman – no.

Man – engineer?

Woman – no.

Man – what do you repair?

Woman – complicated stuff.

Man – you sound like 007.

Woman – ha ha, I do?

Man – of course, you have answered my question and I am none the wiser now than I was before you answered it, about your profession.

Woman – you are a smart one mister. You are the wordsmith.

Man – I concede. You are smarter.

Woman – I like that.

Man – I'm happy that you are happy, but I do not think you are in the right kind of mood at this moment.

Woman – what mood are you talking about?

Man – madam, this app is not for classifieds. This is for consenting adults. Now if you are one, we can take it ahead, otherwise let us drop it here.

The woman was thinking, 'this dog is smart. And he's guessed it right – I was boxing him, but he's thrown the box back at me. Let me give him a bone… who knows, I might get a good boner. ☺

Woman – ok I will come clean. I'm here in Delhi, but about to get on a flight to Dubai. It's a conference I can do without, but hey, there's only as much as you can control. Let's stay in touch. I will surely want to meet you once I am back.

CHAPTER 16

Vandana is Nowhere Near Wooed and Now Raaj is Angry (Almost Two Years Ago)

Raaj was not angry. He was furious. In their meeting at his place Ravi confessed in the presence of Bhanu that he stole Vandana's number from Raaj's phone. Raaj erupted with the majesty of a volcano that had been activated after a long period of dormancy.

"This is how you repay my loyalty and kindness? Dirty bugger, mangy dog."

Ravi remained quiet. All three of them were sipping beer, which was nowhere close to chilling the conversation between them.

"Vandy had me left, right, centre, top and bottom. And I kept on defending you. And look at you. A piece of work you are! You backstabbed me?"

"Khanne, yaar, don't be so melodramatic," Bhanu intervened.

"You shut up, Bhanu. You always tend to take his

side when I am having him." Then, turning towards Ravi, Raaj asked, "Do you have anything to say?"

"Everything is fair in love and war. I backstabbed you, I am sorry. But hey, look at the bright side, I did not stab your behind," Ravi said, winking.

Raaj's rage was now uncontrollable, "Yeah, it is your love and war, and I am the one taking all the bullets in my behind. Bloody idiot. I am on the verge of getting my professional and personal relationship spoiled with her and you are quoting metaphors. Why did you have to call her at all?"

"Raaj, you know I only called her to check about Ajit Mishra and nothing else."

Raaj was about to erupt again but quickly sensed that, Bhanu interjected with a question of his own, "So did she help? I mean, did she give you any answer?"

"It wasn't a very tasty conversation. But I can tell you that if there is fire, it is in equal amounts on both sides."

"Do explain," Raaj said angrily.

"Yaar, *dekh*. I had taken the number from your cell, and…"

"Stop your BS. You have to tell me first: how and when did you take her number from my cell? How do you know my screen password?" Raaj interjected sharply before Ravi could begin to narrate how the conversation between him and Vandana went.

"You remember that day at your place when we

were all planning how to fix me up with Vandana?"

"Yes," Bhanu and Raaj both answered together. But Bhanu was smiling because he knew what had happened, and Raaj was inquisitive because he did not know what had happened. What Bhanu did not know was that Raaj had caught him smiling just now from the corner of his eye. It was Bhanu's turn to get a tongue-lashing from Raaj.

"Bhanu, you mangy dog, why are you smiling? Am I the only doofus in this room who does not know how this happened? You also know how it happened?"

Bhanu looked at Raaj. Raaj was exceedingly angry at being left out of this little secret. He felt like punching both the guys on their noses, but was controlling his violent self. Bhanu decided to just nod in the affirmative without saying anything.

"Wow, now this is something. Both my friends knew and executed their dirty plan without bringing me in. Dirty dogs. Mangy dogs."

"Ravi, check if there's some more beer in his fridge," said Bhanu.

"Shut up! No one will move till I get to know what I need to know!" yelled Raaj.

"In fact, Raaj," said Ravi, "this is exactly how it had happened. You had gone to your kitchen to fetch a few drinks, and before you came back, I unlocked your phone, took Vandana's number and saved it."

"How did you know my screen password?" asked

Raaj, alarmed.

"It is Simi's birthday!"

"I know what it is. And of course you know it, too. I am asking how did you know that is what it is, you bloody oaf."

"Khanne, cool down, buddy, cool down. I will explain everything. No more secrets. So till that day I did not know exactly what your password was, but I just took a chance. On many occasions I had seen you pressing this 4-digit number, the first two digits of which were the day of her birth—01. Since it is a 4-digit number it was only logical to guess that the next two digits represent the month. I took a chance and it worked."

Before Raaj could say anything in reaction, Bhanu picked up the strings, "You said both sides are on equal fire…"

"Ah, yes," said Ravi, and turning towards Raaj, he asked, "can I explain, my lord?"

Raaj nodded and added that he'd like to hear the minutest of details so that when this came up again between Vandana and him, he's able to handle the discussion.

"Ok, so she took my call without knowing who I was. When I introduced myself, she fell silent for a discernible amount of time and I had to check whether she was still on the call. She said she was, in a terse tone, and wanted to know what it was regarding. I narrated to her about my meeting with Mr. Mishra and then told her about my pursuit of IHE and how important this account had been for me. Then, I told her about the call she had made to Mr. Mishra wherein I saw her face flashing on his cell and realised that she was related to him. Finally, I came to the point. All this while she had been listening silently; it was only after I made this point that she erupted. I requested her to let me know what kind of a person Mr. Mishra was—what works with him, what doesn't, etc. She started after this and, without raising her voice, conveyed her anger. She was aghast that I could call her up after our last meeting. She felt that I was very opportunistic and disrespectful of all people. I had to deeply apologise to her. In fact, I had to keep on apologising to her. Bloody egotistical maniac."

Ravi paused to take a few sips of beer. Raaj finally smiled at the jibe Ravi took at Vandana in the end, and Bhanu asked, "So how did the conversation end? And why did you say that there's fire on both sides?"

"So she gave me a long moral lecture—you guys know how women are—about how I had been vain in our first meeting, boastful, disrespectful, commenting on things I had no or little knowledge about. Towards the end she said she really admired my guts because till now no man had shown the courage to ever get back to her after receiving a piece of her mind, especially in the way she delivered it to us in that restaurant—boiling and fuming. I then intervened and told her how badly I had felt that day, and that to this day I regret the things I said. I added in fact that I had been thinking of apologising in person, maybe meeting up over coffee, but then this IHE meeting happened and instead of first meeting and apologising I started asking her about this. So I told her that if I looked at it all from her set of eyes, what she felt and what she was saying, opportunist and all, did sound right. And I added that there was one thing which she must understand and know for sure—that I was the least bit disrespectful towards her and that she was under no obligation to tell me anything about Mr. Mishra, for he was her relative anyway. I think she did cool down quite a lot after this, for she mentioned that she could have considered meeting me had I told her that I wanted to apologise in person, which is what makes me believe *ki aag idhar bhi hai aur udhar bhi*," Ravi said, winking, "but now that I had called her up like this, seeking inputs on Mr. Mishra, she did not even want to see any text from me, let alone me calling her up or we both meeting at all."

The room fell silent. Raaj had cooled down and was admiring the taste of beer in his mouth. He held the beer bottle in his hand and kept on staring at it. Bhanu and Ravi, on the other hand, locked their eyes, talking to each other non-verbally. Bhanu understood what was on Ravi's mind and decided to lead the conversation with Raaj.

"So what's on your mind, Raaj?"

"Hmmm? Nothing, Bhanu. Ravi's got me badly screwed. For no fault of mine I'm in her cross hairs, and she can be quite a charging bull in such matters. I must add here that she was convinced that I had traded her number, but I was able to convince her that I hadn't."

"And she believed you?"

"She did."

"That makes things easier, no?"

"A trifle, yes. But I also made a mistake."

"Which is…?"

"She knows now that the chance meeting in the restaurant was not a chance meeting after all."

"And you were cursing me!" shouted Ravi.

"You shut up. You have no right to speak," retorted Raaj.

"Guys, just shut up. I think we may have a way out here," Bhanu interjected, "She is convinced that Raaj did not give her number to Ravi. She is angry though that Raaj planned the lunch; she's also infuriated that Ravi called her for help with her mama ji without building bridges with her. And yet, as she said, she would have met Ravi in case Ravi had approached her to apologise."

"Your point being…" said Raaj, suspiciously.

Bhanu turned towards Ravi, "Remember I had suggested that if Vandana travels for work, we could set things up if Raaj can only help us with dates."

They both turned towards Raaj, and Raaj yelled, "BUGGER OFF. *Saalon*, am I the only dimwit on this planet?"

CHAPTER 17

Overflow (Present Day)

The drive back home for Ravi was filled with mixed emotions. Four connections on Sofu engulfed him with excitement like never before. He was reasonably sure that at least one out of the four would be a good connect and would lead to ding-dong. And then messages from Suchita. He had never expected to meet with Suchita like this. She had been his girlfriend in engineering college and was two years senior to him. They had come close to each other during ragging days and the closeness had continued. It had evolved into a very special friendship wherein both special friends wanted to be together whenever they had any free time on campus. And when two special friends spend time together like that, it doesn't take long for them to be noticed by other people on campus. Initially, it's one off, and they explore being with each other; then, they are together more often; then, the frequency of their being together increases to the point that almost every moment they are free, they are together—largely in the college canteen. That is the stage in which other friends of theirs, start turning suspicious about their relationship status—love or friendship? Sightings happen, rumours are spread, questions are asked, the special friends deny anything more than friendship, more rumours are spread, special friends start getting seen outside college, still more rumours are spread, special friends start meeting in residences and during few such meetings one special friend's vehicle is seen parked outside the other special friend's residence by a random classmate, and a lot more rumours are spread. Finally comes a stage when their close friends confront them in a very friendly manner, *fundas* are given, *fundas* are shared, discussion happens around love and life, and special friends confess! The whole campus gets to know, 'I told you so' conversation picks up, excitement picks up, professors and support staff get to know, mischievous looks are exchanged between random classmates and special friends, word spreads that the special friends are a couple now and are out of bounds for others.

The question, '*What did Suchita want?*', was doing rounds in Ravi's mind. And he had no answer to it. His mind was running in multiple directions and all directions were leading to ding-dong. Did Suchita know that Vandana and Ravi were lovers? Did she get in touch just like that? Was she married? Was she going through a similar phase in life as he was? Was she still in love with Ravi? Does she want to meet him? If she wanted to meet him, should he meet her at all? Should he share with Vandana the fact that Suchita had messaged him? His mind was filled with questions he had no answers to. Ravi reached home with all those questions and found some more messages from Vandana, including pictures clicked at the international terminal.

Suchita's messages were:

'Hey handsome.'

'You haven't changed much, you look pretty much the boy you were back on campus.'

'Haven't reached home?'

'Hello???'

He kept on staring at those messages. He didn't find anything that would raise his eyebrows, but the first two looked flirty. Should he reply to her, should he not? Should he reply now, should he reply later?

He then looked at the list of four—Aditi, Sabia, Mahek and Samiksha. He had already deleted Sana since she had asked for money. Not that Ravi could not afford to pay for ding-dong, but he felt paying for fun wasn't what he wanted to do. If it is mutual it is more enjoyable, is what he thought. Sabia had mentioned that she was in Delhi only for a night, and the time now was close to midnight so there was no point reaching out to her for ding-dong, but then, hey… she would be the quickest. Confusion!! Mahek was the challenger, and Ravi wanted to see what lay ahead. Samiksha, of course, was making his imagination reach the moon and back. He sent messages to Sabia, Mahek and Samiksha, a 'Hi' to all three.

Out of sheer courtesy, he also replied to Suchita.

'Hi Suchita. It has been a really long time. And I never thought I'd bump into you after so long and like this. How have you been?'

There were still two hours for the flight to take off. He was wondering if Suchita and Vandana were together. And if they were, what would Vandana make out of this if she knew that Suchita was messaging him. But then, what the heck, he had told Vandana all about it, and they were only catching up.

Vandana messaged – 'She looks good, your Suchita'.

Ravi felt as if his mind was skewered! He had to be careful in responding. Vandana was a mature and self-confident woman, but when it comes to protecting their own turf, women can be very territorial and protective.

'Hi' came the message from Mahek. 'How are you Ravi?'

Right now, it was Vandana who was his priority.

He responded to her – *I'm sure she does if you say so, but then she's no more mine, Vandy, and I am no more hers.* ☺

'I am good, Mahek. How are you?'

'You are replying now? Where were you lost, handsome?' - Suchita had responded to his message.

"Yeah, I was driving. At home now.' - Ravi responded to Suchita.

'I am good, Ravi. I have less time with me, so let me know what's on your mind.'

Ravi was wondering as to what reply he should send to Mahek when he got another message from Suchita.

'How has life been for you, in these many years? And why weren't you in touch?' - asked Suchita.

Ravi was trying to choose appropriate words with which to reply to Mahek. From her message, Mahek seemed to be someone experienced at this game, whereas Ravi was new. He was still thinking of the words he wanted to use. Of course he was looking for something mutual, consensual, short-term, pleasurable, repetitive. In short, no strings attached.

'Ravi, I don't want you to get me wrong, but I am pretty excited to see you after such a long time. So can you just spare a few minutes before boarding is announced?'

Ravi saw the message above from Suchita. He was

happy to be in demand. Vandana, Mahek and Suchita were all messaging him at the same time, but it was also proving to be difficult. He wasn't able to sort the chats and formulate the messages he wanted to send. It was like shuffling between a bus, a train and a plane in quick succession and not knowing which one to board next!

He wanted to chat the most with Mahek, but could not afford to keep his girlfriend waiting, and he now also had his ex-girlfriend texting him with intentions that he wasn't very clear about.

'Life has been both rewarding and punishing Suchi. I wanted to get in touch with you, but you had gone far away.' ☺

'Sleeping, are we?' a message came from Mahek.

'Not sleeping, Mahek.'

'Then? Getting cold feet?'

'I hadn't gone so far that I couldn't return Ravi. I just felt at that time that we should give time to this and see if it stands the test of time.' - replied Suchita.

'No Mahek. Not getting cold feet at all. Just wondering how to take this ahead. Where would you want to meet?'

'R, tell me na, what should I get for you, from there?' – messaged Vandana.

'Then I do not think it failed the test of time. I

think our resolve failed.' - he messaged Suchi.

'Honestly V, nothing. Just come back and let us plan out something here.' – replied Ravi.

'What's your poison, handsome? And is Ravi your real name, at all?' – asked Mahek.

'You mean we should have been more resolute to pull it through?'- asked Suchi.

'Yes, and should have taken it to its loving conclusion. But what's done is done' replied Ravi.

'Wheat beer. You wanna choose a spot based on what I drink? Yes, my name is Ravi. Why, yours isn't Mahek?'

'No problem, baby, I'll pick up something of my choice.' – messaged Vandana.

'☺' is all that Ravi replied to Vandana.

'Nopes, my real name is not Mahek. Why would I use my real name here?'

'Means what? Your pic also isn't yours?'

'You are right, Ravi. You are right. So you are going around with this chick? She's a good-looking girl. Nice choice.' – replied Suchita

'Not at all. It is a friend's. And she doesn't know that I have been using it. LoL.'

'Smart' – replied Ravi to Mahek. Whereas Mahek, or whatever her name was, was fully covered and yet behind a shroud, he was not only naked but the spotlight was also on him.

'Not fair, Mahek. Tell me about yourself.'

'Oh she's great. She's simply great. And my choice has always been good. You know that.' – Ravi texted Suchita.

'Why? You want to get married?'- retorted Mahek.

'You seemed to be in a hurry, where has all that hurriedness vanished now?' – Ravi was taunting Mahek.

'R, the flight has been announced, will get going now' – messaged Vandana.

'Love you, V. Have a safe flight and happy landing' – replied Ravi.

'I did not vanish anywhere. I am in a hurry. Off to somewhere,' replied Mahek.

'What? So what's the deal then? I thought you were in a hurry to ding-dong.' – Ravi continued to taunt Mahek.

'Hey, God bless you both. Good catching up, though we have a lot more to do. Flight's been announced.'

'Have a good trip' replied Ravi to Suchita. And then he wondered to himself about this catch-up game Suchita was playing. Both Suchita and Vandana were extremely pretty and intelligent women, for Ravi never went for just the beauty, he equally valued the brains. Suchita and Vandana were on the same flight. Suchita was Vandana's boss. Who knew what they would talk about, how Vandana's professional relationship with

Suchita would proceed in the context of Suchita being Ravi's ex-girlfriend, and how Suchita would behave professionally with Vandana given that Vandana was his current love interest. Ravi was in an awkward position, but not as awkward as the next message from Mahek would put him in.

'Of course I love that, but please understand that I got a lot more requests than what you would ever, and I had to choose based on whatever little conversation I could have had before I boarded this flight to Dubai. I'll be back in three days. Stay in touch.' – Mahek replied to Ravi.

CHAPTER 18

Meeting 2.0 (Less Than Two Years Ago)

"Both you idiots conned me into doing it," Raaj was yelling into the phone. Bhanu and Ravi were intently listening to him from their sides.

"No, bugger," replied Bhanu, "you are only helping a bro."

"Yeah, Bhanu, I know your tactics. Don't take this *haramkhor's* side. I just hope he doesn't ruin this anymore."

"Raaj, don't talk like this," said Ravi, "I will manage it smoothly. I swear on Neelam auntie ji."

"You cheap prick! You are swearing to convince me, yet you are swearing on my ma?" yelled Raaj. Bhanu burst out laughing.

"Bro, I can swear on my mother as well, but I know you won't agree. And you know how much I love auntie ji. I would never swear on her about anything I do not mean."

Raaj knew Ravi was right. In the two years that they had been together in post-graduation, Ravi had spent more time at Raaj's place than in the hostel. And that had brought him close to the Khannas. Mrs. Khanna had treated Ravi just like her own son in every aspect of a parent-child relationship.

"Boss... whatever, just do not screw it up this time," said Raaj, "and do not let Vandy know that I gave you this information."

"Don't worry about that, Raaj," said Bhanu, "Ravi is more worried about the hole Hyatt is going to blow in his pocket."

The three of them laughed at that. Vandana was traveling to Mumbai for a meeting with one of Stellar Creatives' customers. It was a film production house that was planning online marketing strategies. It was an overnight trip. Raaj had shared Vandana's flight details with Ravi. While common sense would suggest that Ravi and Vandana shouldn't be on the same flight, Ravi had planned it otherwise. He would board the same flight and only make his presence apparent to Vandana when they 'bumped' into each other at the hotel, avoiding any eye contact till then. The only chance of bumping into each other in the flight was if they were seated next to each other but that was also taken care of. Raaj had mentioned that Vandana always booked the window seat for herself in the forward section. So if Ravi was some seats behind by the window, there was a good chance that they wouldn't bump into each other in the flight, even if Vandana took a stroll along the aisle.

It was an early morning flight scheduled for a 6:00 a.m. departure. They had to reach the airport around 4:30 a.m. Ravi and Vandana both used to plan their schedule in such a way that they reached their destination with a good amount of time in hand. Vandana must have reached the airport at 4:28 a.m., for it was 4:29 a.m. when Ravi reached and he could see Vandana alighting from her cab and starting to move towards the departure hall through Gate 3.

'Thank God,' thought he, 'you saved me by a whisker. Please be with me today, God.'

So far so good. Now, it was time for the second phase of the plan—to let Vandana know that he was on the same flight. Vandana had done a web check-in the previous day, so she was headed towards the baggage drop counter of the airline. Ravi had chosen the emergency exit window for himself. Not all airlines allowed emergency exit seats to be booked online owing to DGCA regulations. The emergency exit seat was only to be provided to strong, able-bodied passengers. So Ravi had to walk towards the counter to get his boarding pass.

If he positioned himself one or two counters away from the baggage drop counter, kept his profile facing towards the baggage drop counter and his eyes on his phone or towards the airline staffer, there was a chance that she would observe him there. While that was still no guarantee of her concluding that Ravi was on the same flight as hers even if she spotted him, since the airline counters would not just process Mumbai flight but other flights at the same time as well, Ravi left it to her smartness to figure that if both were there at the same time flying the same airline, the odds were that their destination was also the same.

The Gods were really with Ravi that day. The baggage drop counter had a longer line than the other counters. By the time Vandana's turn came to drop her check-in baggage, Ravi had reached the counter that was two counters to the left of the baggage drop counter. He handed his ticket print-out and ID card to the lady on the other side of the counter and stood facing completely towards his right, looking at his phone until the lady at the counter called out his name and handed over the boarding pass to him. He wasn't sure whether Vandana had seen him/sensed his presence, but he did not want to take direct chances anyway. So even when Vandana passed by him staring into the cover of the book she had in her hand, he ignored her to make sure she didn't find him looking at her.

On the way to the security check area, he put some deliberate distance between himself and her. Vandana's security check did not take long, anyway. The ladies' line is usually much shorter than the men's line. Vandana was headed for breakfast after the security check, and so was Ravi. They both went to the premium lounge—both had credit cards that gave them membership benefits to the lounge.

'All I have to do is to keep my eyes away from her. Easy!' he kept on reminding himself. And that was the most difficult part really. Her dressing sense was immaculate. That besides, she was a naturally gorgeous woman. On this occasion, she was wearing a charcoal grey shawl-collar asymmetrical skirt suit, earrings with large black stones studded in them, and 4-inch slingback black stilettos. Her fair complexion was standing out completely. Her shoulder-length shiny hair had been straightened and left loose.

'*Ghanta easy*,' thought Ravi, 'she is looking so damn attractive. Just cannot take my eyes off her.' But he had to; if he wanted his plan to work, he had to keep his eyes off her. So he waited till she filled up her plate and kept sitting still even when she walked past him to take a seat at one of the long tables in the lounge beside which she had kept her cabin baggage. He then got up and walked towards the buffet spread, filled up his plate and sat around the same table as hers, but on the opposite side.

She was eating her breakfast and reading a book. Ravi was also eating his breakfast and reading a business newspaper. He wasn't sure whether she had seen him, but he couldn't look in her eyes to be sure. He was avoiding even looking in her direction, but with his face bent over his plate, from the right corner of his eye he was looking in her direction, trying to get a sense of the direction she was looking in. He wasn't getting any.

'She must have seen me by now,' he thought. Again, there was no way to be sure. But there was something he could do—get up and walk past her towards the buffet spread for a second helping. Maybe she'd look up and see him. He did that but still couldn't be fully sure. Anyway, those were the chances he had to take to come good on his plan, or rather to make his plan come good on him.

Boarding was announced on the Flight Information Display Screen (FIDS) inside the lounge. He saw her looking at the FIDS and getting up. He decided to get up as well and walk ahead of her. That would give her a 100% chance of spotting him, even with a few people in between. With that thought, Ravi got up and walked fast. Sure as hell, a few passengers got up too and were walking towards Gate 39 for boarding.

At Gate 39, there were passengers walking up and down and those sitting on seats or lounge recliners. Vandana took a vacant seat close to the departure gate while Ravi decided to walk up and down, acting as if on a call, talking into the hands-free mic in an imaginary conversation. He had, of course, put his phone on silent lest his pretence got broken. The flight was announced. The announcing staffer called out passengers with seats on rows 21–30 to board first. Ravi cursed him, for he knew what was coming next. And what was coming next was not what he had planned for, but it was a detail he had simply forgotten. To save time and avoid hassles, airlines call out passengers to board in an orderly fashion—those with seats in the back are called to board first, then the ones in the middle rows, and finally the ones in the front rows. Ravi's seat was in the middle rows, and Raaj had tipped him that Vandana liked her flight seat to be in the forward section. So there was no way that she would be seated in the plane while he walked in, giving him ample opportunity to make his presence apparent to her.

Vandana was clearly not in the first set of passengers (who boarded the rear section), and he was clearly not in the third set (which boarded the forward section). So he decided not to board the aircraft when his section was announced. He would board it when the airline invited passengers in the forward section. And when Vandana got up and passed through the boarding gate, he would get up then. Thus, he would pass by her inside the plane when she would be seated. He had noticed that seated passengers did scan the incoming passengers—whether to see if they would find someone familiar, or to check out someone, or for whatever reason. But he hadn't noticed that this was largely a very male trait—few females did this.

True to his instincts, mostly men were looking up

at who was boarding next. Vandana was lost in her book. Ravi, disappointed, went ahead and took his seat, unsure whether Vandana had spotted him or not.

As Ravi was passing by her row, Vandana was thinking, 'What an ass! So many times he passed by me; so many times I went past him. Didn't he notice me, or does he lack the courage or courtesy to say hi?'

CHAPTER 19

Afraid, Scared, Petrified (Present Day)

'WTF,' Ravi was thinking, 'have I landed myself in a soup? Mahek and Vandana are surely colleagues. It cannot be a coincidence that both are off to Dubai for three days. This is bad! I am so jacked! I am deeply and royally screwed.'

Ting-tong, came the notification. He had yet another match on Sofu, or a message from an existing match. But he did not even want to look at it. He was at work, and just was not able to focus on work at all. Shalini had asked him to make a report of the reportees' performance. But his focus was elsewhere. Vandana hadn't messaged him after the good morning message, and neither had Suchita or Mahek. He was reasonably sure why it was so, for they were in the same conference.

'Vandana will kill me. This jackass Bhanu jacked me. *Saala, he's* an expert in all this, but I am so badly screwed.'

He kept on thinking about his predicament in his office. Amidst all this, the fact that Vandana hadn't messaged him after the good morning message was killing him. It was not the fear or the guilt of doing something wrong that was killing him, but the fear of being caught while doing something wrong that was killing him.

***

Meanwhile, the conversation between the man (in India) and woman (in Dubai) was on.

Man – Hi

Woman – Conference, silly!

Man – So?

Woman – So I am busy.

Man – Yeah looks like it, judging by the speed of your replies.

Woman – I was only being respectful. You want me to act pricey?

Man – No way.

Woman – I didn't think so, tiger. Wait till break, I'll message.

***

'Shall I call Bhanu or shall I talk to Raaj about it?' Ravi was thinking. 'Or dump it… Let me first gather my thoughts and think logically. If Mahek and Vandana were good friends, Mahek would have told Vandana about finding me on Sofu. And if Mahek had indeed done so, Vandana would have killed me by now. The fact that Vandana hasn't called me points to only two things—either Vandana and Mahek don't speak with each other, or they haven't yet got the chance to do so. If they plan to speak with each other but haven't yet got the chance to, I am worse than dead. But if they don't speak with each other, I am safe for now. However, I should tread very carefully.'

***

Woman – tell me tiger, I am all ears.
Man – I wish you'd said 'I am all yours'.
Woman – eventually, if you behave yourself. What's the rush, tiger?
Man – come on, babe, stop this game.
Woman – patience will make you reach somewhere.
Man – I am sure. I can be patient, but I have to know what lies on the other side of patience.
Woman – blissful consent.
Man – then you are worth it.
Woman – I know I am.
Man – How is your conference?
Woman – Boring.

***

'Vandana hasn't messaged till now,' thought Ravi, looking at his watch. 'Let me ping her.' He still hadn't checked the latest notification on the Sofu app.

'Hey babe, wassup?'

He waited but there was no reply! He was getting more and more mind-numbed.

'Does she know?' He knew that Vandana did not have the need for her lover's unbroken attention. Even if Ravi didn't call her for one or two or even three days and just messaged her, she would be fine. All she needed to know was that all was well with him.

Ting-tong, he heard Sofu's notification tone once again and decided to check it so as to keep his mind occupied. There was a message from Mahek and a new connect—Rehana. He sent a '*hi*' to Rehana and decided to read Mahek's message.

'Hi player, what's up?'

'All well Mahek, you tell me what's up?'

'All is well on this side. It's a break so I thought I'd chat up.'

'Good thought. So Mahek… you mentioned that you are in Dubai for a conference.'

'Yes I did.'

'What's the conference about?'

'Work, what else? I do not like these conferences much. Will be back the day after. Are you game

for something, or are you just a jay walker? What are you up to?'

'She is so direct,' thought Ravi to herself. He checked his chat with Vandana—still no reply. So he thought of replying to Mahek only and keeping her in play to ascertain if she had blown the whistle on him.

'I am game, Mahek, but the issue is that you know enough about me but I don't know anything about you. I don't even know who you are.'

'That is the game, boy. And it is not my fault that you have used your actual profile here. You will know about me when we meet up. But I can do something for you.'

'What?'

'I can send you a pic without my face.'

'Yeah?? What good is that?'

'As if you are looking for love here.' And with that message she sent an angry emoji. *'Let's be clear we are both looking for fun. At least you will get to see what my body looks like.'*

'You can send, but there's no way for me to know whether it is you or someone else.'

Mahek fell silent for a while. Then she replied, *'you are right. But that is how it will be. And now I must get back to my conference.'*

Ravi checked his chat—still no message from

Vandana. But he was sure that at least till then, Mahek and Vandana hadn't exchanged notes. Otherwise, Mahek wouldn't have messaged him like this, and Vandana would have screwed him anyway.

***

Man – so how can we make it interesting?
Woman – use your imagination.
Man – there you go again. ☺
Woman – ha ha ha. Sorry.
Man – Married?
Woman – no. You?
Man – no. Committed?
Woman – I have someone in my life.
Man – interesting.
Woman – don't you go judging me.
Man – I am not. I just said it's cool that you have a boyfriend.
Woman – you have a girlfriend?
Man – Not at present. So you have a boyfriend. Not that I will ever judge you or judge your boyfriend, for that matter, but why do you want to fish out?
Woman – Yaar, it's complicated.
Man – then un-complicate it.
Woman – Let's just say that I am saving it for him for a later stage. For now, I want to have fun.

Man – great. You are back the day after?

Woman – Yes.

Man – shall we meet up?

Woman – we can. Pick me up.

Man – you have a deal.

***

It was lunch time in Dubai when Vandana's message came – *I am good, babe. How about you?*

'Looks like Mahek and she hasn't spoken as yet,' thought Ravi.

Ravi replied – *I am good. You were busy in the morning?*

Vandana – *Sorry, R, had seen that you had messaged, but I was chatting with someone and then the break got over.*

CHAPTER 20

Meeting 2.0 Contd. (Less Than Two Years Ago)

Hyatt Regency is just over three kilometres from the airport. It is also about an hour away from Bandra Kurla complex, Mumbai's business hub. After landing at the airport, Vandana had to head for a meeting with her customer at Bandra Kurla complex. The schedule was daylong. Stellar Creatives, the company that Vandana worked for, had very perseveringly worked towards convincing this customer to let Stellar handle their online marketing strategy. And they were now in striking range of winning this account. In today's round, the customer had invited three finalists out of the six they had evaluated. Each of the finalists had to run through their solution to the customer's challenge, based on which a high-powered committee would decide, by the end of the day, who would win it. The winner would have to appear in their office the next day as well to finalise the final points of taking over the online marketing strategy of the new films that they were launching.

After landing, Ravi planned to go to the hotel and stay there, and keep an eye out for Vandana and bump into her in the evening. Cautious that they didn't run into each other even while exiting, he did not stand close to Vandana at the carousel. He was watching her from far, unmindful of the fact that Vandana knew where he was standing.

On her way to her customer's office, Vandana was wondering what had brought Ravi here. 'Ravi was dressed in jeans and tees. He could not possibly have come for work, or he would have been dressed like her—in formals. Maybe he is here to meet some friends, but in the middle of the week? Strike out! Maybe he has some relatives here… yeah, this must be the one. A relative's marriage… a relative in distress, maybe! Or maybe he's actually here for work. He will head to a hotel, freshen up, change, and then head for a meeting. Either way, they wouldn't be meeting again!' She could not have imagined that Ravi would also be checking into the same hotel. And since she had already left the airport for her meeting, she knew that they weren't meeting.

'Loser!' she thought, and started focusing on her upcoming meeting.

Ravi took a cab to the hotel after he saw Vandana

getting into her cab. Ravi's cabbie was absolutely shattered when he came to know that Ravi was staying quite close to the airport. He had a good look at Ravi in the rear-view mirror. Ravi, well-dressed, clearly looked like he was from the upper strata of the society. The cabbie was wondering whether he should make the suggestion or not, then in the interest of earning more money, asked Ravi the question.

"Sahib, you are here for how long?"

Ravi thought maybe the cabbie wanted to offer him a drop at the airport as well, and earn more money.

"I am going back tomorrow. Why, what happened?"

"Nothing much, sahib. I was just thinking that all hotels have 12:00 noon check-in time. Right now it is not even 10 am. Shall I take you somewhere else and bring you here by noon?"

Amused at the cabbie's ingenuity, Ravi wanted to know more.

"Where will you take me?"

"A good mall, sahib."

"Will malls be open at this time?"

"Not all shops, but massage parlours would be open, sahib. You must have gotten tired in the flight, sahib. A massage will do you good."

Ravi laughed at the suggestion, but declined. In the next five minutes, they had reached Hyatt. Ravi was able to smooth-talk the receptionist into giving him a room. Once in the room, Ravi was wondering what to do. He had lots of time on his hands. Raaj had told him that Vandana would possibly be back only in the evening. So there was no point in positioning himself in the reception area and waiting for Vandana.

'I will kill Raaj if he has done so,' Vandana thought. Still in the cab on her way to the customer, she had a fleeting thought—what if Raaj only had told Ravi about this trip? But then she remembered how she had taken on Raaj. Knowing the gentle friend Raaj had been to her, she knew Raaj wouldn't do such a thing. Maybe her sixth sense was working overtime here. She was now close to her destination.

The day was moving slowly for Ravi. He wasn't able to decide what would be the perfect opening line. 'Should I just bump into her? Or should I walk up to her? If I bump into her, would it be a good idea to offer to carry her luggage? If I walk up to her, how do I open the discussion? Should I say hi and take it from there? Why the hell is she such a fighter?'

Stellar would be the last company to present that day. Going by the fact that it was almost 12 now and that the first presentation was still under way, it was clear that Stellar's turn would only come post lunch. Vandana's colleagues from her Mumbai office had joined her. Waiting can be nail-biting tense when one is trying to make some sense. Vandana's mind was in two directions today; her attention was divided. 'Did he actually not notice me at Delhi airport, and at the lounge? Bloody idiot! I walked past him. What does he want? Does he want me to walk up to him? Over my dead body!'

'What must I do to win her over?' Ravi was thinking to himself. 'Bloody proud of herself, stubborn girl. And why have I fallen so badly for her? Is it just the looks? Were Suchita and Tara any less? What is so special about her? I am crazy for her like dogs are for cars, except that dogs go behind cars chasing them away, and I am going for her chasing her down. Bloody complicated girl!' Thinking so, he switched on the television. The channel was airing *Saving Private Ryan*! 'Its name should be *Saving Ravi Malhotra*,' thought he.

'And why am I thinking like that at all? I don't even know if he has come to Mumbai for me. He's handsome, he's smart, he is doing well for himself. He can give a secure future to any girl… but why is he so vain? How can he be so disrespectful? And what a bloody opportunist, calling me for information on Ajit mama. Bloody useless manipulative bugger.' Vandana was caught in her own web of thoughts.

'This is such bullshit. This isn't giving me any cock and bull ideas,' thought Ravi while watching *Saving Private Ryan*. 'Let me watch a romcom.' He flipped channels and stopped at one that was playing *Mamma Mia,* which would be followed by *The Proposal*, which would be followed by *It's Complicated*.

It was 4:00 p.m. and Vandana's chance still hadn't

come. She had flipped through her presentation twice and was in no mood to do so again. And where was the room for her to do it? She was in her own thoughts. 'Why am I thinking of him so much? I am not even sure if he's here for me. I think he saw me, but he deliberately ignored me…'

"Vandana," her colleague called out to her, looking at his cell phone, "The customer messaged. We are up in the next five minutes. You are ready, right?

"Yes, I am."

"Great, we need to win this."

"What do you think I am here for?" snapped Vandana. Her colleague wanted to retort, but knew better. He thought Vandana was frustrated by the waiting game. In Vandana's mind, however, a different battle was raging.

It was almost six in the evening. Ravi was watching *The Proposal.* Having watched the last 45 minutes of *Mamma Mia* and *The Proposal* till now, he was none the wiser as to what he should do. And he wasn't even sure whether Vandana's meeting was over. He was not sure whether he should go down and sit in the reception. He wasn't sure what to do, when Bhanu called him.

"What's up?"

"*Intezaar,*" replied our man.

"She isn't there yet? Weren't you two on the same flight?"

Ravi explained his entire day to Bhanu.

"Let me patch in Raaj," said Bhanu and called Raaj. Bhanu updated Raaj with the day's proceedings.

"So what's the plan, Ravi?" asked Raaj.

"I can feel the pressure. I wasn't this unsure when I was proposing to Suchita or Tara."

"You are not sure?" asked Raaj, "What are you not sure of?"

"Words… words… How should I propose to her? What should I do? Why is she so temperamental, bro? I don't even know how she will react when she sees me."

"Oh, gather yourself man," said Bhanu, "I have never seen you so nervous."

"I am not nervous. I am just not able to think of the right words or the right context in which I should approach her, that's all."

"Ok, you are not scared, you are not nervous, you are just stressed! Is that the correct assessment of your mental situation right now?" asked Raaj.

"You can say that."

"Do you have any idea what time she is getting free?" asked Bhanu.

"How would I, *mishti doi*?"

"I asked Raaj, not you," replied Bhanu and continued, "Raaj, can you find out?"

Raaj paused for about 30 seconds, "Yes," he replied, "let me call you guys back. You carry on with the call."

Bhanu and Ravi were discussing possible scenarios, but none of them were fitting here. They weren't very sure what time she would come in. Would she have dinner with her colleagues outside, or would she dine at Hyatt only? Even if she dines-in at Hyatt, would she be alone or with her colleagues? And if she wanted to avoid dining with her colleagues in Hyatt, would she step out for a restaurant or go for room service? Too many variables with one longing heart! Amidst this, Raaj dialled on Bhanu's phone. Bhanu patched in the call.

"Bad news, Ravi."

"What happened, Raaj?"

"The presentation did not go well."

"What? Shucks! She must be feeling bad."

"Yes, she is."

"How do you know?" asked Bhanu.

"I know because of two reasons," replied Raaj, "one, I know her. I know how much she hates losing, for she prepares so well. She normally messages me when it goes well. And two, I spoke with my counterpart. He mentioned that the strategy she had prepared was rock solid and even he had been floored when she had taken him through the presentation before presenting it to the customer. But the delivery of the presentation wasn't good. She was unable to defend two important points."

"That's bad," reacted Ravi, "so did you lose the deal?"

"No. My colleague was able to convince the customer to allow them to get back on those two points tomorrow at 8:00 a.m. But the impression wasn't good.

We are at the number two slot right now."

They were all silent for a while. Raaj spoke again, "She is headed for the hotel, Ravi. And she's coming in hot. She will come in like a volcano in the majesty of a thousand eruptions. Be safe, Ravi."

"This is the only thing that remained. But thanks, anyway. Let me go down and check."

"She will be alone," said Raaj. "My colleague offered her a drop, but she declined and told him that she would prepare for tomorrow."

"All the best," said both Bhanu and Raaj, and the call got over. All three of them knew that there wasn't much to advise at that moment. Ravi would have to do what he was best at—charter troubled, unexplored waters and make it out successfully. He had done it many times professionally, but this was the first time he was doing it in a personal situation.

Ravi reached the reception with a blank mind. At least he knew for sure that she was coming alone.

He was waiting near the reception desk when he saw Vandana, in her business suit, walking straight to the reception, her trolley in tow and her laptop bag on top of it. Her eyes were emitting the angry brilliance of a thousand suns. She clearly meant business. Raaj would have let Vandana be at that moment, but our man gathered himself when it mattered the most, walked towards her and said, "Hi Vandana. Good to see a known face here."

CHAPTER 21

New Horizons (Present Day)

Vandana had been busy with her conference on Day 1. Ravi and she connected for some time in the evening when the conference for that day got over. Vandana had to make a presentation that day about the creative strategies for the top ten accounts. Her session was received well by her peers and superiors. Some of the other sessions didn't go so well and attracted the wrath of Stellar's higher management. Vandana spent some time consoling the poor sods whose presentations had been shred to pieces by Suchita and the other senior executives. Some were asked to rework and redesign. The external speaker, apparently a cat in the advertising world in the Middle East, bored them to death. In a session titled 'The Unlimited Possibilities of Advertising,' he spoke rather on the unlimited achievements of his. The whole session was built around 'I, me and myself'. How Vandana hated such megalomaniacs! But apparently, he was a good friend of the management.

Ravi, on the other hand, did not have much to report to Vandana. It had been a normal sales day with two customer meetings and a focused discussion with Shalini on one of his accounts that was proving to be difficult. That apart, there were loads which he could not tell Vandana about—his newfound excitement with Sofu. Mahek wasn't responding to his messages. Maybe she was busy with the conference or busy ding-donging someone in the conference for all he cared.

He messaged Sabia and Samiksha, sent another '*hi*' to Rehana, and then waited a while. He had finished his dinner long back and was watching a spy movie on the television. He was quite intrigued by Sabia and felt that she would work out the best. She came from another town, was in the city only for a while, was clear in her requirements, and was very beautiful too. Samiksha, of course, was the most aggressive and very straight in the face. Rehana was his latest connect. He was waiting to see if any of them would message. and see if he could get some 'action' before Vandana was back. But all he had were messages from Raaj, Shalini and Anup. He could still open Raaj's message, but no way those from Shalini and Anup!

***

Man: What time are you landing?
Woman: Missing me already?
Man: No… But in need of something that pumps up my adrenaline.
Woman: he he he he.
Man: You can stay at my place.
Woman: where else do you think I will go?

***

Rehana and Sabia replied together.
Sabia – Hi. As the distance meter would tell you, I am more than 4,000 km away from you. But tell me about yourself. Will be in your town soon.
Rehana – Hey. How's you? Tell me about yourself.
Ravi to Sabia – Sounds good, Sabia. I live in Gurgaon, my office is also in Gurgaon, and I go to places all over the world.
Ravi to Rehana – Hey, I am good as well. Where are you?
Rehana – I am about 35 km away from you. Guess where that could be.
Sabia – You are in aviation?
Ravi to Rehana – Looks like NOIDA.
Ravi to Sabia – Nopes. But I give a lot of business to aviators.
Rehana – Bingo, handsome.
Ravi to Rehana – So…

Rehana – So?

Sabia – are you a travel agent?

Ravi to Sabia – ha ha ha ha. No. I am in sales in an IT firm, but we keep traveling a lot.

Sabia – yeah? Fly my airline. Travel with me to some place.

Ravi to Rehana – So can we meet up??

Rehana – of course we can. What else are we chatting for?

Ravi to Rehana – great. So how about now?

Ravi to Sabia – Sure, someday. When are you back?

Rehana – why are you men always in a hurry?

Ravi to Rehana – Darling doll, it is not that we are finding love out of this, so why delay a good time that we can have together?

Sabia – I will be back in India tomorrow, but in Delhi next week.

Ravi to Sabia – that's good, Sabia. Looking forward.

Rehana – Dog!

Ravi – Dog? WTF? Why dog?

Rehana – all you men are dogs.

Ravi – language, lady!

Rehana – Hello, do not teach me language. See what you are asking for. Willing for sex always, ready to jump into bed forever.

Ravi was thinking to himself, 'What a stupid bitch. Sometime back she asked what else we were chatting for. Now she says I am in a hurry and all. Why, just why is it so difficult to understand women? Nana ji was right in advising me to stay away from women. *Do pairon pe chalne wala sabse khatarnak janwar hai aurat, bach ke rahiyo* – he remembered his grandfather telling him that, on more than one occasion. This was clearly one such occasion.

Rehana – Oi mister, where did you vanish? See, it is THIS about you guys that I just do not like! You just do not know how to handle a woman of substance.

Ravi – What? Where is this even coming from? What are you getting so agitated about? And before we go any further, between the two of us, I fail to see any woman of substance.

Rehana – How dare you insult me!

Ravi – Are you crazy? You are the one who called me names, yet you say that I am insulting you, and you are at a loss for words to explain why you got agitated.

Rehana – You are straight away asking for sex.

Ravi – You want me to ask you for coffee first?

Rehana – That's a good idea, and for that you can come right now.

Ravi couldn't believe the chat he was having. 'She

must be crazy,' he thought to himself.

Ravi – Are you stoned?

Rehana – No, you dummy, but a bit of chivalry can do you good.

Ravi – You are unbelievable!

Rehana – And you are just so predictable, just like my ex-boyfriend.

Ravi – Yeah? How long did you let him last? I am happy he is ex and not late!

Rehana – Mind your arrogant language, boy! I am in no mood to meet you anymore. Before I block you forever, say sorry!

Ravi read that message and laughed, 'She really must be crazy. She can go to hell.'

Ravi – Do as you yourself please.

***

Woman – by the way, you never told me where you are from.

Man – two can play a game.

Woman – yeah, sure. But are you sure?

Man – in Delhi.

Woman – thank you.

Man – cheers.

***

CHAPTER 22

Meeting 2.0 Contd. Further (Less Than Two Years Ago)

Of the seven billion inhabitants of this planet, Vandana wasn't expecting to be greeted by Ravi. In fact, she wasn't expecting to meet him in the hotel at all. Ravi's presence had surprised her. Right from the time in the Delhi airport, she had been troubled that Ravi had been on the same flight as her but hadn't even acknowledged her, let alone approach. She had even passed by him a few times inside the Delhi airport but he seemed to not have noticed her. All the way from the Mumbai airport to her customer's office, she had been thinking about Ravi and his indifference towards her thus far. The presentation hadn't gone as well as she had planned for it to, and on her way back she had been suspecting that it was because of Ravi. She had spent too much of her time thinking about Ravi.

Their first meeting might have been a disaster due

to Ravi's vanity, but she had secretly taken to liking him. Of course she could not make it apparent to Raaj after having roasted him, or to Ravi after having hauled him over hot coal. What she had still not figured out was why did she like him? And the fact that she wasn't getting an answer to this question was confusing and enraging her even more. She was angry with herself for not being able to get a logical answer to it. Was it his looks/stable job/intermittent inputs from Raaj as to how well his best pal had been doing professionally? Or was it the way in which he had apologised to her at the Cyber Hub restaurant after being verbally mauled by her?

She didn't know what it was that, despite her dislike of Ravi's manners, had made her hope that he would acknowledge her at the Delhi airport, or inside the flight, or post disembarking from the flight at the Mumbai airport, none of which, by the way, had happened!

While entering the hotel, she was walking with a very determined gait to quickly check into her room, ask for room service dinner, have a warm shower, calm her mind and start running through the slides for tomorrow's presentation once again. And here she was, being greeted by Ravi! Life is clearly not what you plan, but what happens to you!

An ego-boosting thought originated in her mind which completely calmed her senses. Ravi was here for her. This had to be about her. She was convinced! However, she could not show her appreciation of Ravi's presence here. She had to put up a face. Poker face!

"Help me understand how, Ravi."

"We are in a different city, right? A city that neither of us belongs to. So if one comes across a known face isn't one supposed to feel good about it?

"Didn't know you were scared." There was a hint of smugness in her voice. And then the tone turned sarcastic, "Don't worry, I won't let you get kidnapped."

Stepping closer to her without invading her personal space, Ravi said in a very firm tone, "Can we please calm down, Vandy?"

This was again something that she hadn't factored in—Ravi calling her Vandy. Only close friends or close colleagues could call her that. Ravi was taking liberties. She was about to say something, instead, with the same movement of hand as he had displayed in the restaurant, Ravi started, "You have had a long day, and from the looks of it, it hasn't gone any great. I came here just to meet you, Vandy. But it can wait. I can wait. What clearly cannot wait is the thought process running in your head."

'Am I making it so apparent that he can read I am conflicted about him?' thought Vandana.

"What are you talking about?" she asked, her voice reflecting suspicion and curiosity but, clearly calm!

"I am assuming that you are coming in from a

customer meeting or a series of meetings. You are coming in angry, your eyes blazing with anger. Clearly, there's something running on your mind. Something that hasn't gone well."

'Saved,' thought she. 'He doesn't realise that it is he who is creating the conflict.'

"Well spotted. The discussion did not go as we thought it would."

"Hmm. You want to talk about it over dinner?"

"You are inviting?"

"Like I said," said Ravi, very caringly and with an assuring smile, "I came here for you. I want to talk to you. If you are okay going out for dinner with me, please check-in, freshen up and come over. I will be in the lobby. We can then step out for food or we can have it here. I'd actually like to go out, but I think with the task you have at hand, you'd like some time."

Vandana stared at Ravi for a while. She didn't know if he was commanding her or just offering comfort. His words were measured, tone firm but polite, demeanour pleasant… and then it struck her like a bolt from the blue!

Her eyes wide open and face clearly expressing both surprise and suspicion, she opened her mouth to ask a question, "Did he…" But before she could even complete it, Ravi interjected, "He did. But this time before you call him or maul him, please hear me out." They were both speaking about Raaj.

"And this is not the time for that conversation,

Vandana. But I know you need answers. You deserve answers. And you have my word that you will get them. Now, I am really hungry, but you will find me waiting here." Ravi submitted his request with folded hands, gesturing to her to move towards the elevator.

Vandana smiled, went to the reception desk, checked in and walked towards the elevator, smiling at Ravi as she was headed for it—a smile of victory. She might have lost the evening, but was clearly winning the day!

While taking the hot shower, she was also wondering. And while she was wondering, she was smiling to herself. She didn't have answers to all the questions, but she did have some. Raaj had indeed helped Ravi by letting him know her travel plan; how else would Ravi be on the same flight and in the same hotel. Ravi had gone to great lengths to plan this to the tee. He had taken some effort to not look into her eyes even when she was in his vicinity. Then, maybe Raaj had even told him about today's meeting. But what Raaj could not have known and did not know was the confusion and conflict in her mind because of Ravi. Had Ravi entered a small corner of her heart by apologising the way he did at Cyber Hub, or had he only entered her mind, and was yet to go through her mind's critical evaluation before getting into her heart?

Ravi, on the other hand, was waiting for her in the lobby. He had a WhatsApp group with Raaj and

Bhanu. The name of the group was 3 Dirty Dawgs (3DD). Raaj had just sent a text on 3DD.

Raaj – What's up, haramkhor? Are you alive? Is everything ok?

Ravi – Yes, all is good. Everything is under control.

Raaj – Please do what you must, but do not get me jacked.

Bhanu – Ha ha ha ha.

Ravi –Don't worry, it's under control. By the way, she knows that you helped me.

Raaj – Bhanu, Ravi is a dog. He acts like a toughie in front of us, but is a bloody softie when it comes to women. Mangy dog! I will never help him again.

Bhanu – Ha ha ha ha ha

Raaj – Yeah, laugh at my expense. I am the one who'll get laid by Vandy.

Ravi – Oi, I am the only one getting laid by her, whenever it happens, that is. Did she call you?

Raaj – No, but she will roast me when she does.

Ravi – Beta, she will thank you when she does.

Vandana was thinking in between the shower and getting dressed for the dinner. Was it the way he spoke, his confidence, his ability to not panic in a tough situation—a trait her father had displayed many times—that made her like Ravi? When Ravi had called her to get information about Ajit mama she thought maybe he had called to apologise. But he had called to know more about his customer. That had enraged her even more. Earlier, Ravi had apologised in Cyber Hub, but Vandana had never been sure whether he had meant it or he just said it at that moment to placate her. So was that it? Was a deeply felt honest apology what she was looking for? Did she need closure? That could be the reason, but the conflict was not because Ravi had been vain and had made fun of the subjects she had studied back in her B school. The conflict was due to the small string of attraction she felt for him despite Ravi's vanity. How she disliked such men! Yet, she felt something for him. What was that something, and why did she feel it for him, is what had arisen the conflict in her mind. She wasn't able to figure it out yet.

After spending a reasonable time in front of the mirror, she was ready now. She hadn't known that this sort of a meeting could happen, but she had carried clothes from home in case she had to go for dinner with colleagues. She took the elevator to the lobby and stepped out to see Ravi waiting for her.

Upon seeing her, Ravi tried not to give away his feelings, but his eyes, his face, his entire expression cheated on him. Vandana was now very confident of herself.

CHAPTER 23

De-Risk (Present Day)

"Bhanu, this app doesn't seem to be working for me," said Ravi.

"Be patient, Ravi. It takes time."

"How much more, yaar? Vandy is back tomorrow."

"His hand is now in pain, Bhanu," quipped Raaj. The three were dining together at Lakshman Fast Food in Qutub Institutional Area in Delhi.

"Dog," retorted Ravi.

"No, but jokes apart, Ravi, it does take some time. You get all sorts. It is important to establish a connect first. Do not rush into it. I have had so many flopped experiences. I was lucky with the first one though. My first one was an instant hit. But then the next one happened after a month," Bhanu shared his experience.

"So where did it go bad for you?" an intrigued Raaj asked.

"What do you have to do with it?" asked Ravi, "You are on hands-free mode anyway."

The three burst out laughing. Bhanu shared some of his stories with both of them.

'Handsome, where are you lost? No message at all. Caught a bird?' Ravi received this message on Sofu. The sound notification wasn't lost on Bhanu.

"Who is it?" asked Bhanu.

"The question should be what is it?" said Ravi.

"Ok, what is it?" asked Raaj.

"Trouble."

"How come?"

"It is Mahek. Both Vandana and Mahek are in the same conference, and I am scared that if Mahek talks to Vandana, I am done for."

"What is this about?" asked a visibly disturbed Bhanu. Ravi narrated the entire incident.

"Are you an idiot, Ravi?" Bhanu was yelling at the very top of his voice. "Are you a blithering idiot? You know what all you had to do to woo her? She is a tough and very self-respecting girl and you clearly intend on destroying it yourself. I had asked you to have some fun, not tell the whole world about it. You might as well put a placard on your chest about it, arsehole."

"What do I do, Bhanu?"

"Disconnect. And don't just disconnect; delete your profile. Create a fake one now. And I mean NOW."

"Yaar but Mahek is hot…" Ravi was going to say

something but changed his mind looking at Bhanu's blazing eyes. He did exactly what he was told, rather, commanded by Bhanu. In his new profile, he put up a picture in which his face was not clearly visible. Bhanu then asked him to change the pic altogether. He chose the name Ravish. Bhanu banged him left, right and centre till Ravi dropped Ravish and chose another name. 'No Risks' was Bhanu's mantra.

"Bro, I am in no committed relationship, yet I do not use my own pic or name. Are you silly?" Bhanu tried to guide Ravi.

So Ravi's new profile went by the name Kabir Kapoor. Ravi downloaded a random pic from the internet and used that as his profile pic. All info, except that he was based in Gurgaon, was fake.

"Now even if that bitch Mahek tries to create a problem for you, she won't be able to," said Bhanu.

"How?" asked Raaj.

"Because," replied Bhanu, "when you delete your profile/account in Sofu, you get deleted from all your connects' profiles."

"*Array*, I forgot to tell you guys," said Ravi, "Suchita is back."

"What?" asked Raaj

"Seriously?" said Bhanu, joyfully.

"*Fir*… did you…?" wondered Raaj.

"Buddy, there's a complication," said Ravi, "She is Vandana's boss."

"Shucks!" it was Bhanu's turn to be surprised, "why does it always happen with you?"

"Ha ha ha ha, ask me! And my-my," said Ravi holding his phone, "there's a message from her. And oops… here's one from Vandana."

"Now you do not get busy with them," Raaj was teasing Ravi.

"Listen, I have to go anyway," said Bhanu, "Have a long day tomorrow. And it is almost 10 now," he said looking at his watch.

"I came with Ravi, so we will be going back together," said Raaj.

"Sure, but can you drive? I want to keep my hands busy," requested Ravi.

"Fingers, you mean," Raaj corrected him.

"Dog."

After their goodbye hugs with Bhanu, both of them boarded Ravi's ride. Raaj was driving and Ravi was busy texting.

Suchita – handsome, where are you? Avoiding me, because of your GF?

Vandana – Hey, is everything alright? You have been silent. All good at work?

Ravi to Suchita –Suchi, it is so effing complicated. You were my GF, now you are my GF's boss.

Ravi to Vandana – Hey V, nothing much. Just caught up with some avoidable work.

Vandana – No sweat, darling. I was wondering

if all is ok with Anup. I know you handle Shalini well.
Suchita – He he he he. I can understand. Don't worry, sweetheart, I am not here to break your nest.
Ravi to Vandana – Yeah yeah. Anup is under control. How is it there? I was with Raaj and Bhanu at our favourite haunt.
Vandana – You ass. Dare you not take me there soon!
Ravi to Vandana – Jealous?
Vandana – Oh, you know me better. But you also know how I like the place.
Ravi to Vandana – I know.
Vandana – Hey, why are you texting then? Aren't you driving?
Ravi to Vandana – Nah, Raaj is.
Vandana – He's there? Then it is fine… ☺
Ravi to Vandana – so when are you landing?
Vandana – tomorrow.
Ravi to Vandana – Ask a stupid question, get a stupid answer. I meant, what time?
Vandana – I know. ☺
Suchita – Oi, where are you lost?
Ravi to Suchita – Texting your reportee.
Ravi to Vandana – So tell me the time.
Vandana – 10:00 p.m. I had told you, baba.
Suchita – Ah well, you have company.

Ravi to Suchita – You got none?
Suchita – I liked someone after you, but not to the extent of getting involved like you are with Vandana.

"Mangy dog," complained Raaj, "tell me also what's happening. Whom are your fingers tickling? I am getting bored. Feels like I am driving alone."

"*Array*, it is getting difficult chatting with both of them."

"Ha ha ha ha ha ha ha. So what are they saying?"

"With Vandana it is a general chit-chat. Just catching up with her. In fact, she has also been asking me whether all has been good at work since I have been silent all this while."

"So what did you tell her? That Sofu has been keeping you busy?"

"Ha ha… Are you nuts? You know I have been busier with my work, than with Sofu. In fact, now that Bhanu got my profile deleted, it will take me some time to get more connections. Let us see how this pans out now."

"Hm."

"How are things with Simi?"

"Things are good with her."

"When are you guys planning to get married?"

"That's what we have to decide. Our parents will speak with each other in the days to come and then all will get settled."

"Auntie ji is okay with the match now?"

"Yeah, she had some reservations earlier, but dad and I were able to prevail over her. Rather, convinced her."

"Great. I am happy for both of you, man. Simi's a good girl."

"Oh, you bet she is," chuckled Raaj as they were reaching close to their destinations, "And what about Suchita? What is she saying?"

"*Yaar*, that is what I am unable to fully understand."

"Why?"

"She does make flirtatious comments every now and then, but I am not clearly sure what's on her mind."

"Tell me something," said Raaj in a manner of making a suggestion, "Why don't you try with Suchita?"

"Try what? You mean, in a manner of Sofu engagement? Friends with benefits?"

"Yes."

"Not with her. She is the first woman I experienced love with. How can I do this to her?"

Raaj wanted to say something, but before he could, Ravi saw messages from both Suchita and Vandana.

"Give me a minute. Let me reply to my women."

"Sure."

Suchita – Ravi, please do not take it otherwise, but let us meet up sometime if you do not mind.

Vandana – You don't have to pick me up. I'll

manage on my own.
Ravi – I'll be there.
Vandana – No. I will manage on my own.
Ravi – Why? What happened?
Vandana – I have a flight to catch at 7:30 a.m. for Chennai the day after. So I guess my place would be better.
Ravi – Oh.
Vandana – Array there is this customer who has created a ruckus. Seems like I will really have to handle him hard. But don't worry, babe, we will meet once I am back from Chennai. Promise.
Ravi – Handle him hard, but do not make him hard.
Vandana – Dog.☺
Ravi – Goodnight babe.
Vandana – Goodnight R.

"What are the ladies saying?" asked an impatient Raaj.

"I wanted to pick up Vandy, but she has other plans. She has to take a flight to Chennai in the morning of the day after. You know how she is, meticulous and all. So she will go to her place only.

"And Suchita?"

"She wants to meet up, generally."

"I don't think that, Ravi. What is there for an ex to meet you generally?"

"Means?"

"Means, what if she wants it? Or if she's okay with it?"

"You mean friends with benefits?"

"Yes, or ding–dong buddies, or whatever."

"So what do you suggest? It can be a mess-up, *yaar*. Vandana and Suchita are in the same office, she being Vandana's boss."

"Yes, you would have to be extra careful, or decide not to do it at all.

Ravi thought about it for a while. They reached Raaj's place. They bid goodbye to each other and then, before starting for his place, Ravi texted Suchita – *I do not see any problem in that at all, Suchita. Let us catch up.*

CHAPTER 24

Meeting 2.0 Concluded (Less Than Two Years Ago)

Vandana was a naturally beautiful girl. She did not have to do much to look attractive. Right now, all she had done were her eyes, and that too just a liner. She wore a salwar kameez—bright orange kameez with a matt blue Patiala salwar, and light brown *mojaris* with golden work done on them. She had left her hair flowing freely. Whether it was indeed her looks, or his love for her, Ravi wasn't able to decide, but he was dumbstruck. It took Vandana saying 'hey' for his reverie to be broken.

"You are looking good, Vandana."

'Just good,' thought Vandana, 'Idiot!'

"Thank you, Ravi," she said, "I hope I did not make you wait much."

'Wow man,' thought he, 'she takes all the time in the world and then asks me if I did not have to wait much.'

"No. I was reading the newspaper, so I was quite engrossed in that."

'Newspaper, my foot,' thought Vandana, 'hunger is written all over your face, liar.'

"Which newspaper?"

'Yeah like you are really interested in the newspaper,' Ravi thought to himself.

"Business Standard. But seriously, aren't you hungry?"

'See that, now he's coming out clean,' thought Vandana.

"I think we can grab a bite."

"If you'd like Italian, we can go to Stax. For anything else, it is Glasshouse."

"Stax will just do," replied Vandana.

"Stax it is, then," said Ravi.

While walking to Stax, Ravi messaged on 3DD – Guys, she looks great.

Share pic – Raaj's message on 3DD.

They settled down in Stax and ordered food. Ravi requested the waiter to get some bread/dinner rolls with butter for a quick bite.

'Hungry pig,' thought Vandana.

"Vandy, I think by now you know why I am here."

"I'd like to hear it from you, Ravi."

"To meet you."

Vandana smiled, having realised this, when she had

entered the hotel.

"Yeah, so we are meeting."

"Do I need to apologise? Look, I really am sorry for that day."

"Water under the bridge, Ravi. I am sure you did not come this far just to say sorry."

"I did, and I did not."

"How is that?"

"I still have a feeling that you feel that my apology that day wasn't heartfelt. So I apologised to you sometime back. And of course, there is something else as well."

"Like what?"

'As if she bloody doesn't know,' thought Ravi, 'now how many times does a young man follow a young woman on a flight to another city and just wait for her?'

"I want to know if I can get some time, a few moments and more than a few occasions from you to get to know you better."

'He has a style,' thought Vandana, 'bloody salesman.'

"You want to know," she asked smilingly, with the attitude of a queen, "or you need to know?"

'Such a bitch. Knows what I am here for but still has to act tough,' Ravi thought and, staring right into her eyes, bending a little over the table, with confidence he had never known he had in him before, said, "Vandy, have it your way then! You want me on my haunches?

Here I am. I am positively attracted to you and I am turning affectionate towards you. And I am wagging my tail, if you can see."

It was Vandana's turn to return the stare, albeit a stare that was admiring him for his courage. She knew that she was a very attractive girl, no one needed to tell her that. Boys used to roam around her ever since her class 10th[th] days right till her PG. However, such was her class, attitude and style, that they found it difficult to approach her—the fear of rejection, the fear of rejection! What Ravi had just confessed to was such a mood-lifter. Smarting from the day's events coupled with the confusion she had in her mind accentuated by Ravi's 'chance' presence in Mumbai, she had been feeling very low, little realising that the events of the evening were going to perk her up quicker than a passenger jet plane's climb rate during take–off.

"Many times, I feel the need to have you around, seek your counsel, your company. You are bold, brilliant, eloquent, super confident, perseverant, self-respecting, much organised, upright, well-groomed, well-read, and have a modern worldview, yet I feel there is so much to you that I do not know. The more I get to know about you, the more I know how much more I need to know about you, Vandy."

Vandana was positively floored. She had been proposed to earlier, but nothing like this. She had received compliments about how she looked, her eyes, her smile, her hair, her figure, her choice of clothes, her style, her swag and flattery of every other object that would change with time. Never before had a man mentioned the things that Ravi did, things that would never die, things that would only improve with time. Ravi had made her what no other man ever did—genuinely speechless.

"Ravi," she said after what appeared like a lifetime, and then, again, took a very long pause during which Ravi was staring at her lips in the manner of looking for an answer, "I… er… don't know what to say." And saying so, she blushed. She was still looking into Ravi's eyes—clearly, the confidence she had in herself showed—but at the same time, the genuine flattery that Ravi had showered upon her had made her feel shy and a tad insecure, for how could he know all that for sure. Was she giving herself away so easily?

"I am not looking for a yes or no, Vandy. All I need is some time from you. Time in which I get to know you better, time in which you get to know me better, time in which we both get to know each other better. That's all that I ask for."

The waiter was walking towards them, announcing the dishes and serving them. But both seemed to be consumed by the quality of the conversation that was taking place between them.

"May I ask you something, if you do not mind?" asked Vandana.

"There you go, knowing me better," quipped Ravi, and both smiled.

"How much did Raaj help you in this?"

"In what? Executing this trip?"

"No, you said things about me which only someone who's been close to me can observe."

"Vandy, you can be suspicious of my most loved friend, but you cannot give him the credit for observations that I have made."

"And when did you observe all this?" asked a mildly and pleasantly surprised Vandy.

"On three occasions—when I saw you at Raaj's place, when you reprimanded me in the restaurant, and over the call when I asked for info about your Ajit mama."

"But how come?"

"Simple, Vandy. Your eloquence, temper, boldness, and the respect you have for yourself and your achievements were on display in the restaurant. I had rubbed your pride the wrong way unintentionally and was at the receiving end for that. And the way you gave me a piece of your mind just showed your conviction and how strongly you felt about your education, about yourself and about your B school. You must have shown a lot of perseverance there, Vandy, and I am sure you must have received awards and accolades for it too."

The last line put Vandy momentarily on the memory lane. He was right; she had been the topper in all four semesters, and God, how she had toiled for it. So when Ravi had made fun of the lasses of Mass Com and the subjects they used to study, she erupted like a volcano.

"The fact that you could quickly tie up that chance meeting to Raaj's machinations just shows how quick, smart, observant and intelligent you are," Ravi continued, "and the fact that you did not tell me a thing about Ajit mama shows how upright you are, and very interestingly, it told me one more thing about you."

"What," asked Vandy, with a further increased curiosity.

"That, my dear Vandy, you still have not completely forgiven me for the restaurant thing. No wonder that even today I had to start with a very heartfelt and humble apology."

"Don't mention it, Ravi," Vandana was comfortably smiling.

"The way you dress up shows your grooming, the fact that you are organised, and have a modern worldview."

"How come?" asked Vandy with a hint of confusion.

"Tonight seems to be a night of revelations. No sweat. Since I have told you so much, let me share now what I have deduced. Till now I was only telling you what I had observed. Like I said, I have seen you on three occasions. Every time, the way you dressed just showed how organised you must be. Vandy, you are a consummate professional. Profession these days hardly leaves us with the time to spend on decisions related to getting dressed. You aren't in the army anyway where you know that you have to wear the uniform to work every day. Yet, you are impeccably dressed for the occasion. This clearly shows you organise your wardrobe very well. I am sure you did not know today morning when you woke up that you would be dining with a young man who would be very interested in spending time with you. Yet, you brought in a set of extra clothes, maybe for a chance dinner with colleagues that never happened. But even if the intention behind carrying this extra set of clothes was dinner with colleagues, you are able to use it well here. And a woman who has her wardrobe this organised, cannot be disorganised anywhere else. The way you conduct yourself, and the way you take care of essentials just shows how well-groomed you are, a trait that must have seeped in after years and years of practice. And finally, the way you were dressed up today morning clearly shows your modern world view. Now, did I miss anything, or is there anything that I can explain better?"

For once, Vandana was awestruck, and she was honest in admitting it, "I am honoured, Ravi."

'What a dame,' thought Ravi, 'Couldn't she say I am flattered, Ms. Uptight? Had I buttered Anup so much, the oaf would have taken immense pride in promoting me.'

Vandana was picking up lasagne from the serving dish. Ravi messaged in 3DD – *Pat gayi.*

"So, you have a plan for tomorrow?" asked Ravi.

"No, I am headed back to Delhi after my presentation."

"I didn't mean that, dodo..." Vandana could sense a lot of affection and protection in that sentence, "Do you have a plan for your customer, tomorrow?"

How she wished she could tell him that he was the reason why her presentation had been spoiled. But her pride came in the way, at that time! And now that Ravi had bared his heart open and boosted her ego, she was ready for the kill.

"Nothing I cannot handle, Ravi," she flashed a victory smile.

Message from Bhanu on 3DD – *Cheers. We need to party when you are back.*

Message from Raaj on 3DD – *I don't believe this. How do you manage all this? Call us.*

"But I am still waiting for your answer, Vandy. Do we get to spend some time with each other?"

"Yes."

CHAPTER 25

Face to Face (Present Day)

The man in Delhi was at his office working on the tasks ahead of him. But since he had tied up with a woman in Dubai who was returning to Delhi tonight, his mind was elsewhere. The excitement in his head was not to do with sex, which would happen eventually. He had really loved connecting with the woman. He did not know what her age was or if she looked great. What he knew was that she was intelligent, made interesting conversations, most likely unmarried—not that it mattered to him—had someone else in her life but maybe wasn't strongly tied to him, and was hard to get. He just had a hunch that she was beautiful. Clearly, the woman had totally captured his imagination. He kept on staring at the document he had to process, and the time in his watch, which just wasn't moving ahead. The day was boring. Finally, he decided to text her.

Man – Hey.

***

Ravi got a new connect on Sofu, Kavita. 'Is that her real name?,' Ravi wondered to himself and then thought, 'Like it matters, huh!'

Ravi – Hi Kavita.

***

The man in Delhi was eagerly awaiting the woman's reply from Dubai, but there wasn't any. 'Has she developed cold feet? Why does it always happen to me that when I find someone good enough, they just run away?'

***

Kavita – Hi Kabir. How are you?
Ravi – I am good. HBU?
Kavita – All well here.
Ravi – Good to know. What do you do?
Kavita – I am a professor with a university in NOIDA.

Ravi thought, 'Wow, someone interesting. This looks nice.'

Ravi – What subjects do you teach?

Kavita – Economics to undergrad students.

Ravi thought again, 'That sounds very interesting. Economics has been my interest too.'

Ravi – Great to know that. Never connected with someone like you here.

Kavita – Means?

Ravi – It is good to connect with someone so up the value curve.

Kavita – Thank you. Good to know that.

***

Man – Hey, is everything ok with you?

Woman – Yes, of course, why do you ask?

The man thought, 'Yeah, meet me and I will let you know.'

Man – Because you have been inexplicably silent.

Woman – I can explain.

Man – Please do.

Woman – Last day of the conference. Had to do some shopping for myself. As soon as the conference ended around lunch, I had to rush to the mall. Anyway, I'm headed towards the airport now. Should be with you in 6 hours.

Coming to pick me up, right? Or cold feet?

Man – Cold feet? Me? I thought you went cold.

Woman – No chance in hell, boy. See you very soon.

Man – Hey, shall we exchange numbers, just in case for coordination when you land?

Woman – I have a very good feeling about this, and believe me that I will give you my number, but please do not ask for it ever again. I have made some mistakes in the past and wouldn't want to repeat them till I am very sure.

Man – Won't argue with you on that as I have made mine too. But somewhere I thought we were both winning each other's trust.

Woman – Why else do you think I am letting you pick me up and take me to your place? I don't even know you.

Man – Ok, since you are not giving me your number shall we decide on a pillar number/gate number around which you would be standing?

Woman – Not needed.

Man – Then how will I spot you?

Woman – We meet in the lobby of Marriott.

The man in Delhi thought to himself, 'What a piece of work.'

Man – This is new.

Woman – Sorry for the inconvenience, but there are two reasons. One, I do not know you, and two, I have a friend whom I am dropping to that hotel. We can meet post that.

Man – Ok.

The man in Delhi was thinking, 'She is really smart. But she's right and she's smart. She's playing it safe. I do not think she's dropping any friends. That's an alibi to meet me at a safe place.'

Woman – Don't you worry. It's just a matter of a few hours.

Man – Ok, how would I know who you are? Is there a spot in Marriott where you would want me to look for you?

***

Ravi was thinking how to build up the conversation and take it to the point he wanted to. Introductions and pleasantries had already been exchanged. Before he could type, Kavita messaged.

Kavita – so Kabir, what are you here for?

Ravi thought, 'Ah, we are finally talking business.'

Ravi – I am here to connect.

Kavita – Connect for what?

Ravi – What do people connect for, Kavita?

Kavita – There can be many a thing—sex, marriage, friendship.

Ravi – I can understand sex. But do people effectively use this medium for marriage and friendship?

Kavita – LoL. Guess you have had some experiences here.

Ravi – The silly ones.

Kavita – Ha ha. Same here. But yes, people do use it for marriage and friendship. I know a friend of mine who found her life partner here.

'Who goes finding a friend or a life partner here? Bloody losers they must have been,' Ravi thought to himself.

***

Ravi – Vandy, you sure you do not want me to come?

Vandana – Yes babe. Kya hua? Missing me too much? Now don't say yes, I know you better. ☺

Ravi – It would have been good to meet. But hey, I can wait for a day. When will you return from Chennai?

Vandana – Tomorrow 6 p.m.

Ravi – Great. Let us go to our favourite haunt then.

Vandana – Sure. And Ravi, tell me if you want me to get you anything from Dubai.

Ravi – Just come back babe, that's enough.

Vandana – Coming soon. Love you.

***

Man – Hey, busy?

Woman – Sorry buddy. Someone was texting me.

Man – Who?

Woman – Someone. ☺

Man – Boyfriend?

Woman – I won't exactly call him that, but for the sake of a better word, yes!

Man – So how would I know where you are in Marriott.

Woman – If you are as smart as you sound, you will know.

Man – Why do you really act so hard to get?

Woman – Suits me, tiger. ☺

Man – I hope this is the last test.

Woman – It is. See you on the other side of five hours.

***

Kavita – What happened?

Ravi – About what?

Kavita – You went silent.

Ravi – Yeah, was chatting with a friend.

Kavita – Friend or girlfriend?

Ravi – Excuse me?

Kavita – Sorry if that bothers you, but I am looking for something long-term. And it is important for me to know that you are single, and that I am not stepping into someone else's nest.

'Why oh why, does this happen only with me?' thought Ravi, 'I do not even feel like responding to this silly bitch.'

Ravi – Kavita, this is a free dating app. People are here for fun. If you are looking for a husband, try the matrimonial sites. Why are you wasting the time of the likes of us?

Kavita – You are a dog, Kabir. You are nothing but a shameless mutt treating women like objects. Only if we were subjects of your affection and not the objects of your desire, this world would have been a better place. All you men think from somewhere else rather than your brains. Shame on you.

Ravi – Go to hell.

Message not delivered.

Ravi – Go to hell.

Message not delivered.

'What a bitch! She blocked me!' thought Ravi, completely disgusted with his day.

***

Our Man's time to meet the 'Woman' was nearing.

Man was driving very fast to Marriott in Aerocity, the excitement palpable. When he was about a kilometre from the hotel, he texted the Woman on Sofu – *Hey. I am about to reach. Are you in Marriott?*

Woman – *Yes, tiger.* ☺

In his mind he was just playing scenarios of identifying her, having dinner here or at some other place, and then driving to his place with her. After handing his car to the valet, our Man went straight to the lobby. His gait confident but slow, his eyes checking out every living female not in a hotel uniform. That was when our Man saw a very lively young woman sitting on the couch with a travel bag close to the couch, and a hand bag right next to her. She was wearing a blue-green chiffon saree, a big, green bindi on her forehead to match her saree's green shade, and a peacock blue blouse that matched the blue shade in the saree. Seeing our Man walk towards her, she stood up and extended her hand for a shake.

Smiling and shaking his hand, she introduced herself, "Sanjana."

Sensing that it was his turn to introduce himself, he announced his name, "Bhanu, Bhanupratap Bandhopadhyay."

CHAPTER 26

Breakfast, Lunch and Dinner (Less Than Two Years Ago)

"Vandy, I want you to win."

Ravi and Vandy were having breakfast together. Vandana had shared with him the details of yesterday's presentation, the fact that she hadn't been able to do a good job, and her plan to put the situation back where she wanted it—winning the order. She of course had told him nothing about her mind's preoccupation with him and how that had affected her presentation delivery, apart from the fact that there is always the pressure to be better than the competition, and the added pressure due to excessive waiting.

"Of course I will."

"I hope the events of last night have added to your confidence."

"Shut up," she said and smiled.

"So what's your plan for the day, Vandy?"

"The presentation is at 10 in the morning so I will be leaving shortly. We should be able to conclude things by 1:00 p.m. Thereafter, lunch with the team, and then I head for the airport, and from there to Delhi and back home."

"Can we make slight changes to the plan?"

"Like what?"

"Lunch with me here or anywhere else, maybe at the airport itself. Then we fly back together; I'll change my tickets so that we are on the same flight. And then in Delhi I take you to a place which you'll just love."

"Whoa, tiger," said Vandana, smiling, "take it slow."

"I am. It's not like I am going to your home and talking to your old man upon landing in Delhi. Like I said yesterday, some time to spend together. And what's the fuss about? It's the beginning of the weekend tomorrow."

"Sure. I will ping you once I am done with my presentation."

"Cool."

Shortly after Vandana left for the meeting, Ravi took Raaj and Bhanu on a call and narrated the entire incident, right from meeting her when she returned to their discussion at breakfast.

"I am happy for you, Ravi. This is such good news," said Bhanu, "I always knew you'd handle the situation well."

"Honestly, I was slightly scared when he told me

that he told her that I told him about her travel plans," said Raaj, "But I guess all is well that ends well."

"In this case," said Ravi, "All's well that begins well."

The three of them shared a laugh.

"So, what's the plan then?" asked Bhanu.

"We will have lunch together in Mumbai. Not sure where, but we will see. After that we board the flight to Delhi, and upon landing, I take her out for dinner."

"Where to?" asked Raaj.

"You know the place."

"What?"

"There, seriously? On the first date you take her there?" Raaj's reaction was more violent and unapproving than Bhanu's.

"Why, what's the problem with it?"

"Bro it's your first night; take her somewhere nice and classy."

"First night? Are you crazy, bro?" retorted Ravi, "*Bhai*, Raaj, this is the first dinner, not first night. I have no such ambitions just yet."

"I didn't mean it that way. Knowing you, you will consummate in any case only after marriage. But there can be better places."

"Mangy dog!"

Bhanu was laughing. After his lungs had pumped all the air out, he said, "I think it's a good idea, Raaj."

"What can I say? Neither of you had any class."

"It is not that Raaj," said Bhanu, "we have seen the

crowd that comes there. I am sure some of Delhi's finest love stories have begun and blossomed there."

The banter continued for some time. And then something struck Ravi. He asked Raaj to inform him of Vandana's meeting's outcome without letting her know. Raaj was game for it. He did not have to lose anything now, given that Vandy and Ravi were talking.

After a few hours, Raaj messaged on 3DD – *Meeting over. It was a hit. Customer has promised a contract. Vandy is elated. Loving breeze coming your way.*

Ravi was getting ready. He had little time. Vandana would start anytime from there and he hadn't packed up yet.

Vandana – Done with the meeting. Should I come to you first?
Ravi – How was the meeting?
Vandana – Raaj did not tell you? He had called Ashok to figure out what happened.
Ravi – Ashok?
Vandana – His counterpart in Mumbai.

'Man, she is smart,' thought Ravi and then messaged – *I wouldn't know about that.*

Vandana – You want me to believe that? Hey, but honestly, it did feel nice that you are looking out for me. I am not pissed. Coming to the hotel.

Ravi got ready quickly and stepped out of the hotel. He wanted to be back before Vandana could return. They returned almost together. He checked out while Vandana waited in the lobby. The flight was at 4:30 and the time now was 1:45 p.m. The airport was not even 10 minutes away.

On the way, they discussed her meeting. She shared the details very joyously, not sure if the joy was more because of winning over the customer or losing her heart to Ravi. They both got done with their security check and headed for lunch. Over lunch, there were so many things to discuss—college, jobs, best friends, favourite subjects, etc. etc.

Ravi told her that he had liked her the very first time he had seen her—at Raaj's place. That was the day when he really admired her beauty. But the day at the restaurant was when she had captured his heart, mind and imagination. And he had to figure out a way of reaching out to her heart and appealing to her softer side.

Their discussions continued in the flight as well. They both told each other about their families, parents, siblings… Both their fathers were in the army—Brig. Raghav Sharma and Maj. Gen. Basant Kumar Malhotra. Both their mothers were principals in private schools—Sudha Sharma and Reema Malhotra. Ravi had a younger sister. And Vandana had an older estranged sister.

They then discussed their bosses—Ravi told her about Anup and Vandana told him about Jamshyd.

Ravi, of course, had heard a lot about Jamshyd from Raaj. And Vandana seemed to echo that sentiment. A gem, that's what Jamshyd was.

They decided to first go to Vandana's place so she could change before heading for dinner. She simply slipped into jeans, a simple tee and sneakers. They drove in Vandana's car. Ravi asked her if she had ever been to this place he had in his mind, and her answer was no.

The Qutub Institutional Area in Katwaria Sarai, New Delhi, boasts of a lot of hip campuses and roadside eateries—the kind of places that are popular amongst students for their affordable rates. But there is only one LFF there—Lakshman Fast Food, otherwise also known as Lakshman *Dhaba*. That's where they were headed that night. The parathas are beyond comparison, the curries always leave you asking for more, and the boys there are ready to serve you the best they can.

Before their dinner arrived, Ravi placed something on the table and pushed it towards her. It was a neatly wrapped gift.

"What is this, Ravi? Gifts so soon? I really..."

She wanted to refuse. Sensing that, Ravi cut her short and said, "It's for your win, Vandy. Nothing expensive. Just something that you can always remember your win with."

Vandy opened the box and inside found a gold-plated Cross Pen.

"Thank you," she said appreciatively. "When did you buy this? It is beautiful.

"Thought I would buy something before your return from your victory presentation."

CHAPTER 27

New Partners (Present day)

Bhanu woke Sanjana up with a cup of tea, something that Sanjana had not factored in, so she was pleasantly surprised. They were having a pleasant conversation, a warm exchange of words. Last night was very steamy. They had gone to work as soon as they had reached Bhanu's home. With no sense of the time that they had spent in it, they dozed off when they were both spent. Bhanu was always an early riser. When he woke up, he went straight towards the kitchen and not only prepared tea but also prepared *mise en place* for breakfast. His plan was to cook mushroom and chicken omelettes in garlic butter stuffed with fried onions and melted cheese, seasoned with salt, oregano, *dhaniya* leaves, and present it on a plate with a butter toast on either side and hand-beaten coffee. With the cut ingredients ready and tea prepared, he took the tea with cookies and marble tea cakes into the room.

"I must say," said Sanjana, "I am pleasantly surprised, Bhanu. You are a man who seems to take care of his woman."

"I do my bit when I know that the woman I am going out with is a woman of substance. I love to give respect."

"Good with words."

"Remember our first chat?"

"What about it?"

"You had asked me about my profession, and I had told you that I help people make their writing impactful."

"Okayyy…" said Sanjana, "I do remember something to that effect. You are an editor or something?"

"Ha ha ha ha ha."

"Why do you laugh, Bhanu?"

"This is exactly what you had asked—if I were an editor—when I told you that I help people make their writing impactful."

"So what did you reply, then? Sorry, I have forgotten about it, in the sense I do not completely remember, Mr. Wordsmith."

"I did not tell you then, but I am telling you now. I am a litigating lawyer."

"Oh, wow!"

"And you had said that you repair, so what are you?"

"I am a doctor."

"Damn you, seriously?"

"Well, rather you than I, and yes, seriously, I am a doctor. A heart specialist at that."

"Wow," said Bhanu, "I am in august company."

"So am I, and my God, this is so yum," said Sanjana, drinking the tea and eating the marble tea cake.

Bhanu was, of course, confused whether it was the tea cake that impressed her or the tea.

"Which of these is yum?" he asked.

"The tea, of course. You are not just a magician with words; your hands work magic too, Bhanu."

"I believe you got a taste of them last night," said Bhanu, winking and raising both his hands.

"Shut up, dog!" Both of them laughed.

Sanjana worked in a private hospital in Gurgaon very close to where Bhanu's office was. They also lived in the same sector in Gurgaon, sector 69. Both were therefore happy that even for the future, logistics would work out very well. By now, tea had been tastefully and gratefully consumed. Bhanu collected the tea cups, cookies and cake containers and kept them in the kitchen. He handed over a clean towel to Sanjana for her bath.

"Bhanu, you are really a man with manners. I am really impressed."

"Thank you, babe. Have a lovely shower. Geyser's hot."

Indeed, the geyser was hot. Sanjana loved her baths to be long and with warm water. Bhanu was in no hurry himself and was praying that she took long so he could shock her with breakfast. Somehow, this felt different. It wasn't love—it was surely attraction—but it felt very different. Sanjana was not a flip-flop. She was a doctor, could make very good conversations, was exceedingly intelligent and smart, appreciated all that Bhanu was doing for her and clearly did not expect any of that.

Bhanu loved to cook, and was cooking with all the love he had for food. He whipped two eggs for each omelette with seasoning and milk, fried the onions separately till they turned golden-brown and heated garlic butter. The molten butter filled the kitchen with the fragrance of garlic and butter and was turning Bhanu hungry. He spread the beaten eggs on his pan atop the molten butter and waited for the omelette to coagulate at the base but remain a thick liquid paste at the top. At this stage, he sprinkled *dhaniya* leaves, shredded cheese, the golden-fried onions and turned over half the omelette on itself, sealing it completely. On a separate girdle he toasted two bread slices, each on both sides, and spread butter on one side of both the slices. By the time Sanjana was ready, so was breakfast, for both of them.

Bhanu's bedroom opened straight into his dining room. He had guessed correctly—Sanjana was shocked with what she saw at the table.

"Bhanu, I am at a total loss of words. I was clearly not expecting this. After having chats with you, I knew you weren't a wham-bam-thank-you-ma'am type, but I certainly didn't expect this from you. You really know how to treat a girl. Your mother did a great job of raising you in this way."

Bhanu, at the same time, was mesmerised by how she was dressed up—maroon saree, maroon bindi, maroon stiletto pumps, all this coupled with cherry brown hair. Of course, the hair hue wasn't natural; it was a dye. Bhanu had met with many beautiful women earlier, but this one was different. Sanjana's complexion wasn't very fair, but not wheatish either. She had an imposing and sharp nose, large, lively eyes and short hair.

"Well, thank you. It is a very gratifying and humbling experience for a cook if their preparation finds favour with their host. So, please," he said, taking a pause, astonished by her looks while pulling out a chair for her, "taste the food and let me know how you like it."

For the next thirty minutes their conversation was built around food, the work that both had at their offices that day, their resolve to meet again and a lot of other things about the God-created universe. Sanjana proposed that the next time round they meet at her place so that he could get to taste her hand, something that Bhanu gladly agreed to. They also realised that Sanjana's job entailed very little outside travel—only medical conferences or emergencies—while Bhanu's job entailed more travels than hers, but less than many others, say three to four days a month. They also planned to travel to some destination together.

With breakfast over, and Sanjana ready with her bags, Bhanu came to drop her at the door and remembered something.

"Sanjana, can I please have your number now?"

"Of course, Bhanu, so silly of me to have forgotten," said Sanjana, smiling. She gave her number to Bhanu and they hugged each other.

"Looking forward," said one of them to the other.

"Very soon," replied the other.

CHAPTER 28

Love is Followed by a Shock (A Year and Nine Months Ago)

It had been quite some time since the Mumbai trip. Ravi Malhotra and Vandana Sharma were now '*Vanhotra*'. They had planned a get-together with Ravi's friends. Raaj, Simi and Bhanu were waiting in a Cyber Hub restaurant. Ravi had planned a dinner meeting where they all could meet—in the same restaurant where Raaj and Vandana had 'accidentally' met Ravi. Vandana laughed when she heard Ravi's choice of place. But she quite liked the idea of meeting his best friends at the same place in a very different setting. Among Raaj and Bhanu, she knew Raaj and was acquainted with Simi, who had come over to their office a few times when Raaj and she had planned their evenings together. On one of those few times, Raaj had introduced Simi to her. Bhanu was an unknown commodity to her. It was a Friday, so Vandana had rushed home a little early to get ready. It wasn't that she was a fashionista, but she was very particular and mindful about the company and the occasion she was addressing. Ravi therefore drove her home, and after she got ready, drove her back. Raaj, Simi and Bhanu, on the other hand, were reaching there from their respective offices. Bhanu and Ravi knew Simi very well as they would meet on quite a few weekends and other occasions like Raaj's, Bhanu's and Ravi's birthdays.

Raaj was admiring Ravi for the courage he had shown in chasing and wooing Vandana, while Simi was arguing that Ravi did not have to be vain in the beginning for all this to have taken place. It was at that moment that Ravi escorted Vandana into the restaurant towards the table where they were sitting with Hari, the restaurant manager, smilingly waving his hand at him.

Introductions were clearly in order. Ravi introduced Vandana to the group, and the group to Vandana.

"Guys… She's the one, the One-dana. And Vandana, the lady here," said Ravi, pointing towards Simi, "is the proof that while I happen to miracles, miracles too happen to some of my friends."

Raaj and Bhanu and Simi burst out laughing, with Ravi clearly referring to both the ladies as miracles. Ravi then walked over to Bhanu and placed his hands on Bhanu's shoulders, announcing, "and this man here is apparently the best litigating lawyer in the making, Bhanupratap Bandhopadhyay."

Pleasantries were exchanged, orders for snacks and drinks placed, they all settled, and Ravi asked, "So folks, wassup?"

"Before you guys stepped in, I was telling them all the stuff you did for Vandana's and your I-love-you moments," said Raaj.

"But who said that Ravi has proposed to me yet?" quipped Vandana.

"What?" Raaj, Simi and Bhanu yelled together.

"You only messaged on 3DD that you've scored the winning goal," Raaj announced in all his innocence while Bhanu was confused, and Ravi gave the 'look' to Bhanu.

"What?" asked Vandana.

"You didn't know this?" continued Raaj, "He mentioned to us that he had wooed you and you had said yes."

"I got that, but what's 3DD? That's what I said 'what' for," clarified Vandana.

"Oh that?" said Raaj, without realising his mistake, "That's the name of our WhatsApp group."

"Yeah, and why don't you tell her what it stands for?" reacted Ravi, knowing fully well what was going to happen next. Bhanu saw it play out in his mind and was now smiling wide.

"3DD. 3 Dirty Dawgs—our WhatsApp group. He messaged there when he proposed to you in Mumbai," clarified Bhanu.

"What?" asked Simi, and this is precisely what Ravi had hoped for.

"Don't be surprised, Simi," said Vandana mocking them, "boys do take help from their pack in approaching us."

"I did not say 'what' for that, Vandana."

"Then what was this 'what' for?"

Bhanu was laughing by now, Ravi was smiling wide, and Vandana was getting surprised.

"Well," said Simi looking at Raaj questioningly, "someone never told me about 3DD."

Raaj realised a few things here—he had been careless in mentioning 3DD, he had been tricked by Ravi into telling what 3DD was, and that this wasn't going to be his best evening.

When they had formed 3DD, they had decided that they would keep its existence a secret from everyone else. There was no reason for this pact; it was just another of those brotherhood pacts.

"Simi," Bhanu addressed her, "don't start bashing on him now. It is not as if we bitch about you guys on 3DD; it's just another of those harmless, boy things."

"So you were taking guidance from them when you were in Mumbai?" asked Vandana.

"You think so?" asked Ravi, "I mean, Mr. Lawyer last had a girlfriend a hundred years ago, and Raaj is so deeply smitten by his girl, that he hardly has any time for me."

"Don't say anything to assuage me now, Ravi," said Simi, smiling, and then turned towards Bhanu, "and don't worry, Bhanu, I will leave your friend in one piece when I am done with him."

"*Chalo,* at least someone is doing someone," quipped Bhanu and they all shared a laugh together, apart from the drinks and snacks that were rolling in.

It was a great get-together. Vandana and Simi had started bonding and exchanged their numbers. Ravi made use of the moment and quietly made a WhatsApp group for all five of them. He named it Dear Friends. Simi was the first one to notice it and she smiled. There was a lot of talk over dinner—about school days, graduation days and PG days. Ravi made a point to the group that he was going to be very careful about what he was going to say about his PG days, making an obvious reference to his first meeting with Vandana. Raaj had told Simi about it, so again, everyone was all smiles. There was so much that they had to share with each other. Bhanu and Ravi had been a riot during school days while Raaj and Ravi had been so during PG days. Simi had been jealous during their PG days about the amount of time Ravi and Raaj would spend with each other, and made no bones telling Vandana about it.

"You know what," Simi said to Vandana, "the talk about these guys was that they must have been feeling something for each other since they were so into each other."

"Yuck," said Raaj.

"Yuck," echoed Ravi.

"Ditto," remarked Bhanu.

Simi, Raaj and Ravi had been together in PG, so a big part of the conversation was around the three of them and the years they had spent together. Vandana wanted to know more about Bhanu and turned towards him, "So how was it after school, Bhanu? You guys kept in touch?"

"Yes, we did. Not so much physically since we studied different subjects and in different cities, but we were always connected in our minds. We rarely met after school, but whenever we meet, including today, it never feels as if school is over. Ravi and I were like twins from different wombs, always together—joined in mind, body and soul. If there was an instance of notoriety in our class, a teacher with the slightest of observational skills could trace it to us. And then there was such fun, camaraderie and a sense of belonging in getting punished together. We were pricks, real pricks. Did you know we used to sign each other's report cards for each other's dads?" described Bhanu, clearly lost in history.

"What?" asked everyone except Ravi. They were laughing.

"Yeah, had we carried home our report cards with our marks, and on top of them, our teachers' remarks, it would have been a sure-shot disaster," said Bhanu.

"*Saale*, you never told me this," a surprised but amused Raaj said.

"Let me tell you more; Ravi learnt to cook during his grad days," said Bhanu.

"What else could I have done?" interjected Ravi, "Our mess messed up the food big time."

"And while he became a good cook, I became a golfer," continued Bhanu, "Dad was influential so I had access to a few good clubs in Delhi. Though he would never get me a job, on things related to sports and fitness, he was always a pro."

"Did you guys have girlfriends in school?" asked Simi.

"You think?" asked Bhanu.

"No chance, zilch, nada!" said Vandana.

"How about you, Vandana?" asked Simi, "Have you been in a relationship earlier?"

"Yes, I have been," Vandana answered slowly, "Not that I am very proud of it. The relationship did not turn out well." She had earlier told Ravi all about it, as Ravi had also shared about his previous girlfriends. Vandana's remark, however, had turned the mood a little grim, and so as to snatch away the grimness from that moment, Bhanu asked Vandana, "So, Vandana, do you still pull Ravi's leg over your first meeting?"

"No," said Vandana, "I think after the way he approached me in Mumbai and cleared the air over that meeting, it was water under the bridge."

As if to lighten the moment further, Ravi turned towards them all with his right hand over the left side of his lips (Vandana was seated to his left) and whispered aloud and winked, "Apologised, apologised, not approached." It was meant to be heard by all and bring them to a smile, and it did.

The banter continued for quite some time after. And then, as all good things must come to an end, so did this dinner—the introductory dinner. Afterwards, they just strolled for a while in Cyber Hub and started for their nests. Ravi was driving Vandana to her home.

"You guys are a very warm and tight bunch of friends. Keep it that way, Ravi."

"Sure. And one day, let us catch up with your friends as well. I'd love to meet them. And your family, at the right time."

"I am more of a colleague person than a friend person. But yes, I have a close one. Will make you meet her someday."

Instead of driving her home straight, Ravi drove her to Bhandari Pan in Chanakyapuri first. (Their sweet pan is a delicacy. They have a secret ingredient that makes it very tasty.) And the drive at 11:00 p.m. was fantastic, with little traffic. By the time they reached her place, it was past midnight. Since it was the weekend, they thought of spending some more time together after which Ravi would head back home. Vandana offered to fix coffee and Ravi gladly agreed. She opened the door and they both walked in. Before Vandana could switch on the lights, Ravi grabbed Vandana towards himself and hugged her. Before he could kiss her, he noticed a woman's silhouette and immediately switched on the lights.

Vandana looked at her, and before she could say anything, Sudha thundered, "Shut up!"

Ravi realised who this was and opened his mouth to say something. But again, it wasn't Ravi but Sudha who said, "Get out!"

CHAPTER 29

Meeting New and Old People (Present Day)

Ravi was at work. He was planning his meeting with Suchita when a message came on Sofu from Ruby. Ravi and Ruby had connected on Sofu earlier.

Ruby – Hi Kabir. How are you doing? I am going to be in Delhi this week. What are your plans?
Ravi – Hey Ruby. Good to be back in touch. I am here only this week, not traveling anywhere. So let me know how things pan out.
Ruby – Sure.

Post this short chat, Ravi sat thinking about Suchita. He was wondering if he should meet her. The pros were that he and Vandana both knew her. Suchita knew that both of them were indeed going around and were very serious about it. She also did not need any closure as they had closed the breakup back in college only, and despite being connected on some professional networking sites, they had barely been in touch. Knowing her, she would not try to do anything funny or hazardous for Ravi or for Vandana.

He picked up his phone and texted Suchita asking her when they could meet up. Suchita replied after about half an hour about wanting to meet the following day. She was apparently busy with a proposal that had to go by the following day, and she was heavily invested in that.

***

The next day, Ravi and Suchita met at Roots Café in Sector 29, Gurgaon and Suchita began with a compliment, "You have started looking more handsome. You were such a skinny kid back in college."

"Yeah?" said Ravi. "Those were different days. And those were better days. It was always so much easier to live off one's father's income."

"You parasite."

"No, not like that," Ravi protested, "You know what I am saying; you know what it was like. Ask dad for money for anything and as long as it was a genuine need, it was always there."

"Like your bike?" asked Suchita and they both laughed.

While in college Ravi had once asked his dad for a

bike. He wanted the 350CC Bullet. Instead, his father sent him their old geared scooter that no one used back at home. Ravi did not know this till the scooter reached Bengaluru by train. He still remembered the day afresh. He had gone there with Suchita to show off the bike, but when he saw that the vehicle packed heavily in the packaging material resembled nothing close to a Bullet, his heart sank. From the silhouette of the heavily packed material covering his scooter, he could make out what it was. Suchita saw his expression change and thought that it was some mix-up. But when she realised what had happened, she burst out laughing.

"Ha ha ha ha. The Brigadier played a practical joke on you," she had exclaimed then. Ravi's father, who retired as a Major General, was a Brigadier then in the Northern Command of the Indian Army. Ravi had two emotions running through his mind at that time—cynicism for the practical joke that his dad had played on him and the possible shame that his classmates would bestow on him on seeing him ride an old *Chetak* given that he had been bragging about a Bullet to his classmates for since over a month. Not one to sulk or lose his composure for long, he put both these emotions aside, took delivery of his scooter, filled it with petrol and went back to campus.

"What?" snapped Suchita sitting across him bringing him back to the present, "lost in scooter thoughts?"

"Yeah, funny it was, no?"

"Yes, it was."

"You did not make fun of it for long, but the boys pulled my leg on it for about a month. Bloody jackasses."

"How could I?" said Suchita smilingly, "the rides on your scooter were always comfortable whether I rode with you or alone. Besides, I was your girlfriend then and not among the jackasses."

"Those were the days, weren't they?

"They were indeed, Ravi."

"So what happened after?"

"After? After what?"

"After we broke up!"

"It was tough. Took me a while to recover. But once I did, there was no looking back."

"I am sorry, Suchita."

"Bygones."

"Cool. Tell me how your life brought you to Stellar then? What all happened?"

"Long story."

"We have time."

"Like old times?" asked Suchita and winked.

"Ha ha. Yeah, like old times."

"After engineering you know I joined Tech Mahindra."

"Yeah, that was from campus."

"Correct. I was with them for 4 years and then went

for my MBA. I specialised in Brand and Marketing and was picked up by HUL from campus. Stellar was our vendor. I was always in touch with the top bosses at Stellar and enjoyed a good working relationship with them. One professional thing led to another. Jamshyd had left for greener pastures and when Stellar approached me, I agreed."

"Indeed. And in between you never found someone to settle down with?"

"I wasn't looking for anyone, Ravi. After you, I had resolved to totally focus on my career. In fact, as I mentioned earlier, it was rather tough on me initially. But then you know me; I have been bouncing back all my life. *Amma* and *Appa* helped me a lot."

"I can imagine, Suchita. Were they angry with me?"

"Does it matter?"

"Of course it does."

"No, they weren't. *Amma* always said it was my decision either way. *Appa* said he would support me in whatever I decide—getting married or going for higher studies or making a career in engineering. Since I wasn't marrying anyone soon and neither were my parents interested in finding me a match as soon as I had a job, they left it to me. *Appa* guided me well though, in terms of choosing an employer. In fact, he taught me the concept of an employer very well. He said that the way they choose us, we should also choose those whom we want to work with. Took me a while to understand, but when I did, it kind of stuck with me the whole life."

"I never interacted with your mother, but your father was always very wise."

"He is," chuckled Suchita and asked, "so what about you? I know you were going around with Tara in your MBA campus days. How come Vandana?"

"Yeah, that is a nice one, but before I tell you this, how about you tell me how you got to know about Vandana?"

"Later. You tell me about Tara first."

Ravi told her about Tara, his second girlfriend, the one he had met in his B-school. Tara and he had connected over a class assignment and they had chimed very well. Things developed slowly between them. Ravi and Tara both were strong in academics and did take their career very seriously. Their relationship as students was taking a very symbiotic turn. Studies in B-school are assignment and research-based. Many times, this requires gathering data. Ravi was good at gathering data and Tara was good at conducting research, having taken a strong liking to statistical research in her graduation. The projects that they worked on were invariably the best in research and presentation.

Ravi and Raaj had simultaneously developed a bromance amongst them. Plus, Raaj was good at keeping class notes. Where Ravi and Tara relied more on understanding and memory, Raaj relied more on taking detailed notes which he would exchange with the other two. As a trio, they were complete, so it wasn't long before Raaj, Ravi and Tara came together for their assignments. They had become sort of a tag team.

Within this tag team, Ravi was developing a romantic interest for Tara. Cupid struck him before striking Tara. What started as some honest class assignments together, brought them closer as the number of assignments grew. They started spending time with each other, getting to know each other well. This would happen during breaks or planned excursions like movies. One day, when Ravi was sure of his feelings for Tara, he heartily proposed, Tara favourably disposed and Raaj was the first one to get to know. Slowly, the entire batch came to know that 'Ra-Ra' were a couple. Ravi still did not have a bike. So whenever they had to go out somewhere he would borrow Raaj's bike and offer Raaj his scooter for commuting. Raaj would scoff, huff and puff but never let his BBF down except when he also had to go out with his girlfriend.

Ravi told Suchita everything about Tara except why they weren't together. Inquisitive, Suchita asked, "So why aren't Tara and you a couple instead of Vandana and you?" It took Suchita less than a moment to realise that her question had changed the look on Ravi's face, from someone walking fondly down the memory lane to someone who was in sorrow and unexplained anger. Suchita extended her hand to mildly squeeze Ravi's and said, "I have nothing against Vandana, but from whatever you told me..." She was cut short by Ravi's response, "She died, Suchita. Tara died. It was a road accident. I still think about her, though Vandana has filled my life with love in every possible way. Had it not been for that accident, who knows," said Ravi and the mood of the conversation turned sombre.

"I am sorry, Ravi."

Ravi took some time, smiled and said, "Hey, it's cool. And now here we are. So tell me, how did you get to know about Vandana?"

"Yeah, that? Office talks mostly, but in a respectful manner. I got to know more about you from Vandana on the Dubai trip. Both of you used to intently message each other and I thought of messing with you in between."

Both shared a laugh and continued with dinner.

"Say, Ravi," continued Suchita, "are you still, uh, I mean...?"

"On the verge, but not yet in?"

"Ha ha ha ha ha ha, yes?"

"Yes," said Ravi.

"Ah, that means the same deal with Vandana?"

"Yeah, but you really don't have to go there, do you? Tell me about yourself if you are so intent on knowing about me."

"Wasn't really going after boys. Though I did meet a cool guy to hang out with. We made love also, but he wasn't cool enough to think of marrying. Then of course I had a career to build so I had to leave a lot of things behind. You know building a career isn't easy."

"You are right. Ask me. I have been performing well but it seems like my boss is never happy."

"They never are," said Suchita and smiled. "The trick is in knowing what their weaknesses are and providing them support there and not letting them know that you know their weakness. That is what cements the bond. Try it; I am sure it will work."

"Good idea. Will try it on Anup. He's my super boss. My direct boss is a cool cucumber. But tell me something, now that you have reached a certain level in your career, don't you feel like settling down? No family pressure for this?"

"Not much pressure from home, but yeah, now that I have accomplished something, I'd like to settle down."

"You have someone in mind?"

"Why, are you offering?"

CHAPTER 30

Candid Talks (A Year and Nine Months Ago)

All of it happened so quickly that Ravi did not know how to react. It was as if words did not find the way from his brain to his mouth. He was dumbstruck. He did notice though that the resemblance between Sudha and Vandana was striking. Ravi had no doubt who Sudha was. He quietly folded his hands in a namaste and turned towards Vandana and turned back towards the door. While going down in the elevator he was wondering whether he had put Vandana in a tight spot, and whether Vandana would call him tomorrow asking for a break-up. Whatever he knew about her made him sure that Vandana wasn't made of mud that dissolves in a gush of water; rather, she was like the rock that water cannot dissolve and therefore passes by. Nevertheless, he knew Vandana was in a spot and that over time, even rocks are smoothed by water.

"What is this, Vandana?" asked Sudha.

"Ma, you should have told me that you are coming. This is not fair."

"Not fair? What are you talking about? Just because you are busted, this is not fair?"

"Ma, Ravi and I have been getting to know each other better…" Vandana wanted to continue but Sudha cut her short, "And how? By inviting a man up here past midnight and getting intimate with him?"

"Ma, I know you are angry, but hear me out," Vandana was calm and composed, and most importantly she was confidently firm even as her mother was angry and disturbed, "You'll have to give me some time to explain it to you. I want you to understand this in detail before reaching any conclusion. And more importantly, I have taken a lot of time in responding to his overtures in a bid to understand him better. But I hadn't told anything about this to you or papa since I wanted to be sure about everything this time and not get taken for a ride. I would have anyway told you about Ravi in a week or two. It's just that I did not know you were coming here sooner than I was coming to you."

"And this was your way of not getting taken for a ride?"

***

Driving home, Ravi's thoughts were still on Vandana.

He was wondering what if he had decided not to go up and have coffee; it wasn't like they were going to make love anyway. But it was just that they both loved spending time together, talking about the past, present and future. But now he was not sure if there was a future.

***

"Ma, you need to be confident about the values that you have inculcated in us, at least me!"

There was a studied and tensed silence when Vandana said this. Sudha knew what she meant when she said 'at least me'. Both of them were looking each other in the eye. They had been standing and talking ever since Ravi had left. Vandana extended her arm and gestured to Sudha to sit on the sofa. This was going to be a long night and both of them needed to discuss things. Sudha knew her daughter's resolve. She also knew that Vandana was not the one to give up, but then neither was Sudha. Like any loving parent, she wanted the best for her child and did not want her child to get hurt.

"I am confident about you and your sister. I am not confident about boys these days."

"And how do you want to check their fidelity levels, ma?"

Sudha knew that she had no straight answer to this. She was silent, wondering what to say next when

Vandana continued, "Quite honestly, even I do not have the answer to that. There is always that chance."

***

Somewhere, Ravi also knew that Vandana was a tough girl, determined and resolute. He knew that she would stand up for Ravi. But he had also heard from her how resolute her mother was. And the fact that he didn't know what the mother–daughter duo were discussing, was killing him. He was in half a mind to turn back and drive towards Vandana's place and apologise to both Sudha and Vandana, but then apologise for what? He had not done anything against Vandana's will. Loving someone was not illegal.

***

"I do not want to step into your personal life beyond a point, Vandana. You are my little girl who has grown up fast and grown up well. But I know how it played out last time and how badly you got hurt. I do not want you to get hurt like that again."

"So what are you suggesting, ma?"

"That you go slow. Discuss some things with me and your dad. I know you do not speak with your *didi*. But talk to me and papa. We have life's experience behind us and we both can guide you well. I am glad I was alone. Imagine if the Brigadier was around!"

Vandana broke into a smile, and so did her mother. Had the Brigadier, Vandana's father, been around, he would have probably walked into combat with Ravi. It would have been difficult to handle him, no doubt. With both breaking into a smile, the temperature of the house lessened. Vandana went towards the kitchen to make some tea. The mother–daughter duo had midnight tea on umpteen occasions. They would typically watch their favourite movies or shows. Today was different. There was no movie, no show. Today, there was a discussion about what Vandana was doing in her personal life.

While Vandana was brewing tea, Sudha entered the kitchen.

"You were saying that you have taken a lot of time evaluating that boy."

"Yes, I have. It is a long story. Tea is almost ready. Let us take it to the drawing room and I will share the facts with you, in detail."

"Sure, but have you guys…?" Sudha left the question unfinished.

"No, ma…," chuckled Vandana, "Don't start imagining things now. I am telling you everything *na.*"

With the tea brewed, both ladies took their cups to the drawing room. Vandana added the chai masala that Sudha had brought, which added to the flavour and aroma. Vandana had a long chat with her mother wherein she recounted her encounter with Ravi at Raaj's home followed by the 'chance' meeting 'set up' by Raaj and how the meeting ended with Vandana giving earfuls to both Raaj and Ravi.

"I can really imagine you giving it to the boys like that."

"Wait till you hear what happened next, ma. I was impressed by Ravi's guts when he approached me seeking help with Ajit mama."

"What?" said a shocked Sudha. "He knows that Ajit is your mama?"

Vandana narrated the whole incident in detail, culminating with the admonishment that Ravi was delivered at Vandana's hands. Sudha was in splits and laughing aloud. The mood had clearly turned light. Sudha was also admiring her child and listening to the details.

"And he still did not give up?"

"No, ma… He kept coming back like a determined pest," replied Vandana with a smile that displayed admiration for Ravi. "He again approached Raaj, but this time to plan a trip to Mumbai to coincide with my official travel."

"Some guts!"

"I swear," said Vandana, and then as if delving into the past, she asked, "Does he remind you of dad? You had once told me that even dad chased you quite a lot."

"Of course he did. I acted 'so hard to get' once I

knew that he wanted me," chuckled Sudha, "and that would make the whole act of courtship even more pleasurable, you know the chase and all."

"Yeah," reverted Vandana with a sense of pride for her mother, "but while you were doing it for your pride, I was doing it because I was angry."

"You must have been. Then how did you finally get convinced?"

Vandana then narrated the Mumbai incident. Sudha was in splits by the time Vandana had finished narrating the incident.

***

Ravi wanted to be with Vandana in those moments. He knew these were tough moments for both the mother and the daughter. Sudha would genuinely be concerned about her daughter, and of course she was. It was just that Ravi was unaware of the background as yet.

***

"*Dekh beta*, I know both you and *didi* can take care of yourselves; you are two tigresses that the Brigadier and I have given birth to and reared. It's just that what happened last time scares me."

"How am I responsible for that, *ma*?"

"You are not, but then maybe you are!"

Now Vandana fumed, "How can you even say that, *ma*? You know what had happened. That Rohit was a two-timing or a multi-timing scoundrel. But that wasn't the worst. The worst was that he was two-timing me with *didi*!"

"But *didi* didn't know that then. And when she got to know about it, she stopped being in touch with Rohit. You know that. But you never forgave her. The Brigadier was also confused for some time, whether he should be angry or if he should protect the both of you. We had our talks and he came around. And now we have a broken family. It pains me to see my children not in touch with each other, Vandana. You will be a mother one day; you will realise it then."

"*Ma*, I know that you went through pain as well and you still feel it. She is my elder sister, and I feel for her too, but my anger and hurt haven't yet subsided. Maybe my anger has; I do not feel angry at her any more. But my hurt hasn't come down one bit. I am still unable to come to terms. Are you hoping that I go through the same pain as you did when I become a parent?"

"Are you silly? Why will I ever ask that for my daughter? I am saying that growing up is a learning phase for humans both as parents and as kids. You will learn this as a parent that it kills the mother's heart to see her kids not speaking to each other."

Both were highly emotional in that moment and fell silent, walking down their own memory lanes. Once she fell in love with Rohit, Vandana had no inhibitions about being intimate with her man. After all, they had professed their love to each other. Both had told their parents about it. Meeting with both sets of parents was on the cards. Both had to inform their parents about it. Rohit and Vandana were meeting that weekend to discuss how to break it to their families when Vandana got the shock of her life. Rohit had left his mobile unlocked on the table. He got a message on his cell on the Sofu app. Generally, Vandana would not check his mobile. In fact, she wouldn't check it ever. Rohit had also been very protective about his mobile and would always keep it's screen locked. But that was one moment in which he forgot to do it; the call of nature that day was too intense and he did not suspect that he would get a Sofu message as soon as he left his mobile on the table. But he did. He had also changed his mobile just a day ago and had not yet restricted the Sofu app in his privacy settings from displaying notifications on the screen. The app showed a full screen-size notification when a message came along with the picture of the sender. 'When do we make out next?' was the message that had flashed on Rohit's cell from Vandana's *didi*.

"But *ma*," said Vandana after a while, "why did you say that maybe I was responsible for what happened? In the sense that I put my trust in the wrong man?"

"No. I know one cannot know what's hiding behind someone's eyes. I meant something else."

"What?"

"You said that you were both content in every possible way."

"Yes, we were."

"If so, why was Rohit looking outside?"

"Are you suggesting that I was not being intimate enough with him?"

"These things happen not just because of lack of intimacy, but because of lack of connect as well. Anyway, maybe I am wrong in thinking the way I am. I was brought up on traditional doses—take care of your man, keep him happy always, etc. etc. In the heart of my heart, I know he was a loser. And I am glad you are not with him. And now we have Ravi. What do we do about him?"

Vandana was waiting for this and knew that this was the moment. "Meet him, *ma*. And form your own conclusions."

"I think I will. But not here. Send him home. The Brigadier and I would both want to meet him."

CHAPTER 31

It's Raining Sofu Connects (Present Day)

Ravi was driving Anup to the airport. Anup had come to visit customers in which Cyber Dynamics was heavily invested. He liked to drive some of the key relationships himself. These were obviously the most important customers/engagements for the organisation.

"After a long time you have utilised my visit properly, Ravi."

"Thank you, Anup." Ravi returned with a smile, but in his mind was running a different thought, 'He means that till now I have not utilised his visits properly. Can he ever say a good word about me?'

Ting-tong.

"This is how I would want you to plan my visits. These two days that I spent here were very productive."

Ting-tong.

Ting-tong.

"My pleasure, Anup, and I surely will keep the feedback in mind while planning your next visit."

Ting-tong.
Ting-tong.
Ting-tong.

"Good, but what's this notification sound about? Your phone seems to be working overtime. If you work half as much, you can grow like a eucalyptus."

"Come on, Anup. It's about 7:30 p.m. This is when the boys' network starts becoming alive, if you know what I mean," and he winked.

"Ha ha. Yes I know."

They had reached the T3 departure. Ravi dropped Anup and slowly drove away from the departure building. After driving through till the end of the raised road, he parked his car on the side and checked the ting-tongs. He knew they weren't about the boys' network, but about the boy's needs.

Ruby was checking if they could meet up that night for dinner and then take things ahead. This cautious approach was to Ravi's liking as well, since he did not want to commit to anything without meeting with her. That aside, Adriana and Ashley had sent him connection requests. Ruby was a bird that was almost in hand and Adriana and Ashley were in the bush. Made sense to meet Ruby, first.

Ravi – Hi Ruby. I can be there in 10 minutes.

In her text message on Sofu, she had mentioned that she was putting up at Marriott, in Aerocity.

Ruby – Cool. Come over. I am changing, but I should be able to come down in 20 minutes.
Ravi – No sweat, I will wait. I am wearing a green shirt and dark grey pants.

He parked his car and went up to the lobby area. There, he accepted connect requests from Adriana and Ashley. Both were from the UK. 'Wow, I seem to be in luck finally,' thought he. They were both beautiful. One looked mature and the other youthful. 'This is good,' he thought, 'at least I can get one of them. Will see as things move ahead.'

***

Sanjana – Hey.
Bhanu – Hi.
Sanjana – Let us catch up. What do you say?
Bhanu – I am game. What's on your mind?
Sanjana – Catching up. Why? What do you have on your mind?
Bhanu – Doctor, I am the one who plays with words, not you. ☺

Sanjana – Why tiger, I was straight. Seems you are running your imagination wild. ☺
Bhanu – Array baba… you want to meet up for dinner or…??
Sanjana – How is one complete without the other, tiger?

***

Ruby was a young, attractive girl, between 24 and 28 as per Ravi's reckoning. And as she was walking up to him, he saw that she was clearly not the woman whose pic she had used on Sofu, but was also clearly no less in beauty, grace and elegance. They met in the lobby first, and decided to have a small chat there before moving in for a buffet. Ravi had also used a pic that was not his on the Sofu app. But it could be concluded by an independent observer that both were happy with the persons they saw in real life in the hotel. Ruby took a quick liking to Ravi's demeanour and appearance. Ravi asked her about her flight plans after exchanging pleasantries.

"Well, I am here tonight and tomorrow. The day after, I leave for Europe. I was supposed to fly out tonight, but the plans changed, so I thought it would be a good opportunity to catch up with you."

'A lot can happen over two nights,' thought Ravi and said, "That was a good idea. Good to finally meet you."

"Is this your first time, Ravi?"

'How the hell does she know that I've never been laid,' thought Ravi, but he decided to not let her know what he was thinking and asked, "Means?"

"Are you meeting with someone for the first time through Sofu?"

'Thank god,' he thought, and then replied, "No, I have met some girls before," he paused, and then asked, "why do you ask?"

Ting-tong.

***

Sanjana and Bhanu had finally decided to meet at her place. She would keep food ready by the time Bhanu would come home. Bhanu had decided to get something along, so he picked up a bottle of champagne.

***

"Did you get another connect, or did you get a message from an existing connect?" asked Ruby with a naughty smile.

"Whatever it is, I am not checking right now," said Ravi with a smile.

"Thank you," said Ruby in a tone that was appreciative and flattered.

"So, you were asking whether this is my first time. Why do you feel so?" asked Ravi.

"I just had a feeling, that's all," said Ruby and paused. After a small pause, she elaborated, "I had a feeling that you have connected with a few people on Sofu but met with only one. Anyway, it doesn't matter as long as we are clear what we are here for.

"I know what I am here for, Ruby. What are you here for?"

***

Bhanu pressed the bell at Sanjana's flat. Sanjana answered it quickly. Bhanu discovered how graceful Sanjana looked even when she wasn't wearing any make up, or for that matter wearing only home casuals. Sanjana was wearing a tee shirt and a lower. After opening the door and giving him half a hug she turned back quickly and rushed towards her kitchen.

"Make yourself comfortable, Bhanu, I am just about to finish cooking."

In her hurry she did not even notice the champagne Bhanu had brought. Bhanu followed her to her kitchen and kept the champagne in her fridge.

"Wow, you got champagne." Finally, she noticed.

***

"Ravi, I am looking for an intimate relationship that can benefit both of us. Intimacy in this relationship shouldn't be by force, but by choice. It should be at a time and place that is comfortable to both. Let me also tell you what I am not looking for. I am not looking for either of us hounding the other for sex and time. I certainly do not wish to fall in love. I very carefully choose to connect with guys not in my hometown. I love sex and I love casual sex. Something like no strings attached? That's what I am looking for. But while there won't be space for love in our relationship, this relationship has to have respect for each other. When I am in my hometown, I will be very slow in replying. You will have to bear with that."

When he heard her say 'benefit' Ravi hoped that benefit wasn't money. But when in the same breath she added the relationship should be by choice, he felt that the benefit she was looking for wasn't money. He was about to find out that he was wrong.

***

"That was such nice food, Sanjana. I think I might just fall in love with your culinary skills," Bhanu rewarded her food with his compliments.

"Beware, beware, for they say that the way to a man's heart is through his stomach."

"Isn't that a few inches too high?"

"Devil."

They both laughed at that and sat watching Netflix. It seemed like a different evening. Both did have intimacy in mind earlier in the day, but now that they were together and had their dinner, they were simply sitting together holding hands on the long sofa, feet propped up on the coffee table, watching Netflix. 'Was something brewing?' This was the question both had in mind.

Bhanu turned towards her and looked in her eyes, and Sanjana turned towards Bhanu.

***

"So what I am looking for is something very similar," said Ravi, "Mutual respect for each other, mutual respect for each other's time, moments that can be enjoyed together, no love, no piling on each other, and above all, a consensual relationship."

When Ravi said the last two words, he observed Ruby feel the same unease that he had felt when she had mentioned about a beneficial relationship. So, after reflecting on what he had said, she asked, "Explain consensual?"

Ravi did see some disconnect here but decided to answer the question anyway. "We should both have consent for intimacy, a consent that is mutual and devoid of any other expectation. Isn't that what you also said?" asked our man.

"More or less, yes. But I have one expectation."

"Which is?" Ravi was now getting slightly tensed, his eyebrows taut.

"I like to shop for expensive dresses and stilettos. You have got to buy me those."

"Ok, so you are not asking for cash, but kind in return for sex."

"I see nothing wrong or inappropriate in that."

Ravi was eager to answer but paused. He wanted to choose his words carefully. It wasn't because he suddenly had emotions for Ruby, but because Ruby was really worth being intimate with. She was young, beautiful, tall, spoke very well, and from the looks of it, seemed like someone who would really be hot in bed. Plus, she wasn't asking for cash, she was asking for kind. Now kind is like a gift. And which boyfriend does not give gifts to his girlfriend? A part of Ravi was thinking of going ahead and saying yes, while another part was continuously telling him – cash and kind are the same.

***

Bhanu and Sanjana were lost in an unspoken conversation. It was as if their minds were conversing with each other. And both were wondering if it was Cupid, and if yes, what next? It surely wasn't love, or was it?

***

"It is not about wrong or right," deliberated Ravi, "or appropriate or inappropriate, Ruby. It is about the kind of things we want to do and the kind of things we do not."

"What do you mean?"

"See, you are clearly from a good family background…"

"And you are not," cut in Ruby, in a rather agitated state.

"Hey, do not get me wrong. And please allow me to explain. Of course I am from a good family, and so are you. Besides, you are earning well. So why are you offering yourself for something in return?"

"Have you had a girlfriend ever?"

"And how is that relevant?"

"Have you never bought her gifts?"

"That is different. In a boyfriend–girlfriend scenario, no one asks for gifts."

"Yes, because it is expected that gifts would come by, now and then."

"Listen, let us not go down that path. I do not think either of us is trying to woo the other for love now, are we?" Ruby was silent, so Ravi continued, "It is just that I do not have it in my mental make up to make an offer in exchange for sex. I'd rather not have sex than pay for it."

"And now you listen, Ravi," there was a hint of impatience and annoyed firmness in her voice, "I am not a whore, ok?"

"Then why…" Ravi left his question incomplete but understood.

"So that you value what's coming your way."

"Value can be displayed in other ways."

"Such as?"

For a moment, Ravi was left in silence. Ruby had a point. In a relationship where participants participate only for casual sex, how could value be displayed other than getting something for someone. Ravi was clear about how he felt about this, and his next words were going to make it abundantly clear.

"I do not mind getting you a gift, Ruby. I mind being asked for it in return for sex."

Ruby heard it, and it was as if her aggression suddenly vaporised. The changing emotional landscape on her face had Ravi convinced that she was coming around, so he continued, "You are a self-respecting woman from what I can see. You earn well. You are a result of good upbringing. Then why…?" Sitting across Ravi, Ruby raised her eyes and the index finger of her right hand. The gesture was for Ravi to leave his question incomplete.

There was a pause in the conversation. It was as if she was reflecting on what Ravi just said—that he didn't mind giving her a gift, but the act of gifting had to be voluntary, not by conscription.

"I have not thought about the issue like you have. You do have a point, but then I have always received whatever I have asked for. Men are ready to fall at my heels if I ask them to. And please, spare me the moral lecture."

"Well, I am sure they are Ruby, but not this one," said Ravi with his right hand closed in a fist and his thumb pointing to himself.

"So what are you saying? Calling it off?" asked Ruby in a manner of daring Ravi to cancel the engagement that they had been trying to work out the whole evening. This ploy had worked earlier as well; men had not been able to give up on her.

"Ruby, it is not a challenge or a dare. I am sure you will get a million other boys or men who would go to any lengths to please you. But please, do not ask for kind or cash in return for sex. It sounds very…" Ravi left it unsaid, remembering Ruby's gesture sometime back.

Ruby stared into his eyes for a moment. She was angry and was wearing her pride on her sleeve. She stood up, held out her hand and said, "Done. Let me give this up for you. I can make an exception to my own rule."

"So you are cool not expecting anything in return?"

"That's what I said, Ravi. Shall we?" she asked smilingly, gesturing towards the elevator.

It was the moment Ravi had been waiting for.

CHAPTER 32

Vandana's Parents Meet Ravi (Almost a Year and a Half Ago)

The meeting was set up in Cyber Hub. Ravi was hurriedly walking towards the venue. His gait made it clear that he did not want to be late at all. A lot was on his mind, largely excitement, with modicums of fear and uncertainty. And while a lot was on his mind, a lot was on in their minds as well. When they finally met, they all greeted each other with excitement, intrigue, curiosity, warmth and hugs.

"Ok, out with it now. I have been waiting like nuts," said Raaj, "And so has *mishti doi*."

"Of course I will tell you everything, blow by blow. Get me something to drink, bro," Ravi quipped.

Ravi had met with Vandana's parents earlier in the day in Chandigarh. Chandimandir, a small town just outside Chandigarh and in district Panchkula, houses our army's Western Command HQ. Here was the last posting that

Brigadier Raghav Sharma had before his retirement. Both Brig. Sharma and Sudha had fallen in love with Chandigarh—it's cleanliness, it's resourcefulness, the Sukhna Lake, nearness to the Himalayas, Parwanoo, Kasauli, Chail, Shimla were just a few hours away and away from the hustle and bustle of big cities.

Aiming to reach their residence by 11:00 a.m., Ravi had started around 6:00 a.m. from Gurgaon. Idea was to have lunch with Vandy's parents and be back. He had stopped for breakfast in Karnal. There are quite a few dhabas there. In fact, the entire GT Road is lined up with so many dhabas that one can get confused with the drop and go errors. Having had parathas to his fill, he resumed driving and reached the Sharma household by 10:55 a.m.

"Then?" asked Bhanu.

"Well, you know us Punjabis. I instinctively touched her mother's feet," Ravi replied.

"And father's?" asked Raaj.

"He did not let me," replied Ravi, "I had almost bent when he asked me not to, and extended his hand instead for the shake."

"So did you shake his hand?" asked Bhanu.

"Yes, of course," answered Raaj, "our friend is good at shaking."

All three burst out laughing.

***

"Ma," Vandana was on line with her mother, "how did it go? How did Papa and you find Ravi?"

"I think I like the boy. He is sweet. He was a little wary of me I guess, the way I literally pounced on him that day," replied Sudha.

"Kya, ma, were you strict with him today also?"

"Ha ha ha ha, you are being very possessive. No, I wasn't strict with him today. I guess he realised that and did open up at the lunch table. *Chatora hai ek number ka.* I had cooked all that you asked me to, *chat chat karke sab kha gaya.*"

Both women laughed at this.

"They asked me about my background, schooling, college, how we met, etc. You know the regular questions. Vandana had told them about the fact that my dad was in the army as well. Apparently, her old man knows mine—not closely because they've never worked together, but I guess they know about each other," Ravi was briefing his friends.

"So did the Brigadier like you?" asked Bhanu.

"Leave the Brigadier. It is the woman of the house who has to welcome the son-in-law," Raaj expressed his expert opinion, " Did Sudha aunty like you?"

"Bro Vandana's mummy is such a great cook," said Ravi in awe, "I was uneasy when I met with her, but by the time snacks and food came in, I was sold. I now know where Vandana gets all this talent from."

***

"And what did Papa have to say?"

"I think the Brigadier likes the boy. But you know him; he will take his time, say a week or so."

"I know."

"And then of course we have to meet his parents. He said his parents were away on a holiday abroad, visiting some relatives."

"Yeah, his *maasi* and *chacha* both live in the UK."

"Yes, he mentioned. Apparently, they will be returning in a month or so. Good thing that he had informed them about this meeting before coming here."

***

"*Bhukkad*," said Raaj.

"Tell me, what did the Brigadier say?" Bhanu asked.

"The Brig was a serious one. Or at least he acted so. Stiff upper lip, cut-to-cut fauji, just like the General," Ravi said, making a reference to his father, Maj. General Basant Kumar Malhotra.

"Seriously?" asked Bhanu.

"Bro, why are all these fauji dads so serious?" asked Raaj, thinking about his dad and Ravi's.

"So what else did you guys discuss? How did the meeting conclude?" Bhanu's curiosity was killing him.

***

"*Ma*, did you guys discuss *didi*?"

"After a stoic silence, Sudha replied, "No, not yet. This meeting was largely about him. But at some stage we will have to open up. What have you told him so far?"

"Nothing."

"What? You have told him you have no other siblings?"

"Of course I have told him about *didi*, but I haven't told him about the reason for the discord between *didi* and me. All I have told him is that *didi* remains very busy with her research work, which you know is partially true."

"You will have to sort it out with your sister, *beta*. It is not possible that we do not talk about her ever with your in-laws."

"Yes, but they do not have to know what *didi* did."

"Of course not *beta,* but what did she do? She did not even know."

***

"Oh, with her father it was largely the kind of work I do, the working hours I have, the growth opportunities, willingness to work abroad, etc. etc. I quite liked them."

"Hmmm, did they like you too?"

"Well, I spoke with Vandana on my way back. She told me that her mother liked me. Apparently, she had told all our courtship stories to her mother and all those really did impress her," he chuckled and continued, "but her dad will reflect on it for a week or so."

"Meaning?" asked Raaj, "He isn't convinced yet?"

"He takes time. I think he will come down to Delhi and discuss this with Vandana. That's what she was telling me."

CHAPTER 33

Old Flames can be Very Consuming (Present Day)

"You are traveling too much these days," complained Ravi.

"Why, tiger, missing me already?" quipped Vandana.

"Well, of course. But why has your travel picked up so much?"

"I might get the charge for the Western region as well."

"With a promotion and hike?"

"Looks like it."

"Babe, we are getting married in a few months' time. Your travel has to come down."

"Do not worry, tiger, this is temporary. I will manage."

"How?"

"Will hire someone in Mumbai who will report to me. You have my word that before we are married, I will settle this Western region thingy."

"You want me to talk to Suchita?"

"No, why drag her into this?" Vandana asked, irritated, and after a pause said with assuaging confidence, "I will manage it; you know me."

Vandana was scheduled to fly to Mumbai the following day, and both of them were having a conversation around it over a video call. She had an early flight to catch so the conversation did not take long. Vandana slept off immediately, while Ravi sent a message on 3DD.

Ravi – Sleeping?

Raaj – No.

Bhanu – No.

Ravi – Shall we get on a call then?

Raaj – Yes.

Bhanu – Sure.

The three of them got on a call. Ravi shared with them the previous day's development, right from driving Anup to the airport and dropping him off to getting connected with Ashley and Adriana and receiving a message from Ruby to meeting with her in the lobby of Marriott.

He also told them about Shivani, a girl who connected with Ravi earlier in the day while he was in office. Shivani had told him that she came from a small town close to Chandigarh, her background being humble. She was a very hardworking student and was fully aware of the stretch her family had taken in sending her to Delhi for studies. Her dreams were inspiring her to go to Europe for even higher studies, but her family did not have that kind of money. So she was willing to offer sex in exchange for education money.

Bhanu asked, "And you trust her?"

Ravi, "I don't know whether what she was telling was true or not, but it sounded like a good reason for her to ask for money in exchange for sex."

"That's debatable," Raaj reflected.

"How?" asked Ravi.

"Yaar," began Raaj, "first we do not know if whatever she told you is true. She could be lying. It could just be a sob story. Second, if you are asking for money in exchange for sex, then you are what you are."

"My view is different, Raaj," Bhanu interjected. "If she is not doing this professionally, she is not a whore."

"Oh, come on, lawyer. How is she any different from a woman that charges you for sex? Ok, Shivani, or whatever the hell her real name is, may not be from a healthy socio-economic background but what she is seeking is trade, not pleasure," Raaj was hard-hitting.

"Anyway, guys, just so you know, I have even deleted my fake profile."

"What?" they both jumped at him.

"You have just started milking the app, and you are over with it?" asked Raaj.

"Yes. I got what I wanted. Besides, marriage isn't far

away, so that's it."

"Good call," said Bhanu.

After a while the good friends wished each other goodnight and concluded the call. Though Ravi would never meet with her, he did somehow believe Shivani.

The next day, he had a client meeting in Ambience Mall, Vasant Kunj, around 6 p.m. It was a very angry client who had not been giving time to meet with Cyber Dynamics since the last six months. This client's last meeting had been with Anup and Shalini about six months ago and that had ended in disaster. Anup had stopped short of saying unpleasant things, and the meeting was anything but cordial or pleasant. Ever since, Shalini and Ravi had been trying to make amends. Finally, Ravi's charm worked, and Gurdeep Singh from RV Transport Solutions gave him time.

Ravi and Shalini decided that Ravi would go alone. He had a point to prove anyway, and Shalini was completely behind him on this one. The meeting six months ago went bust because of Anup, so if Ravi could bring the relationship back on track, he would have a point to make to Anup.

The meeting went on for about an hour and a half. Post the meeting, after settling the bill, Ravi came out walking and was updating Shalini on call when he saw a silhouette that he only knew too well. He was receiving accolades from both Shalini and Anup on the call. Shalini was so happy that she had patched in Anup on the call.

And while listening to them both, he was following the silhouette to Striker. The silhouette entered the pub while Ravi stood outside, finishing the call.

With the call over, Ravi, in an upbeat mood, entered Striker, and looking for the silhouette, climbed up to the rooftop. He made his way to the table where the silhouette was seated and presented himself. Suchita was pleasantly surprised.

"How come you are here?" she asked.

"Had a meeting. You?"

"Bad day," she said and made a face. "Are you in a hurry?"

"Not particularly. Why?

"I mean, you came to say hi or can we down a pitcher?"

"I think we can down a pitcher."

Both of them exchanged notes of how their respective days went as they drank two pitchers. Ravi's day had started uneventfully but had concluded on a high. Suchita's day had started uneventfully and concluded on a low. Beer and meeting with an old friend, rather an old flame, did elevate her mood. On their way out, Ravi offered to drop her home. Where she stayed was right on Ravi's way to Gurgaon. Suchita would have taken an Uber anyway so she accepted.

The last time they had met, Suchita had mentioned to Ravi that she'd like to settle down. The conversation had ended in a tease, with Ravi asking if she had someone in mind and Suchita asking if he was offering.

"I can think of Anup but he is a few years older than your comfort," Ravi started.

"What?" Suchita was obviously confused since she could not connect the dots.

"Your marriage," winked Ravi.

"Oh, shut up. Whatever you've told me about that oaf, I never will." And they both shared a laugh. Her flat was about eight minutes away, so they could not continue their tease for long. Ravi parked right in front of her ground floor DDA flat.

"I better get going," said Ravi. "It will take me another 45 minutes before I reach home."

"Sure." Saying so, Suchita stepped out of Ravi's car. Ravi stepped out as well and shook hands with her. Suchita gave him a hug and, out of the blue, planted a sweet long kiss on his left cheek, holding his face in her hands. She stepped back, with her right hand still on his left cheek, and said, "Goodnight. Drive safe. Text me when you reach home."

While driving back Ravi was reflecting on what had just happened. He hadn't expected it. He wasn't sure whether he liked it also, though he did not 'not like' it. 'Why would she kiss me?' was all that he was thinking. The fact that Suchita was drop-dead gorgeous and an old flame wasn't helping him either.

He reached home and texted Vandana – *I have reached home.*

Vandana – *So late? Had a long day?*

While he was reading this text, he got a text from Suchita – *Hey, reached home?*

He realised he had sent the 'reached home' text mistakenly to Vandana.

Ravi to Vandana – *yes babe, long day, good day, tired and hitting the sack.*
Ravi to Suchita – *yes.*
Suchita – *Ravi, I am sorry. I don't know what came over me back then. One of those moments, I guess.*

Ravi was relieved to see the text from Suchita and replied – *hey, it's cool. I'm glad nothing happened thereafter.*

Suchita – *me too. Goodnight.*

CHAPTER 34

Green Signal (Almost a Year and Three Months Ago)

Vandana was super excited. Ravi's parents were back and wanted to meet her parents. Also, her parents were coming down to meet her. Her father wanted to pick her brains on Ravi deeply before meeting Ravi's parents.

Brig. and Mrs. Sharma landed at Vandana's place before lunch. They had a hearty discussion with Vandana and then went to meet with Ravi's parents who were visiting Ravi especially for this.

The retired officers had a lot to catch up on and share once they liked each other. The ladies too gelled very well.

Discussions done, Vandana's parents left for Chandigarh. Ravi and Vandana broke the news to their friends. There was happiness all around.

"So, General sahib, let us fix a date for engagement

and another for marriage. We will be very happy if both of these functions can be held in Chandigarh," Brigadier Sharma was on a call with General Malhotra a few days after their meeting.

"Let me check with madam and get back to you on that one," quipped Gen. Malhotra.

"Reema, I was on a call with Raghav. He has requested us to finalise the dates, so I guess you will have to do the talking with pandit ji."

"That's lovely. You asked him to share Vandana's details?"

"You know I am not very comfortable with these things. Ask your son to fetch her details, or speak with Sudha."

"I will tell Ravi to do it. Anything else?"

"Yes, he suggested we hold both functions in Chandigarh."

"I hope you did not say yes to it."

"I did not. I told him that you and I will have to confer."

A week after that, the Brigadier and Major. General spoke again. "Brigadier sahib, next year 5th October seems good for engagement; it's a Saturday. And 19th October for marriage. It's Saturday again. What do you say to that?"

"Sounds good, sir. How about location?"

"I'd say Delhi for engagement, and Chandigarh for marriage. Is that good?"

"Yes, this also sounds good, sir. I will inform Sudha. I think she will also check with our family *pandit ji*. And then I guess Sudha and madam (Reema Malhotra) can coordinate with each other."

"Great. So we will wait for your confirmation on the dates then."

CHAPTER 36

Friends in Need are Friends Indeed (Present Day)

"Now," Ravi explained, "there can only be two options—she deliberately sourced it from someone to come behind me, or someone gave her my number to make her come behind me. "Okay let us look at other things," said Ravi in a sombre tone, "She got to know about Vandana and me. And she took time to come behind me. I am guessing that she got to know about me not in Dubai. It also tells me that Vandana and Mahek are not close friends or colleagues."

"Meaning?" asked Bhanu.

"Had Mahek and Vandy been close friends, I am sure Mahek would know about me from Vandy. Maybe Vandy would have shown her what I look like. Had that been the case, Mahek would have told Vandy as soon as she would have seen my pic on Sofu. Clearly, Mahek is not in Vandy's close group."

Turning towards Raaj, Ravi asked, "I am assuming you would know most of your colleagues, or at least those who work closely with you. Does anyone fit the personality type like hers?"

"Hard to say, Ravi," answered Raaj after mulling over it. "But if we can get to know the trigger, we can predict what she is coming to you for."

"Yes, and therein lies the rub. How do we figure out what has triggered her to come after me, now?"

"And how did she get to know about you and Vandana? What do you think about that?" Raaj asked.

"Difficult but not impossible," Bhanu interjected. "Could have happened accidentally. Vandana and Mahek are colleagues, and Vandana and Ravi call each other and chat with each other. Ravi's image flashes every time he calls her. Mahek could have noticed. I am still wondering what motivated her enough to reach out to Ravi."

"So are we saying, Mahek just wants to make a quick buck? I mean had she been after sex only I am sure she could have gotten it from Sofu." After a pause, Raaj winked and said, "Or maybe she finds you irresistibly desirable."

"Raaj, wanting to make a quick buck is the simplest of all reasons. It cannot be that simple," Ravi answered.

"Normally, the simplest explanation is the correct explanation when a crime is committed. It is just that it stays away from the watchful eye," Bhanu spoke as if reminiscing some real-life experience of being a lawyer.

Amidst all the tension, they were trying to find a few light moments. And while their discussions were on, Raaj had ordered food online. Ravi's doorbell rang and Raaj went to collect food. He had ordered three small pizzas and laid them on the dining table. The three were now sitting at the table.

"Ok, now that we have reached a stage where we have a few unanswered questions, what do we do?" Raaj asked.

"I think we go with the flow," Bhanu expressed his opinion.

"You mean to say we play the game and see how it pans out?"

"Exactly, how else will we get to know what's happening?"

Ravi thought about it and then concluded that what Bhanu suggested was the only way to know what was happening.

"Once we know what's happening, we can try to control it. Before knowing what's happening, how can we control it?" Bhanu reiterated.

"Bhanu, there is only one thing that I am uncomfortable about—that I have no control in this, at least for now."

"That's correct. And that's because she has the initiative and she has stealthily taken it.

"Is there no way that we can get to know her

identity before she meets us?" Ravi asked.

"How will that help us? In any case, you will get to know when she meets you," Raaj said.

"Not necessarily so," said Bhanu. "We have never seen her. You may have seen her, but you do not know who she is. Ravi does not even have her number from before. We don't know whether this is her number also or not. In fact, we don't even jolly well know whether this is Mahek also or not!"

"The more we think about it, the more these 'don't know' will arise," remarked Ravi. "I had checked the number on the web and on number search apps. This number has no reference."

"So maybe she purchased another SIM only for this. She is smart," remarked Bhanu, with a hint of admiration for her.

"Stop admiring her… make a plan to get us out of this."

"You mean I should make a plan to get YOU out of this, Ravi. I have a plan in mind."

"What plan?" Raaj and Ravi asked in tandem.

"I will chat with her, not you."

"*Waah beta*," said Raaj.

"And why?" asked Ravi.

"Trust me, I can handle her better."

"What makes you say so, *mishti doi*?" Ravi asked, wearing his pride on his sleeve.

"Oh, come on, I am not challenging you, Ravi. But

you know I am better at this."

"How?" asked Raaj.

"Ask him what his Sofu score is," Bhanu replied to Raaj with a devilish grin.

"Arsehole," said Ravi with a smirk.

"No, but what's the plan?" asked Raaj.

"Bro," Bhanu started, "the plan is simple. I will chat with her to figure out her motivations and thought process. I am not discounting Ravi's ability to do so, but then he is under stress, and I am not. I can think on my feet while he may find that a little difficult. Beyond a point, in such things, stress sets in. That apart, he can easily trust me. Furthermore, by doing this we are putting an arm's length distance between Mahek and Ravi. That gives us the room to step back and discuss."

"And how will you do this? I do not think you should use your own number."

"And I won't. I am going to buy a new SIM. It's a game two can play." And then, turning towards Ravi, Bhanu said, "All I need you to do is to not answer her calls or texts till I get a new SIM. Whatever the pressure, just ignore it."

"Easier said than done."

"I know. But it has to be this way; there is no better way. Besides, why do you think I told you that here onwards I want to control the narrative. My mind won't be stressed, so I can. Besides, my skills on Sofu." Bhanu left it at that and winked.

"Shut up," said a stressed-out Ravi. Raaj and Bhanu laughed.

Continuing with their pizzas and beers that Ravi had pulled out of his fridge in the meanwhile, Bhanu said, "And in a long time, I haven't had an adventure like this in life. So I am sure it will be fun. Risky, but bold and fun."

"So what will you tell her?"

"I do not have a script in my mind, Raaj. I will have to build the conversation on the fly. This will be a conversation that will make me employ all my skills, all my tact, all my experience, all that I have learned. The bloody bitch!"

There was silence after that. The three finished their pizzas and beer in that silence.

CHAPTER 37

Taking the Bull by its Horns (Present Day)

On his way back, Raaj was wondering whether Sofu's fun had been worth it for Ravi. It hadn't been a good experience for Ravi. And the focus had now shifted to something completely different. It was a fight that had to be won. It was a fight that was threatening to destroy whatever Ravi had built so painstakingly till now. As friends, they knew they were together in this, and they would not lose it. They decided to play this very close to their hearts and be in touch with each other, always. It was Monday night, so they did not carry on their dinner/discussions for long.

Bhanu had bought a new SIM on the way to his place. He had been on a different train of thought than Raaj and Ravi. So far, he had not shared with Raaj or Ravi about Sanjana. He had of course shared with Sanjana that Ravi and Raaj were his closest pals. He had not even shared with Sanjana how he felt about her. They were both sure of it though. Bhanu's thought went to the conversation that Sanjana and he had a few days ago. Bhanu was troubleshooting on her mobile because Sanjana was having some trouble downloading an app. It was an app to catalogue and store the happiest memories in the forms of pictures and other documents. The app was called Memory Store. Bhanu realised that Sanjana's mobile did not have enough space.

"Sanju, I need to remove an app from your mobile. Which one should I remove?"

"Sofu," she replied without batting an eyelid and smiled at Bhanu.

Bhanu smiled back, and before uninstalling Sofu from her mobile, showed his mobile to Sanjana—there was no Sofu on it either. Sanjana was so happy seeing this that she jumped at Bhanu. They both hugged and kissed.

Coming back to the present, Bhanu was thinking about how to start the conversation with Mahek. Upon reaching home he texted on 3DD. The friends had decided to discuss this matter on 3DD so that all of them were in the know.

Bhanu – Ravi, did she message/call?
Ravi – No.
Raaj – Bitch!
Bhanu – can you paste her last message?

Ravi – This needs to be done. I will set up time and day with you. If you keep on following my instructions you are in safe hands. Good day!
Raaj – Bitch!
Ravi – so we wait?
Bhanu – No, we fire a message.
Raaj – Bitch!
Ravi – Why? We can wait till she shoots a text for a meeting or whatever instruction. No?
Bhanu – No.
Raaj – Bitch!
Ravi – your thought behind it?
Bhanu – I do not want to give her the time. I plan to take the initiative away from her. We are improvising on the fly. Let's see if she can.
Ravi – Super.
Raaj – Bitch!

Bhanu was now thinking about how to start the conversation. It was clear that he had to go with the flow, but it was also clear that he wanted to control the flow and wrest the initiative back from Mahek. So should the start be contextual, or just a hi? Sending a hi would be a cold start, wouldn't rattle her much, would make Bhanu's landing on her soft. He did not want to pick up a fight. He wanted to rattle her and shake her out of her comfort zone, and in the process also figure out if Mahek was alone in this or with someone. He had saved Mahek's number before leaving Ravi's place.

Bhanu to Mahek – So then, what have you thought?

He kept his gaze on the screen for some time, but there was no reply. After a while he decided to just let it be. Choosing not to follow up, he decided to call up Sanjana.

"Oi, Sanjana, what are you doing?"

"Nothing much. Prepping up a lecture for tomorrow. I have been invited by my college to address the students."

"Time-pass."

"No," retorted Sanjana with a strong emphasis on the sound of 'O'.

"*Achha baba*, your 'no' does not have to be that strong. I take your point. This is serious business."

"Yeah, you better not joke around."

Beep, came a sound in between the conversation. The sound of that beep took Bhanu's attention.

"I won't, dear sweetheart, I won't. Let me not take your time then. Do a good prep and deliver an impactful presentation."

"Thank you, sweetheart, but I can spare a few minutes."

Bhanu did not know how to respond to that. He knew what that beep sound was about, but he also did not want to sound rude when Sanjana was being so sweet on the call. So he asked, "What is the lecture about, Sanju?"

"Matters of the heart."

"Yeah? Seriously? And is that medical anymore? Send me, babe. Send me to talk about it."

"And ruin my relationship with my alma mater? No chance."

"You know I can do a good job."

'Oh, I am sure, dummy. But they want to hear from a doctor, not Cupid himself."

"Ha ha. Yeah. Ok, now I will get back to the presentation. See you, love."

"Goodnight, sweetest heart."

Bhanu straightaway checked his phone after the call. The reply was indeed from Mahek.

Mahek – About what? Who is this?
Bhanu – You said that you would set up time and day with me.

There was a pause, for Mahek received this message from a new number. But she did calculate that Ravi must be using a different SIM.

Mahek – You seem to be in a hurry, Ravi.
Bhanu – No, I am just curious.
Mahek – Didn't it kill the cat?
Bhanu – Doesn't a cat have nine lives, then?

Mahek – Do you?
Bhanu – We won't know till the time you kill me then, will we? The question is - 'Is that what you want?'

There was silence on Mahek's side. Bhanu was getting eager for her to respond. Mahek took some time. She was clearly caught off-guard, not having expected Ravi to follow up.

Mahek – Listen, Ravi, don't push your luck on this one. I said if you follow my instructions all is safe, and I never instructed you to chat with me. I guess this is where you shut up and wait for my message.

Bhanu was wondering whether he should take a chance with this cheeky woman or keep shut. But he was happy about one thing—Mahek had bought the fact that it was Ravi chatting with her with a new number. Given this, escalating the situation beyond the point of no return could potentially put his friend in jeopardy. He wasn't sure, despite Mahek's threat, whether this was indeed the point of no return.

Bhanu – Ok. Goodnight.

Mahek did not reply. Bhanu took screenshots of the chat and shared them on 3DD.

Ravi – She is threatening.
Bhanu – Yes, and I do not respond kindly to threats. But I decided to shut up for now. Guess I have rubbed her enough for the day.
Raaj – Bitch!

CHAPTER 38

Solid Complication (Present Day)

Ravi and Raaj were very happy. At the same time, they were angry, but not very. But while the anger at Bhanu was friendly, they did not know that quite soon they were going to get mad, very mad. Bhanu knew. And was wondering what then? But it was going to be one thing at a time today.

They were happy because Bhanu had broken the news about himself and Sanjana to them. They were mad at him because he did not tell them about her earlier.

"When were you going to tell us about it? After becoming a dad?" yelled Ravi.

"All this time I had been calling Mahek a bitch when it is actually you who is the bitch."

"Ha ha ha ha, shut up, Raaj," Bhanu said, "I was thinking of breaking it to you the day Ravi told us about Mahek."

"Bitch!"

"No, honestly, I was. But I guess we had to address the Mahek issue."

"Leave that, tell us where and how did you meet her?"

"We met at Sofu."

"What?" exclaimed a shocked Ravi.

"Ha ha ha, what?" echoed an amused Raaj.

"Yes," said Bhanu batting his eyelids, imitating a scene from a random Bollywood flick.

"Man, you have some luck. And I am so screwed. This crappy app has only been putting me in much trouble."

"Yeah, you are right," said a sombre Bhanu. "I never thought I could meet someone like her on Sofu."

"How did you guys realise you were in love? Who proposed?" Raaj was being inquisitive.

"Long story short, we connected for what Ravi lovingly calls ding-dong. But the more we ding-donged, the more we realised how much more we are to each other, apart from ding-dong. It evolved slowly—the longing for each other's company more than each other's genitals. And then came a day when we proposed to each other." And then Bhanu narrated to them the events that he was reminiscing on his drive back from Ravi's place.

"I am very happy for you, *mishti doi*," said Ravi and hugged him.

"Did she reach out as yet, Bhanu?" asked Raaj, inquisitive about Mahek. And that made Ravi a tad bit uneasy. He had been so happy while Bhanu was narrating his romantic journey. The mention of Mahek changed the mood in the room. Mahek was a bull in Ravi's China shop and the bull needed taming.

"Well, she did. Guys, there is something else that you need to know. There is a problem."

"What problem?" asked Raaj.

***

A few hours ago, Bhanu and Sanjana had been together at Bhanu's place. And the following events took place.

"How was your lecture then?"

"Oh, it was fantastic. The kids were so interactive. And more than anything else the kind of thrill you feel delivering a speech at your own college is such a feeling of achievement—the honour you receive, the respect, the regard. It is all so surreal, and yet it is happening there, right in front of your eyes, right in front of you. It's amazing, Bhanu. I am telling you, it is amazing."

"I am sure it is, sweetest heart. I have been there, done that," said Bhanu, proudly remembering the moment when he had given a lecture at his college.

"I swear. And Professor Bhadra gave such a nice introduction about me to the students. I was like, had you said so about me while I was your student, you would have been my favourite professor."

"Why, was he very strict?"

"Very."

"Such professors are always better. They keep us under leash when we are studying, and generally bring out the best in us." Right then, he got a call from his mother. "Hey wait, Sanju, ma is calling."

"Sure."

"Hey *ma*. *Bhalo*? All is good here..." and Bhanu was on a long call with his mother.

Just before Sanjana had arrived, Bhanu had transferred the new SIM to an older mobile that he had saved with himself for emergency usage. He had checked the cell with the new SIM and found it to be working well. While Bhanu was on the call with his mother, the phone attracted Sanjana's attention. It was an old smartphone, almost bordering on 'ancient'. So Sanjana had just picked it up to have a look at it. It was unlocked. And that is when a message came from Mahek.

Mahek – Listen, Ravi, we have to meet.

Sanjana then checked the SMS folder and read the message exchange with Mahek. She observed that all messages were from Mahek only.

Bhanu, when finished with his call, saw that the old phone with the new SIM was in Sanjana's hands, and clearly, she was upset. She was calm, but upset. The look on her face posed a question for Bhanu. But the intensity of her expression forbade Bhanu to say anything. Sanjana raised the index finger of her right hand and opened her lips to say something. But it was as if the words she wanted to use had such gravity that she could not release them from her mouth.

"I won't say I can explain this. But you do have a right to know." Bhanu's voice was very calm, "The last thing I would want is, this to go in a way neither of us wants."

What Bhanu said did have an effect on Sanjana. Her agitated mind cooled down a little. But before she could say anything, Bhanu started again, "If you have read all the messages, you'll realise that the discussion is between Mahek and Ravi."

"And yet there is clearly something more than what meets the eye." She paused, and then as she saw Bhanu pulling a chair to sit next to her, she said, "Not now, Bhanu. We will talk, but not now. Right now I am not sure if I am hurt, or angry, or agitated, or if I even want to listen to you. But one thing I am sure about — I need to be with myself."

***

"And then?" asked Ravi.

"She quietly walked out," answered Bhanu.

"Bad, that's super bad. That's sad, Bhanu. Why didn't you go after her?" asked Raaj.

"Trust me, she needs some space right now. She made it clear. I will make it up to her, I will. I know how to make it up to her. But right now, we need to deal with Mahek."

Ravi walked up to Bhanu and placed his right hand on Bhanu's left shoulder. Pressing it firmly, he asked, "Since when have you not got your priorities right, Bhanu? *Abey*, I am not going to die. This is so good, you and Sanjana. Do not bother about me, bro. Just go and save whatever it is you have with her."

"There will come a time for that. And I will do it. But right now, Mahek wants to meet with you. How do you want to deal with that?"

CHAPTER 39

Friends in Deed are the Friends You Need (Present Day)

"Bhanu, I am calling the shots on this one. Don't be a dick. Go and sort this with her right away. It's ok, the bitch can wait." Ravi pressed on Bhanu.

"*Achha* tell me, how close are you guys to announcing your engagement and wedding dates?" Raaj asked.

"Very close," replied Ravi.

"Then I think we should handle Mahek quickly, Ravi. I do not want this becoming a mess in your life. You have built it very nicely with Vandana, and we would certainly not want to see it getting jeopardised." Raaj's tone was serious.

***

'Is life coming full circle on me?' Sanjana was thinking. 'But what was my fault then? I am sure Bhanu has a reason. It just brought back memories that I have been fighting hard to forget, or at least put on the back burner.'

***

"I think you should simply tell her what's happening here, Bhanu," suggested Raaj, and continued, "come clean. Anyway, you have nothing to hide. Ravi, on the other hand, has a lot to hide and handle."

"Raaj, my feeling is that I should not have done it only in the first place." Ravi was remorseful.

***

'But I will be honest with myself, when I read that message, the thought that Bhanu is a dick, did creep in,' Sanjana was lost in her thoughts. 'I know that he is not a creep though. I am sure there is something to it. But why is my mind continuously going there only, the memories I so want to erase. And also, I am angry at Bhanu.'

***

"What's done cannot be undone. Now let us see how we can move ahead," said Raaj. "Now I know both of you are in a spot, so please allow me to do some thinking here."

"Raaj, it isn't that we cannot think."

"Bro, it is not that. A great man once said—never reply when you are angry, never make a promise when you are happy, never make a decision when you are sad. Now, you guys aren't sad; clearly, you guys are disturbed. And Bhanu isn't disturbed, he just needs to have a word with Sanjana and set things right, that's all. So, let us prioritise. Priority number one, we have to think of the reply that we need to send to Mahek. Priority number two, Bhanu has to come clean with Sanjana. Priority number three, planning what to do with Mahek."

"Guys, trust me, after this I will go and meet with Sanjana. Can we please spend the next half an hour or so over Mahek?" Bhanu persisted.

"Bitch!"

"Exactly!"

***

Sanjana's mind was very much occupied right now. An incident from her past had come to the fore. Besides, she was angry with Bhanu. But the reason for her anger had changed. It had changed from why Bhanu did this, to why he had hidden it from her. She knew of course that Bhanu would explain, but why did he hide from her in the first place? There were just too many questions.

"Bhanu, chat with her like you would have done, as if none of this had happened. As you had pointed out earlier, planning in such cases is difficult, and the chat has to be on the fly."

"Sure, Raaj, but I will still want to chat with a good idea of the outcome we want."

"We want to bust her."

"Look, she wants to meet up. Again, we do not know what's on her mind. So, let me start with an objective to try and know what it is that she wants."

Bhanu – Hey, hi. Sorry, I was caught up with some work. You said you wanted to meet.

Mahek replied after a few minutes – Ravi, I do not like to be kept waiting. It makes me very uncomfortable.

Bhanu – I told you I was caught up. I had no intention of keeping you hanging. You said you wanted to meet. When and where, and this time please also tell me why.

Mahek – You will know 'why' when we meet. As for when and where, let us meet at Leisure Valley Park in Sector 29 in Gurgaon.

Bhanu – Leisure Valley Park is big. Where in the park?

Mahek – Roots Café.

Bhanu – And when?

Mahek – Day after tomorrow, 6:00 p.m.

Bhanu – It is fine. But why can you not tell me what it is about? Is it money or something else?

After about 10 minutes Mahek replied – *If you are so intent on knowing, it is about setting a few things right. Setting them the way they should have been, and not the way they are. No more questions. See you the day after.*

Bhanu – We haven't met before. How will we recognise each other?
Mahek – It's a small café. Now how many single women will be there, Ravi?

***

She realised that her thoughts weren't taking her anywhere and it was best to meet with Bhanu, or rather allow Bhanu to meet with her and let him share his story.

***

"So the meeting's day, date, time and venue are set. How will you take it from here, Bhanu?"

"I am thinking, Raaj. Any ideas?"

"We will have to prepare Ravi strongly. This is not going to be an easy meeting. Do you think she wants to blackmail?"

"She clearly wants something. She said it is about setting a few things right. What does she want to set right? I do not think sending Ravi there is a good idea."

"Then how will we do it Bhanu?" asked Ravi, "Sending you or Raaj won't make much sense since she would know me by face."

"Sending you is fraught with danger, and danger only."

"How come?"

"Ravi, we do not know if she is acting in concert, or if she is acting alone. Mahek said it is about setting a few things right. Has it ever crossed your brilliant mind that Vandana might have found out about you and Mahek and maybe wants to make an example out of you?"

Before Ravi could even process what Bhanu suspected, he was startled by Vandana's call on his mobile. So were Bhanu and Raaj.

"Pick up," said Raaj.

"What options do I have?"

Ravi took the call and walked away from his friends.

***

Sanjana – Bhanu, come over.

Sanjana's message to Bhanu came when Ravi was on call with Vandana.

Bhanu – Right now?
Sanjana – What option do you have?

***

Ravi's call was over. There was a smile on his face, so Raaj and Bhanu knew that there was no cause for worry, at least not yet. But Bhanu's logic had been reverberating in their head. It was not possible for them to know for sure till such a truth presented itself before them that Vandana knew about it, and that Vandana was the one behind it.

"Listen," started Bhanu, but was cut short by Ravi.

"Guys, listen. Vandana just called. Our parents spoke with each other. Venues for engagement and marriage have been finalised."

Bhanu and Raaj congratulated Ravi profusely. Ravi got a call from his mother as well and they spoke about the same thing. Raaj congratulated Vandana and Ravi on Dear Friends. And then the discussion meandered back to the meeting with Mahek.

"Before I tell you what I have in my mind for Mahek, let me tell you something which will take some load off of both of you."

"No, Bhanu, you listen to me," Ravi insisted, "You are in a spot trying to help me. And I am feeling very bad about it. So, you will have to agree with what I am saying here."

"And that is?"

"I will go and talk to Sanjana and clear out everything. That is the only way to set it right, and that way I will also feel happy."

Bhanu smiled and said, "I know her better than you do. And you do not know her at all. In a complicated situation like this there is no point putting an unknown entity in front of her. She is a lioness, quite like your lady. She will eat you up. Besides, she will want to hear it only from me. And, I just told you that I will tell you something that will take some load off of both of you, didn't I? So, Sanjana wants me to come over right now. But before that, let us finalise on the plan for Mahek."

"Sure, go on. Now with a lot of load off our shoulders, let us crack this."

"I will go and meet with Mahek. Raaj, you reach there an hour in advance so that if you see Vandana by any chance, you can text us. I am hoping she won't be there, but cannot be too sure. Plus, it will give us the advantage of knowing who this Mahek really is. She had already clarified to Ravi earlier that she wasn't chatting with Ravi using her real name and image."

"Of course, had there been a Mahek in my office I'd have known," quipped Raaj.

"Bhanu, I am sure Mahek doesn't know you by face, but I am equally sure she remembers my face from Sofu. Won't that create a hassle?"

"It can, but I will handle it. Trust me, I will."

"I am sure he will, Ravi. So I will be there sharp at 5:00 p.m. the day after."

"Bingo," said Bhanu, and then he left for Sanjana's place.

CHAPTER 40

More Shock! (Present Day)

On his way to Sanjana's place, Bhanu had played the entire conversation out in his head. She was no child. And there was no point hiding behind words in this situation. After a long time, he had found someone he wanted to anchor his life with. And he did not want to jeopardise anything at this stage with her. Sanjana deserved to know everything. His task was simple then. All he had to do was not beat around the bush and come out clean. Sanjana knew that Ravi and Raaj were Bhanu's closest pals.

When Bhanu reached Sanjana's place, the atmosphere was neither warm nor cold. One could call it lukewarm. Sanjana did have a question on her face though, and she took the initiative, "Bhanu, before you share things with me, and share them absolutely honestly without any editing, there is something I want to tell you."

Bhanu had a question on his face.

"I know we met through Sofu for a convenient arrangement. I do not think either of us had thought of getting romantically involved. Now, had it been just a matter of convenience, this kind of message wouldn't have mattered. However, since we are romantically involved, it did disturb me quite a lot. Now, I know that the lady addressed her message to Ravi, but even that leaves a few questions in my mind. For instance, were you chatting with her as Ravi, or are you in some way trying to help your friend? And even if you are trying to help your friend, are you taking enough care not to get caught in this in a way that is detrimental to what we have been kindling rather sweetly between us?"

"Those are too many questions," said Bhanu with a calm smile, "and let me answer all of them, though not necessarily in the order in which you asked them, but with the context of what has been happening, why it has been happening and how am I concluding this in a way so that you are convinced that in no way will it even come close to deter what you and I have been kindling between the two of us. Works?"

"I am all ears."

Bhanu was about to start when Sanjana got a call from her mother. She gestured to Bhanu to give her a few minutes and took her mother's call, "Hey *ma*, how are you?"

"I am good. How are you, *beta*?"

"I am good, too. Is Papa better now? He was

running a fever a few days ago."

"Yes, he is much better now. How is your work, doctor *sahiba*?"

"Work is good, ma. It is hectic, but you know I have always loved it this way."

"I know, all three of you have always been like this—you, your dad and your sister."

"What are you saying ma? Have you been any less of a Madam Principal?"

"Ha ha ha ha. *Achha*, leave that. I have some good news to share. I had told you about Vandana's dates earlier; now the venues have also been finalised. Now please ensure that you take leave and come here."

"Ma, we haven't spoken for so long."

"I know, but what is my fault? Can't I see my children together?"

"*Ma*, you know I tried talking to her a lot of times, but how many times did she even give me a chance?"

"Do you realise that despite being the principal of a school of more than a thousand kids who are scared at the sight of me, you are two brats I have never been able to handle?"

"*Ma*, I am not saying no. I'd love to see Vandana getting married, and from whatever you have told me, I think Ravi is a good guy."

The mention of both these names immediately attracted Bhanu's attention. He was now hooked on the conversation.

"He is. Remember how I busted them? But he's such a sweet child. I am sure he will take care of Vandana."

"As I was saying, I'd be happy to see Ravi and Vandana getting engaged and married, but will Vandana be happy seeing me there?"

"Just come to me *beta*, I will take care of the rest. I know she's being unreasonable. And you know when it comes to it, I have a way of getting through to all of you."

"*Chandi mata*," Sanjana chuckled, "I will be there. But isn't it strange that we live so close to each other—she's in Dwarka and I am in Gurgaon—and yet we haven't met."

Bhanu was sure now that the Ravi and Vandana they were talking about were the same that he knew. He wasn't sure now whether this straightened things or complicated them even further.

"*Beta*, life is complicated," said Sudha, "let us uncomplicate it. This is very good news and let us make the most of it."

"Sure, *ma*. I will be there."

The mother and daughter carried on for some more time and then the call got over. Sanjana turned towards Bhanu. Bhanu was smiling.

"What are you smiling for? My mother's call gave you some reprieve to cook up a story?"

"No, but I am shocked. Sweetly shocked, but I am shocked. And what I am about to tell you will transfer my shock to you, though I'm not sure whether the shock on your side will be sweet or not."

Sanjana gave a look to Bhanu that was both questioning and confusing.

"Remember Mahek had a message for Ravi?"

"Shucks, Bhanu, don't tell me!" Sanjana was clearly shocked. Bhanu told her everything from the beginning till the discussion that Ravi, Raaj and he had had just a few minutes ago.

"That's a whole lot to process for me, Bhanu. Is Ravi a cheat? Vandana is my sister, Bhanu, and she's younger than me. I need to know. I will kill him, I swear. Even if he's your best friend."

"Sanju, I will answer that. But now I need to know why you aren't welcome at home."

Sanjana fell silent. The emotion on her face changed from anger to disgrace, and from disgrace to guilt. Bhanu could see that there was something eating her up.

"Rohit was Vandana's love before Ravi. And he was on Sofu too. We were intimate, not knowing that he was going around with Vandana. When Vandana got to know of it, it was close to the time of their announcement as a couple to both families. Needless to say, Vandana broke up with him, and by extension, broke up with me too."

"Did you know about Rohit?"

"No, silly. If I had, why would I..." she left the

sentence incomplete, but Bhanu understood what she wanted to say. She continued, "What probably killed her was that she had been intimate with him as well."

"So, that is why you guys haven't spoken with each other since? I mean, the fact that she felt that partly you are the reason for Rohit two-timing her?"

"Yes."

"And is that the reason why Vandana does not want to be intimate with Ravi before marriage?"

"Likely."

"But what happened between Rohit and you, isn't your fault, though I understand that it's rather complicated."

"Yes, but Vandana never forgave me."

Ding-ding.

Ding-ding.

That was Bhanu's phone chiming. Both Raaj and Ravi had asked him if everything was okay at almost the same time.

"Is that Mahek?" asked Sanjana.

"No, silly. It is my regular phone. Raaj and Ravi are asking if all is okay." Saying so, he messaged on 3DD – '*all ok, will call later.*' Then, Bhanu went towards Sanjana and said, "Bloody hell! It is complicated."

"You bet," her tone was low. And then, as if suddenly the lioness in her had come alive, she roared, "I will kill that Mahek!"

"Why?"

"Bhanu, are you serious? This matter needs to have a resolution and a quick one. If it is not resolved quickly, I don't know how Vandana will react to life. And I do not know how, but somehow, I know if I set this right, I might get the chance to make amends with Vandana."

"Now, that may not be a very good way to think of it."

"Bhanu?"

"Don't you see, Sanju? Things have to be right between you and Vandana, irrespective of this situation."

"But Bhanu, I couldn't help Vandana last time. This time, I feel I can."

"You and I are in the same boat."

"How?"

Bhanu smiled and continued, "When I goaded Ravi towards this path, I never thought such a situation would arise. But it did. Now I have to, and I will see how to deal with it. I want Ravi to steer clear."

A little while ago, Bhanu had told her everything about Ravi's adventures on Sofu, everything apart from Ruby. He chose to omit that for now. There was a pause for some time. Both were looking at each other and thinking of what to do next. Bhanu broke the silence, "Say, Sanju, would you like to meet Ravi?"

"Hmmm?" asked a surprised Sanjana.

"It is eating you from within, the question whether Ravi is good for Vandy or not? Why don't you meet him and settle that? That will also give him confidence."

"And that will also bare him in front of me. Not a good idea, Bhanu. At least not now. Also, given that I am yet to rebuild my relationship with Vandy, let me not step in right now. My first priority is my sister."

"Then there is something else I need you to help me with. And here I won't take no for an answer," said Bhanu.

"Sure. Tell me, what do you want me to do?"

CHAPTER 41

Still More Shock! (Present Day)

The day of reckoning had come. That evening, Raaj and Ravi were to set their plan in action. Bhanu would head to Roots Café straight from work, while Raaj decided to spend some time with Ravi before reaching Roots, since Ravi had been feeling low, very low.

"Bro, I know you are feeling scared and low and repentant. Let's have a pint each. *Thoda dum lete hain.* What say?" asked Raaj. "*Abey dum to wo Vandy mere andar daal degi agar use pata chala to.*"

"So you are upset because Vandy will have your happiness?"

"Yaar, I am upset because I should not have done this Sofu thingy."

"Ha ha ha ha ha."

"Yeah, laugh. And laugh loud. I am high and dry and you laugh."

"Can you help it? Can you change your past?"

"Raaj, I know I cannot. But please understand that I won't stand a chance in front of Vandy."

"So tell me, why are you feeling this way?"

"You know."

"I do not know your trigger."

"Meaning?"

"What was the point at which you decided to junk Sofu?"

Ravi was silent. But Raaj persisted, so Ravi gave in and shared, "You remember I told you and Bhanu about Ruby, over a call? That I met her and we went to her room?"

"Yes."

"After that, everything that I told you was a lie. In reality, it just did not feel right. I could not bring myself to do this to Vandy. God, I love her!"

Raaj looked at his friend, admiring his love for Vandana. "Honestly, Ravi," Raaj walked closer and placed a hand on Ravi's shoulder, "Bhanu and I both thought something was missing, but we attributed it to your 'first time'. So no ding-dong till now?"

"Nopes."

"Ha ha ha ha. Wow. And what was Ruby's reaction?"

"She was furious and frustrated, not that I gave a damn."

"Then why did you lie to us?"

"To shut you up, you teasing dogs!"

Ting-tong.
Tring-tring.

Both their phones chimed. It was Bhanu's message on 3DD – all set, Raaj? You must reach there in 40 minutes.

Raaj – I will. And hey, Bhanu, you and I were right. Ravi did not ding-dong with Ruby that day.
Bhanu – You mean he is clean?
Raaj – Yes. As clean as my undie.
Bhanu – Yuck. But I wish he had told me earlier. I had to hide it from Sanju.

Both Raaj and Ravi didn't get the context of Sanjana here.

Ravi – What?
Bhanu – Later. Time is of essence. Raaj, you scoot now.
"Just break her into two," Ravi told Raaj.
"We will. I swear."

***

The plan was for Raaj to reach there ahead of Bhanu to identify Mahek. He donned a turban and a fake moustache and beard to masquerade as a Sikh so that

Mahek would simply miss him. Also, he would change his clothes from those he wore at work. With all this done, he would reach there by 5:20 p.m. The meeting was set for 6:00 pm. That would give Raaj enough time to identify Mahek whether she came after 5:20 p.m. or before. Bhanu would drop in sharp at 6:00 p.m. and head straight for Mahek.

Roots has both indoors and outdoors seating. Upon reaching the venue, Raaj scanned both the seating areas. He also took a stroll in the garden area just to make sure that Mahek was not waiting there, and doing what he had come to do—scan the area for any unpleasantries or anything difficult. He was also scanning for any troublesome-looking men, just in case Mahek came with those. All he could find was some children playing games in the garden under the watchful eyes of their parents, a few couples, both in the garden and in Roots, a few friends maybe and some random people.

Raaj messaged Bhanu – *Coast is clear so far.*

Bhanu– Keep looking. I am sure she will come.

Raaj – Sure. Will you reach here on time?

Bhanu – We will. Sharp at 6?

Raaj – We?

Bhanu – You will see. ☺

Raaj was having lemonade when he recognised the woman from his office walk-in. It was 5:57 p.m. She came in and took the four-seater table closest to the exit door. Raaj was on the table right next to it. He followed Bhanu's earlier instructions—to immediately update Bhanu and sit tight till Raaj saw Bhanu walk in. Upon seeing Bhanu, Raaj was to move to the next phase. He sent a simple message on 3DD – *It is Ruchi Desai. Belongs to Ahmedabad. Lives here in a PG.*

It was 6 p.m. And Ruchi was seated indoors. Anxiety was visible on her face, as was the fact that she was waiting for Ravi. Now, the indoor area has three doors—the main door to the left of Ruchi's table overlooking the reception desk straight ahead, through which patrons usually enter Roots, and two doors on either side of the reception desk. The door to the left of the onlooker leads to the toilets, while the one on the right leads to the outdoor seating area. Ruchi's eyes were toggling between her cell and the entry door.

Raaj knew that Bhanu was never one to be late, not even by a minute. But in this case, he had tested Ruchi's (Mahek's) limits earlier on chat. It was 6:01 and Bhanu was nowhere to be seen. Ruchi was getting restless. Raaj and Ruchi were seated on the same side of the restaurant on two adjacent tables. Both had their eyes fixed at the entry door to their left, and all they could see was a beautiful lady dressed in Western formals walking towards the restaurant, not a sight they had been expecting for their 6 o'clock rendezvous. Raaj's phone chimed and so did Ruchi's. Bhanu had messaged both. To Ruchi, he messaged – *In the parking lot. Sorry, I got late by just a minute. Walking in.* To Raaj, he messaged – *Look to your right.* Bhanu turned right and found Bhanu walking straight towards him from the toilet side opening. He could not understand. Bhanu gestured to him to be quiet.

The lady who had entered went straight to Ruchi and asked her if she was Ruchi. Ruchi was startled. Raaj saw all this happening and was confused. Bhanu was as cool as a cucumber.

Ruchi was staring at the lady who had walked in, and was thinking what to do as the lady walked towards Ruchi. Before she could even run through options in her mind, the lady said, "I am ACP, Crime, Sanjana, Vandana's elder sister. And I never expected this from you, Ruchi."

Sanjana's voice was low but both Ruchi and Raaj could hear her and both were equally shocked. In fact, Raaj was in a state of both deep shock and deep admiration for Bhanu. Just like Ravi, he did not know till then, that Bhanu's Sanjana and Ravi's Vandana came from the same stock, the stock of Brigadier Raghav Sharma. He thought it was a ruse. Bhanu had that cool smile on his face while he was listening to the ladies' conversation, and Raaj had just one smile of admiration, and hundreds of questions on his face. But he decided to let the play, play itself out. Bhanu had indeed planned this very well and delivered a shock so deep to Ruchi that she was too embarrassed to move. Plus, there was the veiled threat of sitting opposite a senior police officer. Raaj had been running many scenarios in his mind as to how the meeting would turn once Ruchi saw Bhanu and realised that she had been duped. Maybe she would create a noise, shout harassment, or just run away, making Ravi and Bhanu lose all initiative. Or who knew what hell might break loose. But to his utter surprise, not one of those scenarios played out today. What indeed happened was that fear gripped Ruchi so strongly that she was glued strongly and firmly to her chair. Raaj still did not know how the play was going to play itself out. And what Ruchi did not know was that this was not the only shock that Bhanu had planned for her today.

The acronym 'ACP' made Ruchi freeze on the spot. ACP – Assistant Commissioner of Police. Ruchi had not factored this. 'What the hell have I gotten myself into?' is all she could think of, fear written large over her face.

"Let us talk, Ruchi," said Sanjana, gripping Ruchi's hand in an assuring manner, "We are not here to hurt you."

"We?" asked Ruchi feebly.

"Yes, we," said Sanjana, "the person to my left," she gestured towards Bhanu, "is our lawyer. The plainclothes lady you see outside the entry door is a police inspector with an arrest warrant in her hand,

and the person sitting opposite to the lawyer is your colleague and Ravi's dear friend, Raaj." Then, turning towards Raaj, she said, "Lose your makeup, Raaj," delivering the second and final shock to Ruchi that Bhanu had planned for the evening.

Ruchi and Raaj noticed that there was indeed a plainclothes woman standing outside, keeping a watch on all of them with an envelope in her hand. Ruchi knew that she was not only exposed but was badly cornered. Raaj removed his make-up. Ruchi had nowhere to hide or run. This realisation hit her very hard.

Sanjana continued, "You have my word that if you cooperate with us, not only will we not take any action against you, we will also protect you in case you need our protection."

"Um," was all Ruchi could manage before falling silent again and bowing her head down.

Sanjana gave her some time and told her in a very cool, commanding tone, "You will have to tell us more than that, Ruchi."

A fearful Ruchi said, "I don't know where to start, madam."

"Start from the beginning. It is easy. Trust me, you are amongst friends."

Ruchi bared everything. From Raaj's and Bhanu's faces, it was evident that on hearing her complete story, it was their turn to be shocked.

It was Bhanu's turn now. And he spoke to Ruchi,

"Ruchi, this will get complicated. I know this day hasn't been anything close to what you had expected. So take a leave and fly down to Ahmedabad to your parents. We will handle things from here."

Ruchi never expected the lawyer to know where her parents lived. She was visibly surprised. But today was not a day that could be defined as usual, anyway.

Raaj explained, "I told them where you live. And let me tell you one more thing, Ruchi. We won't tell Vandana anything till all this is sorted."

"Please do not, Raaj. She is my boss, and I am so embarrassed at what I have done to her." Saying so, she broke down.

"Please handle yourself, Ruchi," said Sanjana, "I will ask the inspector to drop you home."

"No, madam," said a deeply terrified Ruchi. "I will manage. It is enough for a day as it is. Besides, I have to go to work first. Have to pick up something that I forgot there."

"Are you in a condition to drive?" asked Bhanu.

"I will manage," replied Ruchi, still weeping.

"I will ask the inspector to tail her car till she is home," said Bhanu, looking at Sanjana. Then he turned once again to Ruchi, "Ruchi, not one word of this to her. It is for your own good."

"I got that, sir. I won't betray Vandana anymore."

"And you will remember what to tell your handler if you get a call?" Bhanu reminded Ruchi.

"Yes, sir."

***

Ruchi reached her office. It was after 8:00 p.m. and the office was empty. The policewoman had trailed her and was parked outside. She was under instructions from Bhanu not to leave Ruchi till Ruchi had safely reached home. Ruchi was still feeling very low. She had been promised by her handler that if she followed her handler's instructions to the tee, no harm would come to her. All she had to do was have a conversation with Ravi, record it without Ravi knowing it, and pass it on to her handler. And what had happened today was way beyond what she had imagined. Before leaving Roots she had decided that it was best to resign and go far away from her handler and Vandana. She was consumed in the guilt of having gone behind Vandana's back.

As she was walking towards her desk, she was reminiscing the differences that she had had with Vandana on numerous occasions, and Vandana being a true taskmaster and coming down heavily on her. But not once had Vandana been personal with Ruchi. Ruchi had felt insulted, yes, but never humiliated. The question that kept on echoing in her mind was why did she agree to harm Vandana on a personal level when Vandana had never done that to her. In fact, on a couple of occasions, Vandana had even picked up spirited arguments in the organisation to defend Ruchi.

Having packed her effects, Ruchi was headed towards the restroom for a call of nature. But she knew that while she could relieve herself of the pressure in her bladder, she would be unable to relieve herself of the weight of the guilt on her shoulders anytime soon. She hadn't bargained for what had happened earlier in the evening. And what she did not know was that her day wasn't over yet.

***

"Boss, I never ever imagined this!" exclaimed Raaj after Bhanu explained to him about Sanjana and Vandana. They were all at Bhanu's place.

"Yeah, and can you imagine the surprise Sanjana and I had to go through when we discovered all of this?"

"How do you want to take this ahead, Bhanu?" asked Sanjana, "Ravi would be calling any moment now."

"And how did you manage the policewoman?" Raaj asked before Bhanu could address Sanjana.

"I will handle Ravi, Sanju. I just hope Ruchi does not do anything stupid. Anyway, the inspector is with her." Then turning to Raaj, he answered, "The inspector once needed legal help in a case about her property. Her husband works in my firm. I helped them out profusely without charging her a dime. She would do anything for me."

"And the warrant?"

"*Nakli.*"

***

Ravi was anxious at his place, but decided to wait for Bhanu's call. He was sure that Bhanu would call after the evening was over.

***

While she was in the restroom relieving herself, she got a call on her phone. Upon seeing who was calling, she was petrified. It was indeed her handler. But as per the plan that she had agreed on with Sanjana and Bhanu, she had to take it and talk to her. She was supposed to brief Bhanu afterwards. So she took the call.

"Hi," said Ruchi.

"How did it go, Ruchi?" asked the person on the other side.

"It went the way you planned. Ravi was shit scared. I threatened him with revealing his secret to Vandana. That put him in his place."

"So do you think your meeting had the desired effect?"

"I am sure about it. I hope nothing else is required to be done here."

"Yes, you do not have to do anything else. I will

make my move at the right time. For now, let us see how Vandana reacts when Ravi breaks the news to her. Thank you for your support, Ruchi. Take care." Saying so, the handler disconnected the call and that was a huge relief for Ruchi.

Ruchi stepped out, shutting the door behind her. She was greeted by two very inquisitive and angry eyes. She could feel the temperature of the restroom rise with Vandana's eyes staring right into hers. There was no way Ruchi could have known that Vandana was in the restroom next to hers. Her mind was racing, trying to figure out how much to tell Vandana. This was something no one had expected. Not Ruchi, not her handler, and not Bhanu.

CHAPTER 42

Yet More Shock! (Present Day)

Vandana called Ravi and asked him where he was. Her voice was calm and normal. From her voice and tone Ravi could not guess anything. She just said that she wanted to meet Ravi and was coming over to spend some time with him. Ravi hadn't heard from Bhanu yet and was getting anxious, but a meeting with Vandana was always good as it was about the only thing that could bring a smile to him and also calm his anxiety.

While he was waiting for Vandana, he received a text from Bhanu on 3DD – *all ok. Meeting went well. Trouble warded off. Will explain everything shortly.*

Ravi was relieved, but had a lot of questions. He replied – *cool, will wait for your call. Vandy is coming here by the way. That will give me some peace, I am sure.*

Bhanu was a bit concerned with the timing of

Vandana's visit to Ravi, though he knew that both of them used to meet late at night. He told Sanjana and Raaj about it. Raaj had also checked the messages in the group. The three of them did smell a rat. Bhanu called Ruchi but Ruchi did not respond to his call. Bhanu called the inspector. The inspector told him that Ruchi was driving to her apartment. Since she had told the inspector where she stayed, Bhanu asked her how much time was left to reach her residence. The inspector told him about 20-25 minutes. Bhanu decided to call Ruchi in a while.

***

Vandana entered. Upon seeing her, Ravi's smile vapourised. Her eyes were clearly throwing more heat at him than the sun does on the hottest day on the entire planet we call our home.

"Ravi, you rascal! You couldn't wait till our marriage? How many Maheks have you been with?"

All he could do was muster enough courage to open his lips and feebly pronounce her name.

"Shut up, Ravi," Vandana's reaction was angry and explosive. "You have hurt me badly. Very badly. You have been meeting women on Sofu just to have sex? Are you an idiot? We had everything going so well, so sweet and so perfect. Couldn't you control your desires just for a few months more? You think I do not crave for your touch? You think I do not want to melt in your arms every time when we are alone?"

"Vandy," Ravi made another feeble attempt.

"What?" yelled Vandana.

"I did not do anything with Mahek that you or I would be ashamed of," he said softly with a tone of apology.

"And does that give you grace? Are you a fool, Ravi? Aren't you getting what I am saying? What is it that you are unable to understand? The fact remains that you stepped out. And ok, maybe you haven't done anything with Mahek, but what about others? Only you know what you have done with them."

***

"Bhanu sir," said Ruchi. She had called Bhanu after reaching home, "a bad thing happened."

"What?" asked Bhanu, trying to connect Vandana's visit to Ravi and Ruchi's call.

Ruchi explained to Bhanu the conversation that she had had with her handler in the restroom cubicle not knowing that Vandana was right in the adjacent one.

"Oh my God!" exclaimed Bhanu. "What did you tell her?"

"I told her that the person I was talking to was my sister. And that I had confided in my sister when I got to know that Ravi and Vandana were engaged. And that my sister had advised me to confront him and ask him to come clean to Vandana, or else I would have to do it for her sake."

"You said all this?" asked a surprised Bhanu.

"What else could I do, sir? You know I never wanted to be involved in this at all. I was caught between a well and a valley! At the same time, you had also told me not to tell anyone anything including sharing the identity of my handler."

"Hmmm."

"Sir, have I worsened it for Vandana and Ravi?"

"I do not think so, Ruchi. I think you have done good. Have you booked your tickets for home?"

"Yes, sir."

"Good. I think it is best that you stay away for a few days."

"In fact, I am resigning, sir."

"Hold on to that for a few days. Apply for leave."

***

"Vandy, I know this looks like I have goofed up. But trust me," Ravi attempted to pacify her.

"Trust you? Trust you? Yeah? From the way I see you now, I think if you can trust yourself, that would be news!"

"Vandy."

"No, Ravi. I have no interest in keeping this

conversation going any longer. I had told you about my previous boyfriend. He was a two-timing scoundrel himself, and now, as I realise, so are you. I do not know why Sofu keeps on converting my boyfriends into desirous, footloose, stray people."

There was a pause. Ravi decided to keep quiet this time and let Vandana vent out all her anger before saying anything. What she said next broke him.

"I am done. I am calling this off."

Ravi was tearful, "Vandy, please."

"No, Ravi."

***

"That's bad," said Bhanu. "That's very bad. How are you holding up?"

"You can imagine," said Ravi. "But I thought you had things under control. What happened?"

"Ravi, you want to come over or should Raaj and I come over?"

"I am in no state to drive. You come."

"Sure, give me some time."

Before leaving for Ravi's place, he had to plan how to get this under control.

"Sanju, I guess you and I have to step right in."

"Meaning, we talk to Ravi and Vandana?"

"Meaning, you talk to Vandana. I will talk to Ravi. This will also give you the chance to…" and he left it at that. Sanjana understood what Bhanu meant. While Bhanu had shared everything with Raaj, he had not shared that Sanjana and Vandana were at odds with each other. He also had not shared the reason for the odds. Raaj didn't need to know. But Sanjana understood what Bhanu was saying.

"I think I need to, Bhanu. You are right," concurred Sanjana. "But are you sure that Ravi hasn't messed up?"

"He hasn't, Sanjana," interjected Raaj reflecting on the chat they had had in 3DD, "You have Bhanu's and my word. He had been in touch with a lot of women on Sofu, Sanjana. But not once had he gotten intimate with them."

"How are you so sure?"

"Two reasons. Had he done something like that, he would have told us. And second, he loves Vandana just too much for it. He did reach a point with one of his Sofu connects where he could have been intimate. But where his feet could have taken him, his heart didn't. Believe me when I tell you that he hasn't betrayed Vandana's trust."

"That depends on how Vandana looks at it," Sanjana said, while folding her arms around her chest. "Ok, look," Sanjana continued, "I know both of you know your friend well. And I am hoping that he hasn't done anything silly, but this is my little sister we are talking about. I have to be sure that Ravi is in a place where I can defend him. I know Vandana well. She won't trust Ravi again easily at all. So I am suggesting that I come with you to Ravi's place and I spend time with him before I plead his case with my sister."

CHAPTER 43

Lots More Shock! (Present Day)

It was an hour before midnight. The day had been long and tiring for all. When Ravi opened the door, he expected to only see Raaj and Bhanu. Instead, it was Raaj, Bhanu and a woman he assumed was Sanjana. Introductions were given. Ravi had known that the sisters were estranged, but Vandana had told him not to ask the reason, and Ravi never did. Today as well, he did not bother much about the reason for the sisters' estrangement as much as he did to find out what had transpired at Roots, what happened between what had transpired at Roots and Vandana landing at his place, and why Sanjana was there. He was embarrassed as it was already. He was in a state of deep shock. The questions swirling in his mind were many—Why did Ruchi do this? Why did she want to harm him? Had he done her any harm? What was her motive? What all had she told Vandana? How much had she poisoned her against him? Could he live a life without Vandana? Could he win her back? How would Sanjana help? These, and a whole host of other questions.

Raaj and Bhanu took turns in explaining everything to him. Right from Roots Café to Ruchi's call with her handler, to Vandana overhearing that call, to Ruchi's plan to fly away to Ahmedabad. On purpose, Bhanu did not share the identity of Ruchi's handler with Ravi, along with the motive of the handler. He had saved her identity and her motive right for the end.

"Who is she, Bhanu? Do I know her?"

"Suchita Ramakrishnan."

"What?" said a shocked Ravi. This had horrified him like nothing else so far in his life. He was appalled to his core. In an instant, working at unimaginable speeds, his brain flashed images of Suchita when he saw her for the first time in college, the time they spent together on and off campus, the falling in love, the feeling in love, the breaking of the news to friends, the break up, meeting with her in Striker bar, the hug and kiss after the meeting, and now this. Given his past with Vandana, he never thought Suchita could have had such a conniving nature. Was she even capable of scheming at this level, especially knowing fully well how madly he loved Vandana?

There was shock, silence and contemplation on Ravi's part. "Let me ease that out for you," said Bhanu.

"I will ease it out for myself, Bhanu," Ravi was getting agitated at Suchita, "for now, just give me the facts, and make them as bare as you can. Does not matter if anything hurts me. Nothing can hurt me more than this."

Sanjana was silently observing Ravi through all this, making her own evaluation of him and his character. She knew that she was no one to judge him, but what she also knew was that she had to plead two cases with Vandana—Ravi's and her own.

"Okay, so what all do we know?" asked Raaj in a manner of actually giving an answer, "We know that Ruchi had no motive to blackmail you and that she also had no intent of blackmailing you. We know that Suchita was your lady love back in graduation, and we know now that she was trying to win you back."

"That is something we deduced, not something that Ruchi stated," Bhanu corrected Raaj.

"Yes, you are right. So, getting back to facts, we know that Ruchi reported to Vandana and Vandana reported to Suchita. While in a meeting with Ruchi, on a day when Vandana wasn't there, Suchita saw you chatting with Ruchi. So Suchita had a chance sighting of your profile on Ruchi's phone, the profile in which you used your own pic, you dick! Suchita asked Ruchi what kind of a chatting interface that was, and Ruchi blurted out about Sofu. A few days later, Suchita caught up with Ruchi about Sofu and tried enquiring about you. Ruchi did get a little uncomfortable as apparently, she hadn't shared her Sofu adventures with anyone at work. Then, on another occasion, Suchita asked Ruchi about you. By now, three things had happened—you had deleted your Sofu profile in which you used your own name, Ruchi had sensed that there was something going on between Suchita and you, and Suchita had planned her play because, this time, she asked Ruchi to just set up a meeting with you and tell you to confess to Vandana that you are on Sofu. Ruchi knew that you and Vandana were a couple, and she did feel sorry for Vandana. Suchita capitalised on this, and even though Ruchi initially resisted as she had no beef against you, Suchita persisted and made Ruchi agree to do her bidding, promising her growth at the right time by transferring her to Mumbai in a peer role with Vandana, and also close to her hometown."

Ravi was a mixed bag of emotions at that time—enraged at Suchita, angry at himself, feeling pity for Ruchi, thankful to Bhanu and Raaj, and embarrassed in Sanjana's presence. The first person he turned to was Sanjana, "Sanjana, I am so sorry. I am so embarrassed that it is taking my eyelids a humongous effort to let my eyes look into yours. I don't know what it will take me to win back Vandana's confidence, but I swear I will. And I don't know whether you will believe me or not, but I have never strayed, never. If you do not believe me, I won't hold it against you. I have been stupid,

stupid! It took me more than a year to win her heart, and I won't mind investing a decade more to win it back, but I will."

'This was good,' Bhanu thought to himself, 'Ravi has done half the job for which Sanjana had come over. Now I must quickly step in to do the rest so that Sanjana can convince Vandana.'

"So here is what I am saying," said Bhanu, but was abruptly cut short by Ravi.

"No, here is what I am saying, I will right now go and screw up Suchita's happiness."

"Bro, no," said Raaj, trying to lighten up things, "You got screwed because you were out to screw. No more screwing; let us plan first." Raaj hid his blushing face as he saw Sanjana watching him say this.

"Plan? I will kill her, Raaj."

"Now just hear me out. You do not have to do anything silly," Bhanu intervened, "Back in engineering college, you and Suchita never kind of came close despite her insistence, because you wanted to cherish intimacy after marriage. With those kinds of values, you are a good catch for any woman. So when Suchita saw you on Sofu, she would have assumed a distance between you and Vandana. The fact that Suchita has no romantic inclinations in her life at the moment must have prompted her to see if she could work this out with you, since she knew you anyway. Look at the good things, Ravi. Despite being an easily available thing on

Sofu, you never had sex with anyone! Why? Because you deeply love Vandana. Suchita hugged and kissed you, but you never reciprocated. Why? Because you madly love Vandana," While talking about this kiss Bhanu had one eye on Sanjana, and he knew that his sharing this anecdote had the desired effect.

"She kissed him?" asked a shocked Sanjana.

"On his cheek," Raaj brushed it aside.

"But Bhanu," protested Ravi.

"Boss, just leave all your anger and other emotions aside," Bhanu was not letting the argument go. "It was I who guided you to Sofu," once again Bhanu had one eye on Sanjana, "I should not have. I am sorry to both Vandana and you for having done it. But I would still say that you have stood the test of time. Why weren't you able to bring yourself to get intimate with any of those women, Ravi? Have you ever given it a thought?"

"Raaj and I spoke about it, Bhanu. I know what you are saying. But I honestly want to strangle Suchita right now."

"And for what joy, Ravi? She wanted to win you back. Why, because she sensed a gap between you and Vandana. Why, because you were on Sofu. Why, because I suggested that to you in the first place."

"So what are you suggesting, *mishti doi*?"

"We have to accomplish just two things here. I would prioritise them as follows. First, winning Vandana's heart once again. And I honestly do not think you have lost it completely as yet. She is hurt, and deeply so. And we will need Sanjana's help in this. Second, handle Suchita. Now if I were you, I'd let Vandana do that. If we are able to direct her anger, which is right now on you, on to Suchita, the job is done. Suchita will be receiving what she deserves, and you will be receiving what you deserve."

"*Abey*, if Sanjana handles Vandana and Vandana handles Suchita, what am I handling?"

"Yourself," winked Raaj. And they all had a smile. "Bhanu," Raaj continued, "why do you think Ravi hasn't lost Vandana completely just as yet?"

"Because she doesn't know at whose behest Ruchi did all this. And while that still does not take away the fact that Ravi was on Sofu, fishing for fun, it does bring in an element of help for us," replied Sanjana.

"Sanjana, will you help Ravi?" asked Bhanu.

"Vandana will be very sensitive about this, Bhanu. And some of the things came as a revelation to me," she replied, smiling. Bhanu smiled back. They both knew what she was talking about. Then she turned towards Ravi, "Ravi, are you sure that you are really sorry?"

"Sanjana, I swear that if you and Bhanu agree to it, I will go and kill Suchita right now."

"But that won't help you get Vandana back, will it?"

"Sanjana, what can I do to make you believe that I am sorry, I am angry, I am deeply embarrassed, I made a huge mistake, and I want her back?"

On their way to Vandana's from Ravi's place, Sanjana and Bhanu were having a small conversation.

"You advised your friend to get on Sofu? Was that YOU helping him? You jackass lawyer of little scruples."

"Hey, how was I to know then that it would turn out like this, and that you would be Vandana's sister?"

"Rascal, is that what you have to say?"

"Sanju, I will make my peace with you too, but right now, let us help Ravi and Vandana. You want me to just drop you at Vandana's or be with you there?"

"I am going to kill you after I handle my sister. And I will do it alone. Just drop me there."

"Remember, Vandana does not know about Suchita. Once she knows that, I am sure you will be able to direct her anger away from Ravi."

"That does not absolve him from what he did."

"It does not."

"And it does not absolve you from what you did."

"It does not."

CHAPTER 44

The Shock of Shocks and Peace-making (Present Day)

It was 2:00 a.m., and Vandana was shocked to see Sanjana at her doorstep. Yes, she was feeling lonely. Yes, she needed someone. Yes, she wanted to be held. But this was a shock for her beyond anything she had imagined. It wasn't only Ravi for whom the day wasn't over. The day was going on for Vandana too. In fact, it was only just the beginning. She didn't know that more was about to come.

"*Didi*?"

"Yes, Vandu."

"Ma told you about my marriage, didn't she?" guessed Vandana at Sanjana's sudden presence.

"Yes, she did."

"And I can tell you that if this is the hour you have chosen to congratulate me, well, it is only another bad choice on your part in a series of choices you have made that have affected me. I am calling it off."

"Not till you hear me out. Ravi is not completely to be blamed."

It was Vandana's turn to be shocked. More was to come her way. She did not know why Sanjana said that. Was she taking Ravi's side, or did she know something that Vandana didn't? Vandana had an annoyed, agitated and confused look on her face.

"Ruchi did not give you the complete truth."

The only emotion that appeared on Vandana's face was shock with a capital S. More was about to come.

"And the mastermind behind all this was Suchita."

There, Sanjana had laid everything bare. By now, Vandana was shocked to her tailbone.

"*Didi*, what is all this?"

"You sit, Vandu, let me beat some coffee for you. I know you are hurt," saying so, Sanjana hugged her sister.

It was a long conversation. Vandana went through a phase of discovery through Sanjana's eyes. The coffee, of course, did not last even a quarter as long as the conversation.

After hearing Sanjana completely, Vandana reflected, "*Didi,* it does not absolve Ravi of what he did."

"You are right; it does not absolve him of what he did, and neither does it absolve Bhanu. And I gave it to them royally, and they both took it too. But it also should not make you angry for something that Ravi did not do, and more importantly, could not bring himself to do because he loves you so much."

Vandana went into a thought. *Didi* did have a point. Ravi could not be absolved for what he did, which was getting on Sofu. But he could not be faulted for something he could not bring himself to do, that is, get intimate with some random woman because he was missing intimacy in his relationship with Vandana. And that was good news for Vandana.

"What are you thinking, Vandu?"

"Unable to reconcile. Why did that joker have to loiter around on Sofu, *didi*?"

"Vandu, you both have behaved rather ironically in this."

"Why do you say that, *didi?*"

"You have both been in relationships earlier. And in them, you were ready to be intimate while he was not. In this relationship he wanted to be intimate, while you were not. Do you see the paradox now? Both of you applied self-imposed restrictions on each other, you now and he previously. Your restriction made him uncomfortable, and it made you, only for the lack of a better word, opaque to his needs. Now I am not for a moment advocating pre-marital intimacy. Neither am I advocating against it. These are matters of individual choices that a couple needs to discuss amongst themselves."

"And my boyfriend discussed it with yours? See what happened. I really want to kill him."

"Ravi?" Sanjana quipped.

"Bhanu. He put Ravi on this path." Vandana frowned.

"Leave my man to me. I have already told him I will deal with him later," said Sanjana, smilingly.

"So what are you suggesting?"

"Do not do anything in haste. This cancellation of engagement that you are talking about, think it over from all angles, think of everything, and only then decide."

Sanjana saw that Vandana was in deep thought. So she prodded Vandana further, "Tell me, what's on your mind, besides killing both our men."

"I want to have a word with Suchita. A proper word, face to face, woman to woman."

"Everyone wants to have a piece of her flesh, I see."

"Everyone?"

"Didn't I tell you, Ravi wanted to kill her as well?"

"Oh, he doesn't. Children cannot be sent to do adults' jobs." They both smiled.

"But *didi,* I am still mad at him. Very."

"I know. He does deserve your anger. And he knows that too. But let me tell you this, that I have seen remorse, regret, repentance and shame in his eyes."

"You did?"

And then Sanjana added very softly, "Yes. And

when Rohit happened, all these were there in my eyes too," she broke down, and with teary eyes and a choked throat she said, "You never saw these then, Vandu. But I still have them. Not a day passes by when I don't feel like hugging you and loving you and receiving your love like I used to, earlier. Please forgive me, I am sorry." Saying so, Sanjana held Vandana in a very tight embrace.

Both the sisters were in an embrace, and were crying inconsolably. It wasn't their tears, but years of anger and hurt that were being let go of. They were coming to terms; they were coming to peace. Only two things were left now. And Vandana was going to do both of them.

CHAPTER 45

Closure (Present Day)

"That is not to say I am still not mad at you, you idiot. And I will take time to cool down," Vandana was giving a dressing down to Ravi at her breakfast table.

"I know," murmured Ravi, his head still down with shame, guilt and regret.

Sanjana and Vandana had barely slept last night. Vandana had messaged Ravi to drop in by 9:30 a.m., which he did. Sanjana gave them the space and went to the kitchen to cook breakfast while Vandana and Ravi could talk and reconcile.

"Guys, breakfast is ready. Can I bring it?"

"Yes, yes please, Sanjana," said Ravi, hoping for a respite.

"Yes please, Sanjana," repeated Vandana, mocking and mimicking him, "Why were you so stupid then, if you had to be so scared now?"

"Vandy, nothing I say, and I mean absolutely nothing I say will have the ability to cool you down right now. So I have nothing to say at all. I mean, what reasons can I give? They will only sound lame. I can only beg you for your understanding, your mercy and your love. And honestly, I will understand if you'd like me to just go away and never show my face again."

"And if I say so, will you go away?"

"No chance," said a sheepishly smiling Ravi, "can't let go. I will come behind you till you forgive me."

Vandana smiled, "Forgive, maybe. But forget, tell me how."

"Vandy, I can say that my love will heal the wounds I have caused you, and I can never be sorry enough for causing them. Please, do not call it off."

"Then know this, that I will use it against you as and when I feel like, no matter how old we get."

"Okay, you are allowed."

"Allowed?" asked Vandana, hinting at her anger and surprise.

"I mean I know, but please never in front of kids and grandkids."

Ravi was sitting at the table, hands folded in prayer. Sanjana was laughing and laying the spread on the table. Vandana was smiling. Ravi knew that this was over, almost. The three of them had breakfast together. Vandana had decided to meet Suchita after breakfast, settle the score and come back to her place for lunch with Bhanu, Sanjana, Raaj, Simi and Ravi. After the lunch, both sisters would travel together to Chandigarh to surprise their parents. The engagement was just two weeks away, and marriage was to follow immediately thereafter.

"Am I just not allowed to give my piece of mind to Suchita?" asked Ravi.

"Oh no," said Vandana with a devilish grin, "she's my game, and I am having her alone. You pick up a fight with someone your equal."

***

Suchita thought that Vandana had come into her cabin about work. She was shocked to her core when Vandana opened up.

"You prying, scheming, man-stealing bitch! At least you should have had some shame that the man no longer belongs to you."

Suchita did not know what had happened, but knew that it was no time to keep up any pretence.

"Yeah, and does the man know that he actually belongs to you? When he was with me, at least he never saw other women. What is it that you cannot handle, Vandana? Cannot keep him happy and satisfied?"

Vandana had expected some shame and guilt on Suchita's part, not a fight back. But if it was a fight that

Suchita wanted to offer, Vandana would not shy away from it.

"Suchita, your greed does not even let you see your own arrogance. My man is happily mine, and has nothing to do with you, or Ruchi, or anyone else for that matter. You knew Ravi and I were in love. And you had been in love with him earlier. Had you actually loved him and let go, you should have corrected his behaviour when you saw him straying away. Instead, what did you do? You schemed to make your bread on someone else's dough. And whom did you use for the lame game? Ruchi. Wow!"

When Suchita heard Vandana mention Ruchi, she became aware of the extent of knowledge Vandana had in this matter. She was wondering what had transpired between her call with Ruchi late last evening, and now, for Vandana to know everything. Anyway, she wasn't going to get any answers. So she decided to keep up the ante.

"Get out of my office, now. I do not want to see you here. And while you are going away, think about why your man chose to look beyond you. I did not present him any reason to. He had already decided to stray. And I had no issues in offering him what he was looking for, love with intimacy."

"Do you even know that he had deleted Sofu before you kissed him? And do you know why he deleted Sofu? Because he could not bring himself to step out of his relationship with me. Did he ever approach you? Never.

I'd have loved it had you brought it to my knowledge or drilled some sense into him, but you are such an opportunist bitch. And as for this office, well, this office was my organisation before you came in. And I do not have the habit of leaving what's mine on the table. You may not know this, but today, Jamshyd is joining us back in a role above you and as your boss. And oh, by the way, I had a long conversation with him while on my way here. So not only am I not leaving this room, but I am not leaving this organisation either. Jamshyd wants both of us on line with him now!"

Vandana placed a very strong emphasis on 'now'. It was verbally bolded, underlined and italicised. Suchita now knew that she had lost the game. And if there was anyone not just leaving the office but the organisation, it was her.

***

The lunch table was filled with the atmosphere of merrymaking. All six of them had literally forgotten what the last 24 hours had been like. The table was abuzz with discussions about the upcoming engagement and marriage, and possibly another engagement and marriage, followed by the third engagement and marriage. Raaj and Simi were the oldest couple among the three but weren't married yet. Bhanu and Sanjana were the latest couple, and Vandana was dead sure that as soon as her mother got to know of their relationship, they would get engaged. And why not? Brig. and Mrs. Sharma would be very happy to see both their daughters getting along together, and even happier seeing both of them getting married soon.

"Ravi, let us drive them down to Chandigarh. It will be great."

"I am game, Bhanu, if the ladies do not object."

"And what will Simi and I do here?"

"And what will Simi and you do there?" quipped Vandana.

They all burst out laughing.

"Well," said Raaj, "you know…" and he left it at that.

"Hey," Vandana remembered, "I think it's time we added *didi* to the Dear Friends group."

Ravi immediately complied.

Bhanu continued, "So I was saying, let us go there together. Dad has left his SUV with me for a few days as he has gone to meet my brother in Bengaluru. And if you ladies do not mind, Simi can stay with you, while the three of us monkey around. This is a long weekend of four days."

"Only monkeying around but not Sofu!" said Sanjana.

The plan was cast in stone. Everyone was to meet at Raaj's at 4:30 p.m. and start for Chandigarh by 5:00 p.m.

It was at 10:00 p.m. that they reached the Sharma residence. Vandana had told her parents that she would be dropped by Ravi. She hadn't told them about Sanjana and Bhanu. Her parents, especially Sudha, were more than pleased to see both their daughters together. They were of course surprised to know about Bhanu, but only surprised, not angered. The boys dropped the ladies at the Sharma's and checked-in at a hotel close by.

The next morning, Bhanu's parents reached out to Sanjana's. It was decided that they would attend Vandana's engagement, which was just two weeks away. Raaj and Simi also informed their respective parents. The wheels of marriage were set in motion.

Epilogue

Ravi and Vandana's marriage had been a splendid affair. It took some time before and after the marriage for Vandana's hurt to go away completely, but Ravi, with his persistence, was able to achieve it. It hadn't been easy for him to present his case to Vandana, and it had not been easy for Vandana to forgive him. One of the things that Vandana had told him while forgiving him was that despite the fact that she had forgiven him, she reserved the right to bring up the issue when it troubled her. Ravi had wholeheartedly agreed to that.

Shortly after, Sanjana and Bhanu's engagement was announced. Vandana and Ravi decided to visit Europe for their honeymoon. It was a week's travel. On their return, they were received by Sanjana, Bhanu, Simi and Raaj. By then, Raaj and Simi's engagement and wedding had also been announced.

The next few months would see celebrations, dinners, meals and what not.

At the dinner hosted by Bhanu and Sanjana at Sanjana's place, the newlyweds reminisced about their honeymoon. The other two couples were planning theirs. Sanjana and Bhanu decided on Oz, whereas Simi and Raaj planned for Africa.

"So, no more Sofu, I guess?" Bhanu asked Ravi.

Sanjana gave him a very dirty look while the others just smiled away.

"Boss, I want to live long and also live peacefully. And I'd love to advise other men out there not to experiment with their lives like this."

"And how would you do that, wise man?" asked Raaj.

Holding Vandana's hand and looking into her eyes, Ravi answered, "By writing a book and recounting all my experiments with Sofu."

An excerpt from the sequel of Love Swipe Blackmail

On the operation table lay Suchita, unconscious, surrounded by doctors and nurses. Sanjana was walking fast towards the operation theatre thinking to herself, 'All I have to do is ignore a few things. No one will be able to point fingers at me, and Suchita will never be able to recover.'